An Invisible Woman

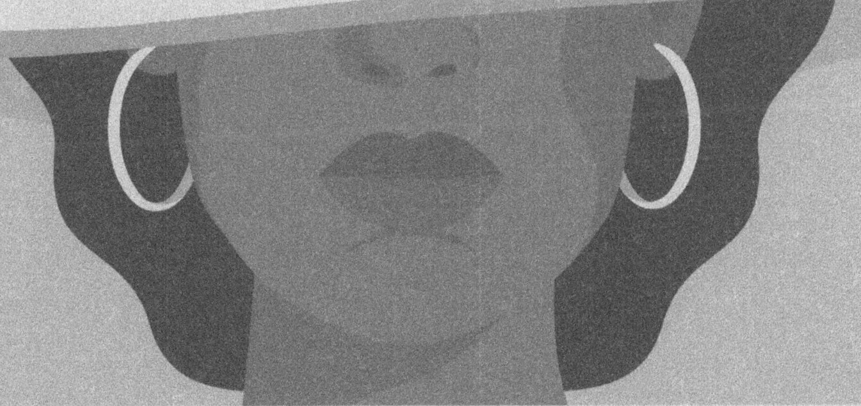

KAREN SLOAN-BROWN

BROWN REFLECTIONS

An Invisible Woman

KAREN SLOAN-BROWN

Prologue

I'm not invisible, but I might as well be. No, it's not because of my skin color. The fact is nobody sees me. White people don't see me, and black people don't either. I'm not noticed when I'm out in public. No one speaks to me. Out of habit, I wear a faint smile, but no one returns it.

It's been that way for most of my life. I can't count the number of my schoolteachers who never saw me when I was growing up or coworkers who didn't acknowledge me or my work. I might as well have been an empty robe on a hanger when I sang in the soprano section of the choir at Mt. Tabor Baptist Church. When I'm out socially, men act as if I'm not there. It's not because I'm basic or plain. In all honesty, I'm an attractive woman, generally characterized as pretty. My invisibility is something that I can't define.

I know I'm not alone in my imperceptibility. My mother was an invisible woman, too. I'm not sure if she passed it down to me genetically or whether it is an acquired trait. There are many women like us. Some resort to drastic measures to increase their visibility. They cover their faces with heavy makeup, get numerous tattoos, wear rainbow-colored weaves and extensions down their backs, have excessive breast and butt implants, or expose their bodies with overly revealing clothing. But I prefer to accept my lot as a poker player accepts a bad hand. I bluff and do the best I can.

A portion of my invisibility is my fault. From the time I was a young girl, I preferred to stay in the background. In school, I was a smart kid, but I never raised my hand in class, despite knowing the answers more often than not. There were many missed opportunities in college when I wanted to participate in the lively discussions that took place between study groups exchanging ideas. I always had something to say, something to contribute, but I stayed quiet. I thought I was shy. Apart from that, I have no other explanation. I've always let others have the spotlight.

The paradox of my invisibility is that I'm always seeing things that aren't there, shadows out the side of my eye, cartoon figures in the clouds, hands reaching out among the branches of trees, and images of people made by the water drips from the condensation inside the shower door. I certainly sympathize with those who see the Virgin Mary in melted chocolate or the face of Jesus on a grilled cheese sandwich.

Please forgive me. I've forgotten my manners. I should introduce myself before I say another word. My name is Chantelle Parker, the only child of a father who died before I was born and my mama, who passed away 19 years ago. I don't have any children myself, at least not anymore. I'm an actuary. I've worked for the Supreme Life Insurance Company for 16 years. For the last year and a half, I've focused all my energy on my career, making money, and trying my best to be seen. I've bought things that I thought would make me stand out: designer clothes, designer bags, designer shoes, and a little red corvette. The irony was that, when people took notice, they only saw the things and not me.

I'm in a major transition right now. My life as I knew it is over. It was blown up by an electronic explosive device—specifically, a computer with internet access—and the pieces haven't settled down yet. So many parts are missing that it's improbable that I will ever be able to put it back together again. Reflecting back over it, I can see things didn't disintegrate all at one time. It was a painful, drawn-out process tearing me down layer by layer. More horrible is the fact that I no longer even recognize myself.

It was only twenty months ago that I was a wife, a mother, and a homeowner with my own unique version of the white picket fence. Today, I am single, divorced with no children to call my own, and there's a "for sale" sign in front of the house I decorated and lived in for close to nine years.

I was young with stars in my eyes, having barely said "I do" when the first bomb exploded. It was a lethal blow, a cause to withdraw, a signal of the end, but I didn't have the sense to retreat. Blame it on my upbringing. My mama taught me never to give up. She would always say, "Anything worth having is worth fighting for." So, believe me, I fought for the marriage in every way I could, even after my husband declined counseling or any type of therapy. It took ten years before I could recognize I was in a losing battle. In spite of that, I continued to fight. It was my husband who abruptly and unmercifully put our long-suffering marriage to rest.

I guess I must concede that the decision to separate was a mutual one, although it was after I was issued an ultimatum that I could not abide. The object of contention was his freedom to indulge in pornography. I refused to accept what I considered as his obsessive fixations on other women. The irony is that I, the invisible woman, was beaten out by other phantoms, images of unknown women he couldn't feel or touch.

He claimed it was all harmless, he was only looking, and that he was just being a man. My main grievance was that, in the midst of that, he stopped looking at me. I'm not sure when it happened. I know he saw me in the beginning. I'm sure of it. I was absolutely vivid in his eyes. However, unbeknownst to me, I began to blur over the years until I was slightly out of focus. Then I blurred a little more until I had faded like the color of an old photograph, and then I disappeared.

Chapter
One

The end of my marriage and the loss of my family and my home was the second time that life pulled the rug out from under my feet and knocked me on my behind. The first time was in the spring of 1992. It was just before my eighteenth birthday, during my senior year in high school. My mama, Frances Parker, and I were living in a two-bedroom apartment on the third floor of the Nicklewood Arms complex in Midtown Atlanta. It was the only home I had ever known. Mama had moved there, next door to her older sister, Betty, when she was seven months pregnant with me, after my father had died in a car accident on his way to work.

"Get a move on!" Mama shouted over the old-school music playing on the kitchen radio. "You don't have time to be late."

Mama's voice calling out to me every morning was one of our daily rituals for as far back as I could remember. She needn't have called me though; I was already awake that morning, staring at the watermark stain on the ceiling, which that day looked like an old man shaking hands with a fluffy dog. It was the familiar smell and sizzling sound of bacon mixed with the buzz of a Motown hit on the radio that served as my alarm clock, signaling that it was time to get up and into the shower. I threw off the sheet that I was tangled in and got to my feet.

"You don't have to iron my clothes anymore, Mama!" I shouted back for the umpteenth time when I saw the freshly starched blue jeans laying across the back of the chair in front of my desk. "I'm not a baby. I'm a senior about to graduate from high school."

"You never get too grown for a helping hand," she said, coming to my door with a dishtowel thrown over her shoulder. "When you get out here on your own, you're going to wish for these days. I wish I had somebody to help me sometimes. It ain't easy out here."

"I don't know why you keep saying that. I'm not going anywhere," I said, half-teasing while I searched in the closet for a shirt. "I'm going to get a job after graduation and help you out around here so you can finally stop working so many hours."

Mama worked for Piedmont Airlines cleaning the planes. She got a job there right after my first birthday. And throughout all her years there, she had worked all the overtime she could get. That meant I was a latchkey kid from the time I started elementary school. Most nights by the time Mama got home, I was already in bed.

Another ritual of ours was for her to read poetry to me: Langston Hughes, Gwendolyn Brooks, but mostly Nikki Giovanni. It wasn't so much that she was highly enlightened on race and social issues or a black revolutionary; it was because she was practically dead on her feet and didn't have the energy to read me long stories.

"You going to need a good job to take care of me, Chantelle," Mama said, fanning herself with the dishtowel. "Your mama's ready to live the good life. You can't do me any favors working by the hour on some penny-ante job. I'm old and tired enough to know that much about this life. That's why I want you to get your college degree. Then find somebody to share your life with. Don't try to do it all by yourself, baby. It'll wear you out. I'm telling you the truth."

"Not again," I said, walking past her to the bathroom in bare feet. "You don't have to keep telling me that every other day."

"Yes, I do. I don't want you to be like me, slaving on a job that don't get you nothing but rough hands."

I looked back at my reflection in the mirror and told her, "Mama, I'm already like you."

I heard her sigh. "I just want better for my only child. That's all I'm saying."

"Stop worrying so much. I've got it under control," I said, closing the door.

"I'm not worried," she said, talking to me from the outside of the bathroom door. "I'm just so happy you got accepted to Spelman. I can't wait. We're going to take that trip out to California before school starts, just like I promised. Life seems so carefree there. I want to be carefree, even if it's just for a week."

I smiled to myself, thinking about the trip, too, as I climbed into the shower. "Yes, ma'am. I'm ready!"

When I turned off the water that had grown tepid, I could hear laughter coming from the kitchen. It was my Aunt Betty and my cousin, Sheree. It was an arrangement that hadn't changed over the years: Mama made breakfast every day, and Aunt Betty made the dinner every evening. So Sheree and I, only four months apart, were raised together like sisters. We're both 5'8, and we share a strong family resemblance. The only difference is Sheree is lighter-skinned, and I'm brown as pecan pie. For most of our lives, you didn't see one without the other, and some people even thought we were twins. Actually, we were like magnets, opposite forces attracting and holding us close.

Sheree is bold and boisterous, and I'm introverted and reserved. I'm book smart, and she's street smart. She's creative, and I'm careful. Still, more than family, we're best friends, balancing each other on the tight rope above the fray of the mean streets of Midtown. Growing up, every summer we'd catch the train to Six Flags and stand in the long line to ride the Mind Bender rollercoaster. We sat together, but Sheree rode with her arms raised straight in the air, cheering, while I tucked myself into a knot, holding my stomach tightly to keep its contents from spilling out. Sheree was always fearless; she dared anybody to step to us or look our way back in the day when kids in Atlanta were disappearing and turning up dead.

"You and Sheree leave here together every morning looking like y'all are going to two different places," Mama said when I walked into the kitchen. "Chantelle looks like she's going to a baseball game, and Sheree looks like she's going to a photo shoot."

"We're going to the same place Auntie," Sheree said, munching on a piece of toast. "I'm just going in style."

"You're not going anywhere if you don't start hitting those books like Chantelle," Aunt Betty added, sipping her coffee as she sat at the kitchen table.

Chantelle tilted her chin proudly. "Correction. My outfit is banging, so I'm definitely dressed for success."

Go ahead, girl!" Mama told Sheree, slapping her on her shoulder. "You're going to have to get Chantelle sharp when she graduates from Spelman and starts working in one of the glass buildings downtown."

Sheree put down her glass of juice. "Don't worry about that, Aunt Frances. Chantelle is going to be straight."

"Excuse me, but I have my own style, thank you," I said, sitting down in front of the plate Mama made for me. "I know how to dress. I just don't see any reason to get all decked out just to go to school."

"My philosophy is, always be on point," Sheree said, holding a fork full of eggs just beyond her burgundy lips. "Who knows? I might get discovered at the bus stop."

"I doubt if anybody is looking for you at Grady High," I said, laughing.

Sheree was unfazed. "Auntie, if you let me borrow your new Mustang, I bet all eyes will be on me when I whip up to the school," she said, raising her perfectly shaped eyebrows.

"I'm sure they would, sugar," Mama chuckled. "I might let you drive it one day, but not for a while. I worked double shifts for three years to pay for that car. You at least have to wait until the new smell wears off."

"Hush up, Frances!" Aunt Betty snapped. "Don't get nothing started because when I get my car, I'm not letting nobody drive it but me."

"Don't be like that, Mother dear," Chantelle said with an English accent. "We graduate in two days, and when I start working, I'm going to need some transpo."

"That's why the Lord gave you those two good feet to walk on," Aunt Betty said offhandedly.

"These shoes aren't made for walking," Chantelle said, looking down at the strappy sandals on her feet. "They are strictly for styling and profiling."

"What are you talking about, crazy child?" Aunt Betty asked, shaking her head.

Sheree lifted one foot in the air. "These babies are for sitting down and crossing your legs."

"You two better get out of here, or you'll miss the 7:45 bus and be late," Mama said, picking up our plates of half-eaten food from the table.

"Being late doesn't bother me," Chantelle said, applying a fresh coat of lipstick. "That way, I can make a grand entrance."

"Help her, Jesus," Aunt Betty said, throwing up her hands.

"I'm not trying to mess up my perfect attendance on the last week of school," I said, standing up and heaving my full backpack onto my shoulder.

"Be safe, peaches. I love you," Mama said, patting me on the back as I hurried out.

Sheree and I headed out of the apartment complex side by side, doing our own things: her, singing with Shanice on her portable CD player, while I repeated trigonometric functions in my head for my final exam. We hopped on the bus right before the doors closed. I sat in the window seat, and Sheree on the aisle. She bounced her head to her music in her headphones, while I stared at the hustle and bustle of Atlanta's streets.

Having grown up around each other, we didn't need to fill the air with constant chatter; that's what Doreen and Lena were for. Doreen was light-skinned, short, and rocked an asymmetrical blunt haircut, and she was definitely the "Brick House" that the Commodores had sung about. Lena was a Whitney Houston look-a-like. She was going to cosmetology school after graduation, even though she could already out-style most of the hair stylists in the city.

Doreen and Lena met us outside Grady when the bus let us off. The two of them were wearing the same color outfits as Sheree was wearing. That's when the odd duo became a quartet, looking like another version of En Vogue with Sheree preening like Diana Ross, Lena sassy and tossing her hair, Doreen stretching the seams of her clothes to the max, and me out of sync and slightly out of style as we made our way into the building.

***

I stood high on my toes trying to see above the crowd of my fellow graduates clamoring like a school of hungry fish when food is tossed to them. Each of us caught up in a frenzy of congratulations and savoring the collective moment before we would all go our separate ways.

"There they are over there!" Sheree said, pulling me by the hand and pushing through the mass of navy and white caps and gowns and proud family members taking pictures outside of the gym. Once we had weaved our way through the crowd to get to them, Sheree started jumping up and down in her heels but feeling no pain. "Mama! Aunt Frances! Hallelujah! I'm so glad that's over with!"

"Hush up, child," Aunt Betty said, smiling and holding her arms high and wide to wrap around Sheree. "I guess you think you're grown for real now."

"Probably," Sheree joked as she struck a pose. "But I know one thing for sure: I won't be getting up at the crack of dawn to catch a bus going to Grady High School anymore."

I slapped Sheree a high five. "I know that's right."

"I'm so proud of you, peaches!" Mama said, squeezing me tight against her chest. "You've made it through high school with honors, and I know you're going to make it through Spelman the same way."

My shoulders dropped a little. "I know that, Mama," I told her for the hundredth time. "You don't have to keep telling me that."

"Yes, I do, baby," she said, looking happy but with tears in her eyes. "I don't want you to forget it. Your education is going to take care of you."

"It'll take care of both of us," I told her, wanting to stay upbeat. "You have worked enough double shifts."

"I know, sweetie," Mama said. "Just a few more weeks of overtime pay, and we'll be up in the clouds on our way to California to do it right."

"That sounds absolutely lovely, sister girl," Aunt Betty teased. "But in the meantime, let's get something to eat."

Sheree rubbed her belly. "Oh, yeah! I've got a taste for some chicken and waffles."

"You're always hungry," I said, shaking my head at her.

"We'll all be by the time we walk to the car," Mama said, pulling her purse from her wrist up to her shoulder.

Sheree sighed. "Not in these shoes, Aunt Frances."

"Yes, ma'am," Mama said, leading the way to the car. "I had to park two blocks away."

I held my diploma tight against my chest and followed Mama in my four-inch heels. "That's okay. Nothing is going to bother me today."

When we got to the car and Mama turned the key in the ignition, the radio, always on her classic old-school station, was playing "Let's Get It On." Mama started swaying and popping her fingers as she drove. Aunt Betty hollered from the backseat, "Yeah!"

"Not in the car, Mama, please," I said, amused at them. Sheree started laughing.

"Oh yes, baby," Mama said, raising her hands high above the steering wheel. "If it wasn't for Marvin Gaye and this song you wouldn't be here."

"I know that's right," Aunt Betty said, slapping her on the shoulder.

Having dinner at Gladys Knight's restaurant was almost magical that night. We were so happy, and the food was delicious.

"I'm stuffed," Mama said. "I don't think I can walk to the car."

"I am, too," I chimed in, rubbing my belly.

"Uh-uh," Sheree said, waving her hand. "Now how are you two gonna look strolling around Venice Beach wearing bikinis with those corn muffins you ate sticking out?"

Mama laughed. "Stop, Sheree! You know good and well I'm not putting on no bikini. I can't wait to see the Pacific Ocean, but I won't need a swimsuit. I can guarantee you those waves won't even get up to my knees."

"Come on, Aunt Frances," Sheree said. "You know I start my new job at Bloomingdales in a week, and I can hook you and Chantelle up with my discount. You both need to be fly in LA, especially when y'all go to Muscle Beach."

"The beach is cool, and I want to take a dip in the ocean," I said, musing. "But I really want to see all the orange trees, the Hollywood Walk of Fame, and then check out Universal Studios."

Sheree threw her hands up and shook her head. "I don't believe you two."

"It doesn't matter to me what Chantelle wants to do or see," Mama said, smiling. "My heart is set on going on a tour of Motown, Hitsville West. I want to see the studio where Marvin recorded his albums. I want to see where all that good music was made. I would love to shake Berry Gordy's hand."

"Now, I wish I could go see that myself, Frances," Aunt Betty added longingly. "That by itself would be worth the trip."

"Please," Sheree said, smirking. "If I was going, I'd spend most of my time shopping 'til I dropped on Rodeo Drive. I might even run into a few tall, dark, and handsome celebs."

Aunt Betty laughed. "Window shopping is about all you'd be doing."

"On that note, I guess we better get up from here," Mama said, snickering. "I can't wait until I can get up in an airplane and fly high in the clouds instead of cleaning them. I've got two shifts waiting on me tomorrow."

I groaned before I slid out of the booth. "Can't you take a day off, Mama? I got the scholarship at Spelman."

"I'll rest when you graduate, baby," Mama said, reaching for my hand. "Then all the hard work will have been worth it."

"Come on, Mama," Sheree said, grabbing Aunt Betty's hand. "I'm going to start saving for our trip to New York for Fashion Week at the end of the summer."

Aunt Betty nodded as she stood up. "All right, child. We'll see."

When we left, not only were we full from eating, but we were full of hopes and dreams for the possibilities that lay ahead of us.

***

It was Thursday night, two weeks after graduation, and I was lying on the couch watching the final episode of *A Different World*. The phone rang five minutes before the show ended. I figured it was Sheree calling, bored and wanting to go to a movie or something. I was just about to answer the phone when the character Dwayne Wayne burst into the church, interrupting Whitley Gilbert's wedding. When I saw that, I let the phone ring. I had to see if Whitley was going to go through with the wedding and marry Byron. I kept my eyes glued to the TV, the phone still ringing. Knowing Sheree, she would probably be knocking at the door in two minutes like she usually did whenever I didn't answer her call.

I smiled to myself when the knock on the door came a few minutes after the episode ended. After all that suspense, I was still going to have to wait until the next season to see which guy Whitley chose to marry.

Pretending to be exasperated, I snatched the door open. "What is it?"

It was Sheree and Aunt Betty standing there looking horrified. My heart instantly started beating so hard I could feel the pulse deep within my ears at the sight of their tear-streaked faces.

"What happened!" I screamed, scared out of my mind.

"A man from your mama's job just called me," Aunt Betty said, between her heaving breaths. "He said she collapsed at work about an hour ago."

"Oh, my God, no!" I said, covering my mouth and beginning to shake as my panic grew. I rushed back to the sofa, jammed my feet into my sneakers, and hurried back to the doorway where they were standing. "Let's go. I've got to get to the hospital."

Aunt Betty took my hands in hers and squeezed them tight. "Baby, sit down for minute."

"I don't have time!" I said, snatching my hands back. "We need to go now!"

Sheree wrapped me up in a hug with one arm around my neck and the other around my waist and whispered in my ear. "She's not going to be all right, sis. She's gone."

"No, NO!" I screamed, grabbing my stomach as I doubled over. The pain was so bad that I thought my insides were falling out. "No, it's not true! She's coming home. She wouldn't leave me."

"Come on, baby," Aunt Betty coaxed, pulling me toward the couch.

"This can't be real. I don't have anybody else!" I cried pitifully, shaking my head in dismay.

"Don't say that, Chantelle!" Sheree hollered over my wailing. "Me and Mama are here for you. You know that."

"I can't believe it. I can't believe it," I mumbled over and over through the tears and mucus pouring into my mouth.

"I don't either, sis," Sheree said in a softer voice, sitting on the other side of me.

"Jesus! Jesus! Lord have mercy!" Aunt Betty yelled out with her fists balled up.

The three of us sat side by side, holding one another tight and rocking in unison for what seemed like an eternity. Sorrow encircled us on that couch like the wind tossing a tiny boat in the midst of a terrible storm. I wanted to surrender to the agony. I wanted it to consume me, take me out of misery, and let me die, too. It was Sheree and Aunt Betty calling on Jesus that held onto me and kept me from going under.

***

The doctor at the hospital, who never told us his name, said that Mama died of a heart attack. But I knew my mama had worked herself to death, shift by shift, week by week, year after year. It wrecked my nerves and made me feel guilty because most, if not all, of her sacrifice was on my behalf. All my life, she had never let me want for anything. I thought I would have had the chance to make it up to her, but now I never would. Aunt Betty made all the arrangements, while I tried to escape the heartache in my sleep. I hated being awake; it was too painful.

On the morning of the funeral, two days after my eighteenth birthday, which passed unnoticed, I laid in bed staring at the water spot on the ceiling that, on that day, looked like a huge bird flying above an empty boat. I smelled the bacon and heard it sizzling, and I heard the music playing on the radio. I closed my eyes and strained to hear the sound of her slippers shuffling across the floor. I wanted to believe that the last five days were a nightmare and that I had finally awakened.

Then Marvin Gaye was singing "Let's Get It On." That's when I knew she was gone. Whenever that song came on, Mama would smile to herself, pop her fingers, and sing along as if it was duet. It was her and Daddy's theme song. She would surely have been in my room by the second verse, teasing me and saying that, if it wasn't for that song, I wouldn't be here.

I drug myself out of bed, showered, and got dressed in the pale pink dress Mama had bought for me to wear on Easter. My head felt so heavy, I didn't have the strength to raise it, and I couldn't eat a bite. My head was still bowed as I followed Aunt Betty's feet down the steps into the limo that was waiting for us. In a daze, I sat between her and Sheree. I felt like a forgotten book leaning between them; they were the ends that refused to let me fall.

"Come on, Chantelle, say goodbye to your mama for the last time," Aunt Betty said after the viewing was over, grabbing me by my hand. Sheree stood up on the other side and lifted me to my feet by my elbow.

"I don't want to," I said quietly, feeling all the eyes on my back.

"I need you to help me then," Aunt Betty insisted. "That's my baby sister up there."

Instead of resisting and making a scene, I walked up to the blush-colored casket and closed my eyes. I didn't want to see my mama like that. I wanted to remember her dancing around the kitchen with a spatula in her hand, singing to a Smokey Robinson song. Pain intensified in the hand that Aunt Betty squeezed tightly as she stood beside me moaning. I felt a tinge of relief when Sheree guided us back to our seat on the front row.

That day, and for the next six weeks, I refused to allow my watery eyes to focus. I thanked the Lord for Sheree, who was there to lead me around like a blind woman everywhere I had to go. It didn't seem right after all those years of working for Piedmont that Mama's insurance policy was just enough to cover the funeral costs and pay the balances on all her bills. When it was all said and done, Mama had left me with the contents of our apartment, her 1991 white Ford Mustang that she'd spent six years saving for, the $1,700 we were going to use on our vacation to California before I started college, and $3,000 for college expenses.

***

Grief was my constant companion as I sat for hours in front of the TV. Sometimes it was on, other times it was off, and I just stared at my dim reflection on the dark screen. I only left the couch when I had to or when Sheree would come drag me off of it when it was dinnertime. Somehow, in the back of my mind, I thought that this spot on the sofa facing the TV was the place where everything went wrong. Maybe if I stayed there, one day I could rewind this awful drama like a tape in the VCR, and Mama would come home from work as she always did. I waited with my world frozen in animation, closed off in our apartment, as the sweltering days of August plodded on for the rest of Atlanta.

"We got the hook-up, Chantelle," Sheree sang, busting into the apartment on a Friday night. She was dressed club-ready in a violet jumpsuit, with Lena and Doreen close behind her. "We brought you something to eat from Big Mama's."

Sheree never got tired of trying to cheer me up, so I did my best to meet her halfway. "I guess I am kind of hungry," I said, scooting to the edge of the couch.

"How're you doing, girlfriend?" Lena asked, plopping down beside me in her skintight red minidress, while Doreen and Sheree walked into the kitchen.

"I'm hanging," I said, forcing my lips to form some semblance of a smile.

"You need to let me give you a touch-up," she said, running her fingers through my uncombed hair. "I can't have my girl looking a mess when you strut on campus at Spelman."

"I guess so," I said, rubbing my hand over my hair to smooth it back down.

I could hear Doreen's legs rubbing together as she switched her hips into the living room with a plate of food in one hand and a glass of sweet tea in the other. "You have lost weight, Chantelle," she said, looking down at me with sad eyes. "You must not be eating enough to feed a bird, but I know you're gonna want to eat some of this. I've got you some fried chicken, barbeque ribs, potato salad, turnip greens, and sliced tomatoes."

"Thank you," I said, taking the plate from her and putting it on my lap. The food smelled good, even though the aroma had to fight its way around the scents of three different perfumes that encircled me.

"I know you're hurting, sis," Sheree said, sitting beside me. "I can't stand coming over here and not seeing my Aunt Frances, but she wouldn't want you to be like this." I nodded as I forced myself to take a few bites under their watchful eyes. "We want you to go out with us tonight. You've been in this apartment all summer."

I shifted a mouthful of food to my cheeks so I could talk. "I'm all right. Y'all go on out, and have good time."

"You need to get out of here and get some fresh air," Lena said. "Just for an hour or two."

I took a swallow of the tea to wash the food down. "I'm not good company right now," I said, glancing around at each of them. "I don't want to spoil the vibe."

"If we leave you here, it's going to spoil the vibe even more," Doreen said with one hand on her round hip.

"Y'all are already dressed. I'll go next time," I said, wishing they would let it go.

"Stop making excuses," Sheree said, nudging me. "Get up, take a shower, and bring your gloomy ass out with us. Besides, we look too good to be riding on MARTA, and that Mustang is sitting outside collecting dust."

I didn't want to go, but I gave in, knowing they weren't going to stop asking until I said yes. "All right," I said, stomping out of the room.

I took a quick shower, pulled my hair back in a bun, put on some Levis and a sleeveless blouse, and stomped back into the living room. Sheree shook her head slowly and twisted her glossy lips to the side. I knew she didn't approve of my outfit, but under the circumstances, she was going to let it slide.

I realized how much they wanted to be there for me when I insisted on driving with the windows down and the sunroof open. It was a hot and muggy evening, but none of them complained. The air freshener hanging from the rearview mirror moved back and forth with the warm breeze that blew some of my sadness away as we sang to the radio. By the time we got to the club, my heart didn't feel so heavy.

The club was packed. It took a while for us to get a table. We had just sat down when a guy came over and asked Sheree to dance. Lena saw some other friends and went to socialize with them. Then Doreen's jam came on, and she sashayed onto the dance floor. I was at the table all alone, but I didn't feel like dancing. Truthfully, it made me mad to see that everybody was going on as if life was all beautiful when it wasn't. After a while, Sheree came back to the table with a beer for herself and a soda for me.

"You okay, sis?" she asked, sounding concerned.

I looked into her eyes and said, "Yeah, I'm good."

"Then I'm good, too."

Another guy came over and extended a hand, asking Sheree to dance, but she shook her head. I was glad she turned him down. People are wrong when they say misery loves company. More aptly, misery needs company. We sat there sipping our drinks and staring out onto the dance floor.

Chapter

Two

"**K**eep your mouth closed, and be still. I'm trying to keep this line straight," Sheree fussed as she outlined my lips with a berry-shaded pencil.

"I don't know why you're doing all this. It's not a big deal," I said, speaking through my teeth. "I don't need a full face just to sit in class. There are no guys there to impress."

"Please, Chantelle. How many times do I have to tell you? It's not what anybody else thinks of you; it's what you think of you."

"Exactly. I think it's what is inside my head that counts, not what I look like."

Sheree rolled her eyes in exasperation. "It's inside and out, sis. They both count. Plus, I promised Aunt Frances that I was going make sure you looked right when your classes started, and you best believe that's what I'm going to do."

"I know that, and I appreciate you hooking me up today. But the truth is, Mama was more excited when I got accepted to Spelman than I was."

"Now you look like a star," Sheree said, standing back and admiring her handiwork in making me more than presentable.

"It's about time. Now I can get something to eat," I said without bothering to look in the mirror. I could smell the bacon Aunt Betty had cooked for breakfast.

"I can't believe you're going to mess up your lips after I got them perfect," Sheree said, following me into the kitchen.

"Do you want me to go hungry?" I laughed, heading toward the kitchen.

I had moved in with Sheree and Aunt Betty a week ago. Spending so much time alone was starting to wear on me. There was no one to talk to, no one to listen to, no one to see me, and nobody for me to be aware of. Sometimes it made me feel like that tree that falls in the forest: If no one hears it, does it make a sound?

"I thought I was going to have to come in there and drag you both out this morning," Aunt Betty said, sipping on a cup of coffee.

"That was Sheree styling me," I said, sitting down at the table beside her.

"And you needed it," Sheree teased.

"Well you look very nice, Chantelle," Aunt Betty said. "Frances was so proud of you. I wish she could be here to see you go off to school today."

"I wish she was here, too, Aunt Betty," I said wistfully.

Sheree sat down at the table with us, and Aunt Betty bowed her head and blessed the food. When she raised her head, she said, "Anyway, I'm glad you moved in over here with us. I didn't feel good about you staying in that apartment all by yourself. Besides, it didn't make sense to keep paying that rent. Family has to stick together."

I nodded. "I spent half of my time over here anyway. This is home for me, too."

Aunt Betty rested her hand on my arm. "As long as I'm here, you're welcome here. But if you change your mind, you know you can stay on campus with that scholarship you got."

I stared down at my food. "Yeah, I know."

"Aunt Frances riding your back about studying all the time sure paid off," Sheree said, nudging my arm.

I closed my eyes to see her again. "I can still hear her in my head telling me to make good grades, go to college, and get myself a good desk job in a tall building downtown with central heating and air."

"Yes, yes, yes," Aunt Betty said, nodding. "I can hear her saying that, too."

For the first time, I was determined to follow her words to the letter without question.

***

I was definitely in my element at Spelman. I majored in mathematics and minored in accounting to give myself more options. I had always liked numbers. They are practical, logical, and unchanging. It doesn't matter whether you add, subtract, multiply, or divide them; in the end, the answer is right or wrong, no blurred lines. I got a sense of security from that absoluteness. It was that undeniable certainty that I wished was as easy to calculate in the rest of my life.

I worked hard and aced most of my classes. I felt as if I owed that to my mama. Some nights when I was studying, I could almost feel her presence looking over my soldier. There were times when it was so strong that I would glance over my shoulder and expect to see her. Once, I thought I saw her out of the corner of my eye. All the same, being on the dean's list every semester gave me the affirmations that I used to get from Mama: that I was special, smart, and unique. It was a confidence builder. I discovered I could shine brightly, even without anybody seeing me. I didn't need public accolades. I was the satisfied poker player holding a royal flush, knowing that I had this game won.

I wasn't antisocial during my time in college. I'm not a loner. I like the company of people. I still hung out a lot with Sheree, Lena, and Doreen whenever I could. There was also a nerdy clique that I hung out with to go out to eat or to catch a movie. In spite of my being undistinguished on campus, I somehow formed several quality friendships. Oddly enough, my closest friends have been gregarious and flamboyant like Sheree. It's not that I'm drawn to them like a moth to a flame; rather, I'm the gravity that draws them. The pull is my ability to serve as the harmonic background to their spirited melody or as the subtle shading that allows them to be the focal point of a vibrant painting.

That's how it was in the spring semester of my sophomore year during Freaknik. The news reported that more than 100,000 young black people had come to shut down the city. The party was going to be in full effect. Sheree wanted to be front and center at Piedmont Park. It was all about being seen. The traffic was already out of control when I picked her up at Nicklewood Arms. Lena and Doreen were there, too, waiting for me. So, there we were, heading down Peachtree Street in my mama's white mustang. They all looked fly, and it felt like the old days when we were headed to a nightclub with fake ID's.

"The number of cars on the street is crazy!" I said to Sheree. "I don't think we'll even be able to make it to the park." There were cars with license plates from all up and down the East Coast. Young black men and women from HBCU's, among other places, had come to Atlanta in full force. They were riding high in convertibles with the tops down, through the openings of sunroofs, on the hoods of their cars, and in trunks and hatchbacks.

"The ATL is the only place to be this week!" Sheree said happily, rolling down all the windows, even though it was damn near 90 degrees.

"The brothers are out," Lena said, checking out a jeep full of black guys hanging from every window, yelling at the ladies.

Doreen saw a car with the top down and three women gyrating in the backseat, pulling up their tank tops, and flashing their breasts.

"These negroes are wild as they want to be!" she said, pointing in their direction.

I looked over the top of my sunglasses in amazement. "They have no shame."

"That's what time it is!" Sheree said, laughing. "Get as far away from your hometown and anyone who knows you, and act a complete fool. Let loose for a minute. Then go back home, and praise Jesus."

"You are out of your mind," I told Sheree, shaking my head.

She laughed again. "I'm not the one out here showing my pocketbook and everything in it."

Then the traffic came to a standstill, and a party broke out around us. There was heavy bass rocking the Mustang from every direction. Boom boxes and car stereos were at the maximum volume. I stayed behind the wheel while Sheree, Lena, and Doreen got out. It was an impromptu booty-shaking contest. The guys in the jeep next to us hollered as if they were at an intense ballgame and their team was winning. Some were even bold enough to smack a few behinds in their enthusiasm. The heat of the moment in Hotlanta had taken them all by storm.

That was my first and last Freaknik. It had gotten out of control. Abandoning all inhibitions has its risks. Things got violent, and more than a few women were victims of sexual assaults and rapes. After that, I spent my spring breaks on campus studying, so Sheree couldn't talk me into going. During my senior year, I did break down and let Sheree borrow the Mustang so she and her crew could go. They brought it back detailed to the tee, but if that car could talk, I'm sure it had a story to tell.

***

My plan stayed on course. Four years after I started at Spelman, I graduated with Mama's words still in my head: "Get yourself a job in one of them big office buildings downtown." I had my eye on the tallest building in Midtown, the Bank of America Plaza, as my ultimate goal. I had already spent a total of 18 months there as an intern and knew that was where I wanted to be.

It was the morning of my job interview. Sheree and I were sitting in the parking lot of Bloomingdales.

"You look fly," Sheree said, giving me a onceover before she went in to work. "That job is yours."

I gazed at my reflection in the rearview mirror. "I don't think they'll be hiring me for my looks," I said, blotting the thick coat of lipstick with a tissue.

"You'd be surprised how much your appearance matters in the business world, Chantelle. The better the impression you make, the faster you move up that corporate ladder and the less work you'll have to do."

I tilted my head and gave her a side eye. "They already know what I have to offer."

"I'm sure they do, but it doesn't hurt to use everything you've got to get what you want."

"I don't want to play games. I'm a professional," I said with attitude. "I just want to get the job and get paid for all the work they had me doing for the past three summers at a discount."

"I heard that," Sheree said, raising her hand to give me a high five before she reached for her purse to get out of the car. "You better get a move on; you don't have time to be late."

My heart fluttered hearing her say the words Mama told me every morning. I took a few deep breaths before I sped out of the mall parking lot and jumped on I-85 toward downtown. I merged in with all the cars and their passengers with determined faces, staring ahead as they raced to their destinations.

Thirty minutes later, I got off at my exit, drove two blocks, turned into the parking garage, and parked in a visitor's space. I rode the elevator up to the fourteenth floor. I had come here so many times as an intern, dreaming and planning for this very day. It wasn't nervousness that I felt; it was the uncertainty that comes just before the dice are thrown in a board game. Things could go to my advantage, or I could be setback to square one.

I passed Joanne Newberry's office on the way to my interview, and she gave me a thumbs-up. I nodded with a confident look that I didn't feel inside. Joanne had been my mentor for all the summers I had spent there as an intern. She was white and twenty years older than me, but we had a good rapport. She reminded me of the principal at my middle school: forceful but exuding warmth like the sun. Even though our backgrounds were completely different, she told me that she could see herself in me. Then I passed the vacant office next to hers, the one reserved for her permanent assistant, the position I wanted to fill. I had all the qualifications and a track record to show management, but there wasn't another black person in the department. I would be the first.

There were two other team leaders I was scheduled to speak with before my interview with Alex Levine, the senior director of the division. I had met both men a few times while I was an intern, and those interviews were typical. Neither of them made eye contact. They each commented on my admirable transcript, referred to my experience as an intern, and asked me about long-term goals. Both spent a half hour telling me about their career paths and achievements. There was an hour break between the time I was to meet with Alex Levine. Instead of eating, I went out to get some air.

It didn't occur to me where I was while I was walking until I found myself in front of Gladys Knight's Chicken and Waffles restaurant. I hadn't been there since graduation with Mama, Sheree, and Aunt Betty. I hesitated for a minute; then I walked in and stood in line for a table. I didn't want to sit down. I just wanted to look at the booth where we had sat that night, to remember that perfect moment in our lives. Still in line, I glanced at my watch to check the time, and when I looked up, I saw the back of a woman headed to the restroom. Her hairstyle, her frame, and the way she moved was exactly like Mama. I rushed through the restaurant to follow her, but when I opened the door to the restroom, there was no one in there. Flustered, I hurried back to the plaza for my interview.

***

"Come in, Ms. Parker," Mr. Levine said without looking up after his administrative assistant ushered me into his office. "Please sit down." Unlike the other two interviewers, he didn't stand up or make any effort to shake my hand. He looked like an older version of Richard Gere with glasses. I watched as his eyes scanned the pages of my CV in the open file lying on his desk. "You definitely look impressive on paper," he muttered, turning the pages. "That's in addition to the recommendation I've received from Ms. Newberry."

"Thank you, sir."

"Being that you have worked here as an intern for three summers, I'm sure you are familiar with the company. My associates have assured me that you are capable and conscientious and would be a valuable asset on our team. Is that right, Ms. Parker?"

"Yes, that's correct, sir."

"Then I have no objections to your becoming a new member in our division. I haven't heard any complaints here at the office, but my wife tells me I'm not the easiest man to work under," he said with a chuckle. "However, you'll find that hard work is rewarded here Take a few days to mull the offer if you like. Human Resources will be in touch."

"Thank you, sir," I said again. After a long pause, unsure if I should attempt to make more conversation, I stood up and walked slowly toward the door. I paused as I turned the knob, glancing over my shoulder, but he never looked up. It felt surreal.

Joanne was on the phone when I passed by her office. I gave her a thumbs-up, indicating that things had gone well. I hid my smile as I pushed open the heavy glass door on my way out and contained myself on the elevator. When I reached my car in the parking garage, I relaxed my lips, let a smile spread across my face, and then let my mouth hang open. After three separate interviews in one day, I had gotten the job offer to be an actuarial analyst at Supreme Life Insurance. I was elated and encouraged that my five-year plan was not only on track, but ahead of schedule. I had accomplished my second goal of landing my dream job; my first was graduating from Spelman College.

A week later, I was sitting in my office-with-a-view on my first official day. I thought about what Mama had told me about getting a job in a tall building downtown with my own air-conditioned office. My eyes watered with the memory. I was where she wanted me to be, except she wasn't where I needed her to be. Then I saw something glide across the window. I thought it might be a window washer. I walked over to the window, but there wasn't anyone there. No hanging ropes or scaffolding. I wiped my wet eyes; they were playing tricks on me again.

Chapter
Three

A year later, I had money in the bank, credit cards, and a wardrobe that Sheree approved of. If everything at work stayed on track, I would be moving up to actuarial associate. I was officially an adult, and I refused to continue living my life in obscurity. I wanted the whole world to know that I was available for dating, marriage, and promotions and that I was bringing a plateful of talents to the table. On May 24, the evening of my twenty-fifth birthday, I made up my mind to go out on the town alone and reintroduce myself to the city. It was a Thursday, ladies' night, and I didn't want to be blocked out or shaded by Sheree or any of my friends. It was my own personal debut.

The temperature was seasonably warm that night. I strolled into the Cosmopolitan Club to the tune of Aaliyah's "Back and Forth," feeling confident and looking cute in an electric blue dress and metallic gray strappy heels. My hair was flat-ironed straight, with a part on the right side, and my makeup was on point. I took a panoramic view of the room and saw that most of the tables had at least two people sitting at them.

Although I was committed to being totally unreserved, I wasn't going to intrude on perfect strangers. I weaved my way through the small clusters to get to the bar. I would certainly need a drink to loosen up and blend in with the revelry of the club. When the bartender made his way over to me, I ordered an apple martini. Hopefully, it would provide me with an extra shot of courage and charisma to usher in the new me.

The DJ had been laid back, but he was obviously ready to get the party started when he played "Hip Hop Hooray" by Naughty by Nature. He changed the vibe throughout the room with that cut, commanding everybody in the place to get on their feet. The whole club answered his call as they swirled onto the small dance floor like a horde of bumblebees buzzing around a honeycomb.

I stood at the bar, bouncing from my ankles up to my shoulders. I wanted to join the migration, but I needed an invitation. No one asked me. Why couldn't they see me over here flossing in my best dress? I sighed, ordered another martini, and rocked and grooved along the edge of the bar. The music was loud, and the mass of people in the center moved in unison, jumping up and down with joy in attempts to obey the DJ's urging to reach the roof.

I closed my eyes for a moment as I imagined how I would have taken center stage of that 12-foot by 12-foot square they called a dance floor. Then I had the unfamiliar sensation of being watched, and I opened my eyes. That's when I saw him. He was seated at one of the tables with two other guys. He winked at me and smiled. I graciously returned the smile without parting my lips before I turned back toward the bar.

I felt embarrassed. I wondered how long he had been watching me. I could still feel his gaze deep on my back like two hands caressing me. Suddenly, I felt naked and told my body to stop moving to the beat under my feet. Then the DJ blended in his next record, refusing to let the crowd retreat to their seats. It was my jam, "Whoomp, There It Is" by Tag Team. I forced myself not to react. That's when I felt a hand grab mine and pull me around. It was him, leading me out on the dance floor.

My first instinct was to play demure and pull away, but this might have been my last chance to grace the dance floor. Besides, he looked good in the dim light, and he smelled like he had just gotten out of a hot shower. When we got through to the middle of the mass of gyrating bodies, he turned around, and we made eye contact. He let go of my hand and started to groove to the beat. I liked the way he moved; it was smooth, sexy, and inviting. I turned my back to him and started to shake my hips and my shoulders. This moment wasn't about him; it was about me getting a chance to shine in the purple and white lights that flashed across the room like shooting stars.

When the song was over, I was flushed from doing my thing, along with the alcohol running through my veins. I turned to walk back to the bar. I didn't know he had followed me until I felt the heat of his body behind me.

"Can I buy you a drink?" he asked, smiling like he was Billy Dee Williams and I was Diana Ross.

"Thank you," I answered, being sociable.

"You know you're the prettiest lady in here," he said, staring into my eyes as he motioned for the bartender.

"Is that right?" I said, breaking his gaze and looking around.

"Absolutely. The rest of them fade in your shadow."

I chuckled at his line. "I don't know if I have much to do with that. It's dark in here."

The bartender interrupted before he could respond. "What can I get for you?"

"What are you drinking?" he asked, tilting his head to the side.

"Apple martini," I said to the bartender.

He nodded approvingly. "Sweet for the sweet."

I shrugged my shoulders and looked away. Now was the time for me to decide if I was interested or to look for the nearest exit. Out of the corner of my eye, I could see that he was handsome enough, but I needed to know if he had anything else going on. I still hadn't heard of the city where you can take good looks to the bank. *What the hell*, I thought, making up my mind. I came in here being bold, so why should I stop now. The bartender set the drink down in front of me, and the man handed him a ten-dollar bill.

"I usually don't accept drinks from strangers," I said, picking up the glass.

"My name is Teddy, Teddy Griffin," he said, smiling.

"I'm Chantelle," I said before I took a sip.

"It's a pleasure to meet you, Chantelle. Now we're not strangers anymore."

I chuckled. "You told me your name, but I still don't know anything about you."

He kept smiling. "We've got all night to get to know each other."

I threw my head back and laughed. He joined me, laughing too. Then he took the drink out of my hand and put it back down on the bar.

"At least I can get you back out on the floor," he said, taking my hand.

I got my groove on for three more songs as he watched my every move. I was thrilled by watching him watching me. Then the DJ played a slow tune. He pulled me close before I had time to turn away. I could feel his perspiration mixing with mine. We were in the middle of a crowded dance floor, but it felt as if we were alone, just us. This man had seen me and had touched me. It was intimacy. It was the gift I had wanted to receive when I walked into the club that night.

Now it was time to make my exit. I felt like Cinderella at the strike of midnight. It was time for me to go back to my life.

"I've got go," I whispered near his ear.

"I'll go with you," he said, the last word sounding like a question.

"Come on. You know better," I said kindly but firmly.

"You've got me all wrong, Chantelle. I just want to spend some time with you. I'll take you wherever you want to go."

"That's nice, but I can't. I've got an important meeting at work in the morning. If everything goes according to plan, I can take a step up the ladder."

He nodded in approval. "I heard that. Why don't you give me your number, and we can celebrate your new promotion?"

"What if I don't get it?"

"You will."

"How do you know?"

He smiled at me again. "I'd give it to you."

"Thanks for the vote of confidence," I said, smirking.

"No thanks needed, just your phone number," he said, handing me a pen.

I wrote my number on a napkin from the bar, gave it to him, and walked out of the club, hiding the wide smile I felt behind closed lips and gritted teeth. That evening had given me a new sense of confidence and self-worth. I was alive, moving and breathing, not a two-dimensional piece of décor in the background of someone else's life. Perhaps I was special after all.

***

The shadow of branches from the tall oak tree outside my window danced across the wall beside my bed. I was watching the abstract show and wondering if I wanted to get up or not. I needed my mama to holler out to me and get me moving, but that wasn't going to happen.

It was early, around 6:00 AM, but the sun was already high in the sky. This day would determine if I had a future at Supreme Life or if I was back in the job market. I was the best they had in the department, and after last night, I wasn't about to be passed over. I had just turned over on my side to snuggle in for another ten minutes of sleep when a mosquito buzzed by my ear. I threw off the sheet and rushed into the bathroom for my shower before he could draw blood.

I dressed quickly and quietly, not wanting to wake up Sheree and Aunt Betty. I didn't want any breakfast or conversation that might make me any more anxious than I already was. I held the bolt tightly on the door as I unlocked it on my way out and eased it shut. I took a deep breath once I had made it to the car.

I beat the morning rush on the interstate and got downtown in record time. I even got to have the ride on the elevator all to myself. Inside my office, I closed the door and sat down to make a list of why I deserved to be an associate. I was on reason number four—the databases and statistical models I had created—when Joanne knocked on the window and motioned to the clock, letting me know it was time for the meeting.

I walked in step beside her outside the long hallway. We passed row after row of coworkers huddled in their cubicles. We finally arrived at the office of our senior director, Alex Levine, at the end of the hall. Out of the nearly three years I had been working for the company, I had only met with him once, and that was during my initial interview. His administrative assistant smiled politely when we arrived.

"He's expecting you. Go on in," she said, opening the door to his conference room.

"Come on in, Ms. Parker," he said, grabbing my hand tightly in both of his before he pointed to the chair on his right. That enthusiastic welcome caught me by surprise. I sat down, and Joanne sat next to me. "First, I want to tell you how pleased we are to have you here at Supreme. Ms. Newberry has proposed that we elevate you to the associate level." He paused and looked at me for a response.

"Yes, sir," I said with my list clasped in my hands under the table. "It was my goal to continue working here after I graduated from college, and I have enjoyed being part of the success of this company."

"Chantelle has excelled here as an employee over the last year, and I expect even greater things from her in the future," Joanne added.

Mr. Levine nodded and lifted his cup of coffee. "It has been our policy that our analysts have three to five years' experience before they move up to the associate level."

Joanne interjected as he drank his coffee. "I understand that, sir, but Chantelle is an exceptional asset to the department. She was a key contributor on several important projects as an intern for three consecutive summers and has consistently been invaluable as a leader demonstrating efficiency and creativity."

"I am aware of Ms. Parker's contributions," Mr. Levine said firmly. "The competition for premiere persons in this business is fierce. Considering her limited experience and what she has been able to accomplish in such a short span, I concur with you, Ms. Newberry. Congratulations, Ms. Parker, your position will be changed to actuarial associate, and your salary will be adjusted accordingly."

"Thank you, sir," I said, rising to me feet and shaking his hand. "You won't be disappointed."

"I'm sure I won't be," he said, standing up.

Joanne gave me a quick hug. "I'll stop by your office in a few minutes."

I walked out of the conference room completely dignified, resisting all urges to jump up and down to celebrate. The windows of my office kept me and my excitement contained. I picked up the phone to call Sheree and then put it down. I wanted to tell her and Aunt Betty in person. I sat down and tried to work on some figures, but I couldn't concentrate.

"Congratulations!" Joanne said, walking in the door, smiling.

"Thank you so much for stepping up for me."

"You deserve it, Chantelle. You make me look good, so I've got to take care of you."

"I appreciate that so much," I said, standing up.

"It will be more responsibility for you, and I know you can handle it. The best part is your salary increase. How does $60,000 sound?"

My heart jumped. "Like sweet music! I can't believe it!"

"At this level, you can see there aren't too many women around. We need to help each other if we intend to crack that glass ceiling.

"You can count on me," I said, sincerely.

"Well, meet me out front in an hour."

Joanne took me out on a two-hour lunch to celebrate. When we got back to the office, I still couldn't get much work done. My emotions were on high. I kept thinking about how happy and proud Mama would have been. She could have finally quit her job. I would have been able to take care of both of us. When Joanne suggested I leave early, I didn't need her to tell me twice.

All the way home, I could neither pull in nor contain my smile as I drove along Peachtree Boulevard. I sped through a yellow light, and then something made me slam on my brakes. It was my mama standing at the bus stop.

I was overwhelmed. A car was riding close on my bumper, so I made a right at the corner to circle the block. When I got back around to the bus stop, there was a bus there, and the waiting passengers were already aboard. When the bus started rolling, I followed it. As it accelerated, I drove faster along the side, trying my best to look into the windows. I couldn't see her among the riders. She wasn't there. My eyes were playing tricks on me again. I pressed down on the gas pedal and let the horses of the engine gallop forward, taking me home. I wasn't going down that other road.

***

"You don't have to say a word!" Aunt Betty exclaimed, looking up from the catfish she was frying when I walked into the kitchen. "It's all over your face. You got that job, baby! I'm so proud of you! I know Frances is up there in heaven shouting right now."

"I wish she was here," I said earnestly, thinking about the woman at the bus stop. "Where's Sheree? I can't wait to tell her."

"She's still at work. She'll be getting off soon," Aunt Betty said, wiping her hands on a towel and giving me a hug.

The affection in her embrace only made me miss my mama's touch even more. But I didn't want my thoughts to linger in that place. I was determined to concentrate on my good news.

"I'm going to drive over to the mall and pick Sheree up," I said, too excited to sit still. "Do you need anything?"

"No, I can't think of anything. Oh, yeah, I almost forgot. There's a message on the answering machine for you," she said suspiciously.

"Thanks," I said, praying that it wasn't anybody from Supreme Insurance saying my promotion was a mistake.

With clenched fists, I walked into the living room and tentatively pushed the message button and waited. I relaxed as I recognized his voice.

"Hey, Chantelle, its Teddy. Call me back. I want to take you out and celebrate. My number is 919-7518."

I sat down on the sofa and dialed the number.

"Hello," he answered.

"Hi, it's Chantelle. I got your message, and I did get the promotion."

"I'm not surprised."

"Yeah, right, I wasn't sure about it myself."

He laughed. "So, where do you want to go tonight?"

"I don't know. I need a minute to think about it."

"No need. All I want you to do is put on another one of those dresses you had on last night," he said smoothly. "I know where I want to take you."

"Is that right?" I asked, chuckling at his self-confidence. "Okay, how will I know where to meet you?"

"I'm picking you up," he said, matter-of-factly. "What's your address?"

"I live in Nicklewood Arms."

"I know where it is. What's your apartment number?"

"I live in Building H, Number 11."

"I'll be there around 7:30. Is that okay?"

"Yeah, I'll be ready."

"Then I'll see you in a few hours," he said, hanging up the phone.

I couldn't believe it; I was smiling again. Maybe it was my birthday gifts from God, but I was definitely on a winning streak. I changed out of my suit into jeans and a t-shirt before I waved at Aunt Betty, who was eating fish and watching *The Oprah Show*.

The weekend traffic on the interstate was already jammed and creeping along one car length at a time, but it didn't bother me one bit. I popped in my new Erykah Badu CD to hear "4 Leaf Clover," turned up the volume and the A/C, and enjoyed the ride.

At the mall, I parked outside Bloomingdales near the women's clothing section where Sheree worked. The smell of high-end perfumes and colognes hit me as soon as I stepped through the second set of glass doors. I perused the contemporary style section, taking note of the well-dressed manikins and the outfits they displayed, looking for an idea of what I was going to wear for my date later on in the evening. Then spotted Sheree finishing a sale with an older white lady sporting so many diamonds and jewelry that I wouldn't be surprised in the least if she was carrying a million dollars or more in her Louis Vuitton monogrammed handbag.

"Start a dressing room for me, girl," I said, sneaking up on Sheree after the woman walked away with her packages.

"You got it?" she asked, wide-eyed and excited with her hand in the air.

"Oh, yeah!" I said, slapping her a high-five three times.

She started to dance. "Give me 20 minutes, and we are gonna hit it hard tonight. Hell, yeah!" she cheered. "Your birthday and a new job!"

"Tomorrow," I said hesitantly, not wanting to be a killjoy. "I've got plans for tonight."

"Oh, really? Are you keeping secrets now?" she said, sounding somewhat indignant.

"I met this guy last night."

"So that's what happens when you sneak off by yourself," she said with folded arms. "Do tell me all about it."

"Not much to tell, at least not yet. His name is Teddy, and he's going to take me to dinner."

"Oh, there's a lot to tell, girlfriend. Don't even try it. How does he look, where does he work, and what does he drive?"

"He looks all right, and that's all I know about him," I answered, feeling like I had come to school without my homework.

"I should go with you to check him out for myself," she said, seriously considering it.

I put my hand on my hip for emphasis. "Have you forgotten I'm grown?"

"Excuse me," she giggled, looking down at me. "At least let me do your makeup."

"As long as you don't go crazy."

"I got this, sis," she said waving her hand at me. "Go on and pull the car around while I clock out. These heels are killing me.

"I thought you said the price of beauty is never too high," I said, walking away.

"It's outrageous as hell, but I'm gonna keep paying it," she said, locking up her register and twisting away.

I shook my head in amusement as I made my way out of the store.

***

Sheree backed up to check out her work. "Chantelle, you are fine as hell tonight. Your hair is banging, and I have beat your face to death."

I got up and faced my reflection in the mirror. It was only vaguely familiar because of the coral-colored off the shoulder dress I was wearing. "You've got me looking like you."

"That's right. Like I said, you are fine as hell tonight."

"Maybe this dress is too much for a first date."

"For you, maybe, but it's cool. And since you won't let me go out with you, I want you to take my cell phone," she said, stuffing it in the narrow clutch. "We don't know this guy. You might need to call the law or me. And if this brother steps out of line, then that's his ass."

I had to laugh. Sheree always had my back, my front, and my sides. At that moment, I wanted to hug her and thank her, but she didn't go for sentimental mushiness. I understood it. Raised by single women, we all had to be strong without a man around to fight our battles.

"Your new friend is here!" Aunt Betty shouted from the living room.

I took another quick look at the woman in the mirror. I had to admit she was fine as hell.

"I look too good, Sheree," I said, feeling subconscious. "I don't know if I even want to impress this guy like that."

"First off, there's no such thing as looking too good. Second, you're not going to get married; you're only going to dinner. So, stop tripping. You think too much for me."

I couldn't help but laugh again. "You're right. I'm tripping." I grabbed the clutch Sheree insisted I carry, which matched the shoes she lent me.

"Now let's go and see what kind of mess you have dragged up in here," Sheree snickered, leading the way out of the bedroom.

Three steps behind her, I walked into the awkward triangle between Teddy, Aunt Betty, and Sheree.

"You look spectacular," Teddy said, his eyes only on me.

"Thank you," I replied, checking out his linen suit. "This is my Aunt Betty and my cousin, Sheree."

He reached out his hand to Aunt Betty first. "It's very nice to meet you, ma'am." Then he turned to Sheree. "It's a pleasure to meet you, too."

"Where are you from?" Aunt Betty asked abruptly, detecting an accent.

"I'm from Baltimore; I came down here to go to school."

"Where's that? Sheree asked.

"I'm a Morehouse man," he said proudly. "I graduated four years ago."

Aunt Betty nodded with approval. "What made you decide to stay in town? You're a long way from home."

"Yes, ma'am. I went into business with a few of my frat brothers flipping houses. The real estate market here is real hot right now."

"Uh-huh," Sheree said, giving him a onceover. "So, where are you taking Chantelle out this evening?"

Teddy turned back to look at me. "Dinner at Stoney River and anywhere else she would like to go."

"That's sounds nice," Aunt Betty added in a no-nonsense tone. "You seem like a gentleman, so I know I don't have to tell you to how to treat a lady."

"No, ma'am," Teddy said, taking my hand. "You don't have to worry. Nothing but respect. She's in good hands, trust me."

"She better be," Sheree said, cutting her eyes at him.

"I'll be fine," I said with a smile toward Aunt Betty and then Sheree as we walked to the door.

When the door was closed behind us, Teddy said, "They're very protective of you."

"Yes, they are," I said, nodding and thinking about how they had been there for me. "We're really close."

Teddy took me by the elbow and guided me to a black BMW. I would have guessed that was what he drove, classy and sporty. He opened the car door for me and closed it after I got in. I checked out the interior as he walked around to the driver's side. The car was spotless.

"You look beautiful," he said, stroking his fingers along my arm once he was in the car beside me. "I'm glad you called me back. I really wanted to see you again."

"I thought I'd take a chance," I said casually. "My mama always told me good things come in threes. Yesterday was my birthday, today I got the promotion I wanted, and so now I'm wondering what the third thing will be."

"I already know what it will be," he said, driving out of the apartment complex.

"Oh, really? How's that?" I asked, chuckling at his cockiness. "Are you psychic?"

"Maybe I am. I knew I wanted to be with you from the moment you walked into the club. I'll do whatever you want me to do. I just want to hold you."

"I'm going to need you to pump the brakes," I said, holding up my hand. "You're moving too fast for me."

"Relax, Chantelle. I'm not talking one night. I'm talking about something that will last. I want to be good to you. I want to make you happy."

I figured it was a line, but I was still slightly taken aback. "You don't even know me. We just met last night."

"I've been out here in these streets for a minute, and there's not much out here. I know what I want in a woman, and that's you."

"Why me?" I asked curiously.

"You've got it going on. You know it."

The truth was I didn't know that, but he was giving me a new perspective on myself.

"We'll see," I said, looking outside of the passenger window. "Right now, let's just have a good time tonight."

I thought he had come on too strong at first, but surprisingly dinner was comfortable and fun. We drank a whole bottle of Merlot with our prime rib steaks. He talked a lot, but he was funny, and I liked his quirky sense of humor. When we left the restaurant, I was enjoying his company.

Once we were in the car, he kept rubbing my arms and then my legs. I hadn't been out with anybody like him. I felt as if it was crossing a line, but the fact that he couldn't keep his hands off me made me feel like the sexiest woman in the world. I knew he was staring at me, but I kept my eyes on the cars that passed by the window, wondering what his expectations might be.

When the car stopped, and we weren't in the Nicklewood apartment complex, I got a little nervous. It was the wine from

dinner that kept me mellowed out. I wanted to say something, but I
didn't have words. I had once fantasized about a night like this, and
I wanted to see how far I could go. He got out of the car, opened
my door, and extended his hand. I didn't think or ask a question. I
swung my legs out, took his hand, and followed him into his house.

Teddy closed and locked the door behind us, still holding my
hand as he led me to the kitchen. He poured a couple of glasses
of wine from the refrigerator, still holding my hand. He gave one
glass to me. I took a sip. He tapped my glass with his and took a
sip. My hand was beginning to sweat inside of his. Gently, I tried
to ease it from his grip.

"Don't pull back," he said intently, pulling me closer to him.

He kissed me too long and too passionately for people who only
met the night before. My conscience began to bother me. I didn't
know how to react. What if my mama was looking down on me
right now? I needed to wait. I wanted to play hard to get and save
myself for the subjective 90 days. I wanted to resist his touches
and his kisses, but my body was so hungry it ignored my better
judgment. It felt so good to be desired, even though it scared me a
little.

When Teddy made love to me, he consumed me. In a way
it made me feel as if he was taking something from me that I
couldn't get back. He held onto me all night and even in the
morning. That's how it was in the beginning.

Chapter
Four

I can't say Teddy swept me off my feet. More accurately, he picked me up and put me in his pocket. We were together every day for the rest of the summer. His house didn't have a lot of furniture in it—no pictures on the walls, no plants decorating the rooms—but it was spacious and spotless. It didn't feel like the home of a single guy. We both worked long hours, and even though he'd given me a key to his place, I was rarely there when he wasn't.

I had done a pretty decent job of dodging Sheree and Aunt Betty, leaving early and coming home late, until we were all at home on Labor Day. I knew I had an earful coming when I heard the bacon sizzling and the radio playing. I got out of bed, brushed my teeth, and headed to the kitchen to face the music.

"Well, it's good to see you this morning," Aunt Betty said, her tone full of sarcasm. "I almost forgot what you look like. You've been flying in and out of here all summer before anybody can say more than two words to you. Then you stay gone for days on end."

"I'm sorry, Aunt Betty," I said, knowing I wasn't right.

"I'm worried about you, child," she said, throwing the dishtowel over her shoulder. "I know how it feels to be young, but you don't have a lot of experience dealing with these men out here. I don't want you to get hurt."

"If she does get hurt, she won't be the only one," Sheree said, coming in the kitchen and dropping down in the chair across from me.

"I'm all right," I said, scraping some scrambled eggs on my plate. "I know you both think I've gotten carried away, and maybe I have. This is a new thing for me. I'm enjoying myself, and I'm happy."

"I just wish you would date some other guys sometimes," Sheree said. "Don't get so serious too fast. Explore for a while. Find out what more there is in the ocean before you settle for the first fish you catch."

"That's right," Aunt Betty added. "This Teddy doesn't need to monopolize all your time."

"I hear you both," I said, staring into my plate.

***

I didn't listen to Sheree or Aunt Betty. I kept spending as much time with Teddy as I could. A month later, on his birthday, I wanted to cook him a romantic dinner. I used my key to let myself into his place to surprise him.

When the food was almost ready, I checked the clock and saw that he would be home soon. The table was set, but it was missing something. It needed something extra to add to the ambience. I was searching for candlesticks when I opened a drawer filled with dirty magazines. Not one or two; there were more than I cared to count. It shocked me at first. Then I thought I might be overreacting. After all, this probably wasn't something unusual for a single man. I closed the drawer, and I took some comfort that most of the females in the magazines were black. I sat down at the table to wait for him to get home.

Suddenly, my plan to prepare a romantic dinner at home now seemed like a bad idea. The upbeat vibe I felt at the grocery store had gotten bogged down by my discovery. The planned celebration could have easily turned into an argument.

Sautéing the shrimp, I changed my mind over and over on how to handle the situation. I wanted to ask about the magazines. Why so many? When did he look at them? I had so many questions. Was I invading his privacy, and was I overreacting?

When I heard Teddy's key in the lock, I decided to hold my tongue and not ruin his birthday celebration.

"That's why I'm so crazy about you," he said, coming into the kitchen and giving me a quick kiss on the lips. "You look good, and you can cook, too."

"Happy birthday," I said, forcing a smile to my face.

"Thank you, baby," he said, taking off his jacket and putting it on the back of his chair. "I figured we were going out, but this is even better." He took a seat, and I fixed two plates and brought them to the table. "I'm ready to eat, too," he said, nodding in approval of the food. "We had a couple of showings, and I didn't have time to stop for lunch."

"I had a crazy day, too," I said, pushing a shrimp around on my plate.

"Did you see the news? They finally found out who set that bomb in Olympic Park."

"No, I didn't. Did they catch him?"

"Not yet, but they're searching for him," he said, his mouth full. He kept eating, relishing the meal, and making conversation about his day until his plate was clean. "Thanks for this dinner," he said, rubbing his tummy. "It was delicious."

Most of mine was still on my plate. Every time I saw him take a bite of food, I thought about him drooling over the pictures of the women in the magazines. That was just enough to keep me slightly nauseated.

I swallowed and said, "You're welcome. I'm glad you enjoyed it."

Then there was a moment of quiet between us. I didn't want to say much more. I was still trying to hold down all the questions that kept rising in my throat. He scooted his chair back from the table and stood beside me.

"You're the best thing that ever happened to me, Chantelle. I love you, and I know we can build a fantastic life together." He reached into his pants pocket and pulled out a small black box, opened it, and took out a diamond ring. "Will you be my wife?"

My heart started to beat fast, and my hands shook. The same heat I felt while cooking the shrimp seemed to engulf me. It was like being on the rollercoaster at Six Flags again as my exhilaration and anticipation mixed with fear.

"We haven't known each other that long," I said, the fear taking over. "That's a big step. Don't you think we should wait to get to know each other better?"

"Why should we? We already know we want to be together. What are we going to wait for?"

I searched my mind for a response. "I haven't even met your family yet."

"You're going to be my family, the most important person to me," he said, taking my hand. "Give me the best gift I could ever get for my birthday. Tell me you'll marry me."

There were only two answers left: yes or no. I didn't want to say no. I didn't want to lose him, even though I wasn't sure if I was in love with him. I was almost sure he was the one for me, except there were a few things that worried me, things that made me want to back up. That was my nature. I was always so careful, analytical, never leaving anything to chance. I figured I had missed out on so many experiences playing it safe. This time I decided to throw caution aside.

My voice trembled. "Yes, yes, I'll marry you."

I was in a daze as he slid the ring on my finger. Then he took my hand to help me stand, and we kissed. My heart continued to beat fast and high in my chest. I wondered if he could feel it through my dress and his shirt. I was as excited as I was scared.

⋇ ⋇ ⋇

Later that night, I lay beside Teddy, with his shoulder as a pillow under my head, thinking that was the way it would always be. He shook me gently, but I wasn't asleep as he pulled his arm out from under me and sat up.

"Look, baby, there are some things about me that might make you change your mind," he said, sounding stressed.

The butterflies in my stomach took flight. I immediately thought about a friend I went to Spelman with who had married a guy she met in jail during a visit there with her church. He'd told her that he was locked up for writing bad checks at his job. It turned out later that he was in for murder.

"Have you killed anybody?" I asked timidly.

He shook his head. "No, no, it's nothing like that."

"Is it criminal?"

"No, I haven't broken any laws."

"Is it financial? Do you owe a lot of money?"

"No, it's nothing like that. It's about my baggage from past relationships."

I tried not to show how leery I felt. "What about them?"

"Sometimes it's complicated for some people to move on. It's not easy to break away."

"What do you mean?" I asked, sitting up. I needed to make sure I heard everything he had to say.

"Ties between two people are hard to let go."

"Is it in the past as far as you are concerned?"

"Yes, for me it is."

"Then as far as we're concerned, we can leave it in the past," I said, wary of what he was saying to me.

"Sometimes you can; sometimes you can't."

"If you're talking about relationships before you met me, I can't hold that against you."

"I don't really want to talk about it right now," he said, sliding back down in the bed. "I just want you to know you're the only woman I want and the only one I want to spend the rest of my life with."

I was still sitting up. "I have a serious question for you."

"Go ahead."

"Is this a situation that, if the shoe were on the other foot, you would still marry me?" I asked, digging to see how deep the issue was.

"Absolutely. As far as I'm concerned, I'm making a commitment to you, for better or worse, come hell or high water."

"Then why don't you just tell me what it is?"

He pulled me down next to him and kissed me softly on the lips. "It's not important right now. This night is all about us."

***

I stumbled into the living room, feeling dead on my feet after work.

"Well, look what the cat dragged in," Aunt Betty said, cutting her eyes at me.

I blushed, embarrassed about spending so many nights at Teddy's house. I knew the words that were spinning around in her head, even though she didn't allow them to fly out of her mouth. She didn't have to. I had heard them so many times growing up, "You wasn't raised like that." That's why I was so relieved to give her the news.

"Hi, Aunt Betty," I said, sitting on the arm of the sofa to give her a hug. "How are you doing?"

"I'm doing fine," she said sarcastically. "What about you?"

Sheree walked in the room before I could answer. "What's up, girl? I see you still riding 'Love's Train.' "

"Stop it. I know I have been scarce lately, and I'm sorry if I've been disrespectful, Aunt Betty. But I want you both to be happy for me."

"I'm happy for you, sis," Sheree said. "If you like it, I love it."

Aunt Betty chimed in. "It's just you went so fast into this thing, and we don't even know this boy. Like I said before, you don't have that much experience dealing with these men, and that bothers me. Why don't you slow it down for a minute?"

I eased down on the sofa next to Aunt Betty, my knees touching hers. "I can't do that, not now. He asked me to marry him, and I said yes."

"Lord, have mercy!" Aunt Betty said, looking up at the ceiling. I couldn't tell if she was pleased or disappointed.

I turned toward Sheree, who was leaning against the frame of the doorway shaking her head. I exhaled, and my shoulders rounded as the air went out of my chest.

"Go on, sis, do your thing," Sheree said, breaking the silence and coming over to give me a hug. "You know I got your back. If y'all love each other, it's all good."

"You know I support you," Aunt Betty said. "I just don't know why you have to marry the first man who turned your head. I wish you would give yourself some time."

"She will, Mama. They're not getting married tomorrow," Sheree said, trying to calm things down. "They just got engaged."

"We don't see a reason for us to wait," I said cautiously. "We want to have a December wedding. I was thinking about Christmas Eve."

"Chantelle, are you pregnant?" Aunt Betty shouted angrily.

"No, ma'am. I'm just in love," I assured her.

"How do you know?" Aunt Betty demanded. "You ain't been in love before."

"I don't know. I just know I want to be with him."

"Go on. You're grown. I can't stop you," Aunt Betty yelled, getting up from the sofa and leaving the room in a huff. I started to follow her. I needed her to understand how I felt.

"Don't listen to Mama. She'll be all right," Sheree said, grabbing my elbow. "We've got things to do to get you ready by Christmas."

"There's one thing I wanted to talk to you about first," I said, lowering my voice.

"What is it?" Sheree asked quietly, concern on her face.

"Yesterday, while I was cooking dinner for Teddy, I found a drawer full of magazines. They were all of naked women, a lot of them. It made me kind of uncomfortable."

"Wow, sis, I don't know what to say. Men like to look at those things. After you're married, he won't need to look at them." She pushed me on the shoulder and laughed. "At least you don't have to worry about him being on the down-low."

"I guess it's not a big deal. You're right," I said, forcing a smile.

***

Sheree was my maid of honor, and she was the best that anybody could have had. She found my venue, found my dress, and planned the reception. For my bachelorette party, she hired two strippers, and I got drunk for the first time in my life.

The odd thing was that Teddy and I were spending less time together. He seemed to be preoccupied with his business and was on edge most of the time when we did get together. I was covering most of the expenses, so I wasn't sure what was bothering him.

Several times, I asked him if he had changed his mind or wanted to postpone the wedding. He always insisted that wasn't the case.

Aside from that, there were several nights when I stayed at his house and the phone would ring in the middle of the night. I knew they weren't business calls. He'd answer quickly and go outside of the bedroom to talk.

"Is that your past coming back to haunt us?" I asked once, after he came back to bed.

"Yeah, it is, but it's nothing that you need to worry about. I'll handle it."

I closed my eyes, but I wasn't asleep. I kept thinking about the calls. I had seen the area code and checked the city. I knew it was another woman and that she lived in Baltimore. With her living out of state, I didn't feel that she was a threat to me. I only wondered what she hoped to gain. It was obvious that he wasn't moving back there.

Despite all the concerns, we were married on Christmas Eve. The wedding turned out to be more than I had ever dared to dream about. Neighbors, church members, friends from college, Joanne, Mr. Levine, and several of my coworkers from the company all came to the wedding. The strange thing was Teddy's guests only included a few of his frat brothers and their dates but no family.

Teddy and I spent the night at the St. Regis Hotel, and Aunt Betty cooked a fabulous Christmas dinner for us before we boarded a plane for a honeymoon in Cancun. I was torn in two directions when the plane took off. I wouldn't be coming back to Building H, Apartment 11, at Nicklewood Arms. That complex was the only home I had ever known. Now I had taken off full-speed ahead into a new life with a man I had met just a little more than six months ago. It was as thrilling as it was scary. All the pieces of my life were coming together.

***

The honeymoon was breathtaking. I had never been out of Georgia, much less the country. The attention from Teddy made me feel like the most beautiful woman in the world. I was totally fascinated by his attraction to me. I felt fortunate. Out of all the men in the world, I had found my soulmate.

But for some reason, I got the blues on our last night in Mexico. I was brushing my teeth, and I saw something gold go down the drain. I turned off the water and looked closer. There was nothing in sight. My rings were still on my fingers. I touched my ears; I hadn't lost an earring. I couldn't figure out what it could have been, and now it was gone. I considered calling the front desk about a plumber, but what would I tell them to look for? I shook it off. It was probably my eyes playing tricks on me and the anxiety I was having about being a full-time wife.

On the flight back to Atlanta, we had been in the air for about an hour when it suddenly occurred to me that we hadn't talk about our expectations, finances, or where we would live after we got back. Then one of the flight attendants said, "Keep your seatbelts on, ladies and gentlemen. We'll be passing through a storm, and there may be a bit of turbulence." The rain started a few minutes later. The speed of the plane made it look like thin random wet lines. I stared out the window, wondering where the next raindrop would fall.

Chapter
Five

I've heard the expression about the honeymoon being over when real life creeps back into the fantasy of a perfect romance. However, saying that our return to Atlanta was a shock back to reality is an understatement. It had barely been a week of heaven before I was transported to another realm throughout a month of revelations. It all began with an emergency call from Teddy in the middle of an end-of-month conference meeting at work. I rushed back to my office to speak in private.

"What's happened?" I asked him, begging the Lord that nothing was wrong with Aunt Betty.

"I can't talk about it on the phone," he answered stoically.

"Has there been an accident?" I asked, praying that there hadn't been.

"No, stop panicking. Nobody died."

Relief dripped down in a stream of sweat from under my arm. "I'll be there in an hour," I said, hanging up the phone. I reached for my purse and grabbed my coat from the hanger, slipping on one sleeve as I hurried out of my office.

Joanne was standing just outside the door. I'd left it open while I was on the phone.

"Is everything all right?" she asked, concern in her voice.

I kept moving past her. I didn't have time to talk. "I think so. I'll let you know tomorrow."

I ran down the hallway to the elevator and kept punching the down button over and over again, as if that would make it come faster. I stepped back and took another breath, telling myself to relax. Teddy had assured that me no one had died. If anything was wrong with Aunt Betty, Sheree would have called me by now.

I shifted my weight, and then the elevator finally opened. Just as the doors were closing, I thought I saw a woman there wanting to get on. I pushed the button to open the doors, but there was no one there. It made me nervous. Whenever that happened, it made me feel that my mama was trying to speak to me.

A steady downpour started as soon as I got in the car, but that wasn't going to slow me down. I sped through the traffic the best I could, crossing in and out of the high-occupancy lane. I had barely shifted the gears into park in the driveway before I jumped out of the car. I didn't bother to grab my purse or my umbrella to protect my hair from the rain.

I burst in the front door to face the disaster head-on, but the house was quiet. I darted past the living room and into the kitchen, looking for Teddy. I found him in the kitchen sitting calmly at the table. On either side of him were two little boys dressed in matching jogging suits, looking at me with big, frightened eyes. One of them had a runny nose.

"What's going on?" I asked, totally confused.

"These are my sons," he said matter-of-factly and then nodded toward them, "This is Julius, and this is Jeremy."

I looked at the two boys in disbelief. I felt as if I was about to collapse. Somehow my legs moved forward, and I leaned against the back of the empty chair at the table.

"What are you talking about?" I asked, not comprehending.

"These are my kids," he replied boldly, as if I should have known.

On the verge of hyperventilating, I could only whisper, "This is crazy! You never told me you had children."

"So many times I wanted to, Chantelle, but it never seemed like the perfect time. I wasn't sure how you'd react, and I didn't want to risk what we had."

"Teddy, I can't believe this! You should have told me. I had a right to know."

"You're the one who said that my past didn't matter to you."

"This isn't your past! This is right here and now!" I yelled.

One of the boys began to whimper, and it seemed to set off an alarm for his brother as he joined in and began to cry at full volume. Teddy got up from his chair and picked up the one who was crying the loudest and held him to his chest, while he patted the other one on his back. I still couldn't believe what was happening as I stared at them.

"Look, I'm sorry," he said sounding frustrated. "I should have told you about them, but I didn't."

"Just stop!" I said, raising my hands in the air. "Why today? Why like this? I don't understand."

"Jaycina, their mama, came by about an hour ago and left them here. I didn't have any idea she was coming."

I frowned in confusion. None of this made sense. All I could do was shake my head.

"Why did she leave them? When will she be back?" I asked, perplexed.

"I don't know; it might be a while," he said. "She brought their things."

I followed his eyes to the pile on the floor in front of the dishwasher. There were two backpacks, one Lion King and one Toy Story, both overstuffed to where they couldn't be zipped. Mentally, I couldn't process the scene. I needed to get out of there so I could think.

"I can't deal with this right now. I have to go," I said, turning on my heels.

Grateful that my keys were still in my hand, I stormed out the same way I came in and jumped back into my car. By the time I got on I-85, my eyes were so full of tears I could barely see the speedometer needle as it moved higher and higher. The sight of the three of them at the kitchen table kept flashing in front of me. I needed to get as far away from that vision as fast as possible. I pressed on the gas and flew back to Nicklewood Arms like a homing pigeon with the directions embedded in my brain.

Running up the stairs, damn near hysterical and crying like a baby, reminded me of the day that some boy had snatched the locket from my neck when I got off the school bus. Mama had given it to me on my thirteenth birthday. Sheree hadn't been there with me because she didn't feel like waiting around for me at the library again. But when she saw me racing up the stairs, she stopped me and demanded to know what had happened. I told her, and she stomped all the way to the bus stop, dragging me behind her. The boy wasn't there, but she told his crew that he'd better have my chain back by the next day, or he was going to be sorry. I don't know what went down, but when I got out of class the next day, Sheree was spinning my locket around in a circle and smiling.

Back to my present pain. I banged on the door, even though I had a key. I couldn't get myself together enough to find it on my keyring or use it. I banged on the door again. Sheree jerked the door open, ready to go off. She was stunned into silence for a moment by the sight of me. I know I looked like a crime victim.

"What the hell, Chantelle!" Sheree screeched, looking alarmed and pulling me inside the door and over to the couch to sit down. "What happened to you?" I kept crying, and Sheree started getting upset. "Mama! Chantelle is in here crying!"

Aunt Betty rushed into the room. My eyes were closed, but I could hear her house slippers scooting across the floor toward me. I'd rushed there wanting to tell them all about it, but suddenly I felt more embarrassed than betrayed. They both had warned me to wait before marrying Teddy. Aunt Betty sat down beside me and rubbed my back, trying to console me. I concentrated on the warmth and soothing feel of her hand, and the movement helped to reel in my emotions.

"What the matter, sugar?" Aunt Betty asked softly close to my ear, while Sheree stood in front of me ready to fight.

I tried to wipe my runny nose. "It's Teddy," I said, shaking my head in disbelief.

"Is he hurt?" Aunt Betty asked patiently.

"No, I'm the one that's hurt!" I shouted, too ashamed to look her in the face.

"What did he do?" Sheree demanded, bawling up her fist.

"He's got two children, twin boys, not even three years old."

"What!" Sheree shrieked, waving her arms. "See? I knew he wasn't right!"

"My Lord!" Aunt Betty said, shaking her head and still rubbing my back. "This is a shame. He should have told you he had kids from the beginning."

"He knew what he was doing, Mama!" Sheree said angrily. "That boy knows he tricked Chantelle. He was trying to get somebody to help him pay that child support."

"How did you find out about this?" Aunt Betty asked, bouncing her leg nervously.

"He called my job and said it was an emergency. When I got home, they were at the house."

"Was his baby mama there asking for some money?" Sheree asked, sounding disgusted.

"I don't think she wants money," I said finally, getting over my initial shock. "She wasn't there. She dropped them off at the house with their clothes and toys."

"Oh no she didn't!" Sheree said, starting to laugh. "Well, whenever you're ready, we can go back over there and get your things because that is some bullshit.

"Watch your mouth, girl!" Aunt Betty said, "I'm having a hard enough time trying to hold onto my religion."

I finally looked at Aunt Betty. "I don't know what I want to do right now. I can't think. This whole thing has blown me away."

"You don't have to figure this out right now," Aunt Betty said. "Just stay here tonight. Give yourself some space to make up your mind."

Sheree took a step closer until I looked her in the eye. "What is there to think about?"

"Calm yourself down, child. It's not that simple," Aunt Betty said, taking the pressure off me. "She's married to the man now. She can't just walk away like it never happened."

"I don't see why not," Sheree argued. "He married her under false pretenses."

Listening to them go back and forth was giving me a pounding headache. I needed a restart button to change everything that had happened in my life. Every time it felt as if I was winning, there was always a setback. I needed the world to slow down so I could catch up. If that was too much to ask, could I at least get some peace and quiet?

I pushed myself off the couch. "I'm going to lie down for a while. I'm beat."

"Do you want me to fix you something to eat?" Aunt Betty asked, patting me on the hand.

"No, ma'am. I'm not hungry."

I made my way down the hall, walking like a woman who had been turned inside out, holding onto the walls and feeling for the doorway to the room where I had lived after my mama died. Still wearing my coat, I fell across the bed, mentally and emotionally exhausted.

Sheree walked in about a minute later. "Here, take a hit on this," she said, handing me a small bottle of Hennessy.

I leaned up on one elbow and poured a big gulp in my mouth. I swallowed it and then poured another mouthful. "Thanks," I said, falling back on the pillow.

"I've got your back, sis," she said, leaving.

***

Teddy nearly blew up my cell phone and left messages all through the night, but I wasn't ready to talk. I barely slept, and when the morning finally came, my face was puffy, and my eyes were practically swollen shut. I looked sick, so I called out from work. For the rest of the day and all day Saturday, I laid in bed like an invalid. I didn't shower or eat. Aunt Betty and Sheree checked in on me every few hours to make sure I was okay.

On Sunday, I finally nibbled a few bites of food as I sat up in bed and stared at the wall. The scene with Teddy and his boys replayed over and over in my mind until the shock had worn off. Then I got out of bed and took a shower.

Early the next morning, I was ready to face the world, but not Teddy. Sheree did my hair and makeup and let me borrow a dress with a bright flower print, and I went to work.

When Joanne saw me walking past her office, she hopped up from her desk and followed me into my office.

"My goodness, Chantelle, I thought about you all weekend," she said, before I could take off my coat or sit down. "Did you get my message? Is everything all right?" she asked, staring into my face as if the answers were written there.

"Yeah, everything is okay," I answered, avoiding eye contact. "Teddy had a couple of family emergencies to deal with, but it's all better now." If I sat down, she would, too, and she would want to hear every detail of what had happened. "Has Levine requested the report for the Coca-Cola plan yet?" I asked, switching the subject from my personal business to work business. "I've got it ready."

"That's fantastic. You're ahead of schedule as usual," she said, still scrutinizing my face.

"I'll give it a quick review, and then I'll send it to you," I said, taking off my coat.

"Okay," she said, getting the hint that I didn't want to talk. "There's no rush. Take your time."

When Joanne closed the door behind her, I turned on my coffeemaker. I watched it percolate and drip into the pot. When it finished, I poured coffee into a mug I had bought on our honeymoon, and then I finally sat down to mull over my predicament.

***

Four days later, I had finished analyzing my short marriage and the risk assessment on my options. I had contemplated leaving and then staying and what I stood to lose and what I might gain. Early Saturday morning, I showered, put on sweatpants and a sweatshirt, and drove back to Buckhead to talk with my husband.

I pulled my car into the driveway beside Teddy's car. I walked slowly to the front door, a stark contrast from the last time I was there. I took a deep breath, used my key to unlock the door, and stepped inside. Teddy was standing there with one tear-streaked-faced boy in his arms, and he was holding the small hand of the other.

"So, you decided to come back," he said with a hint of rudeness. The expression on his face was a complicated mix of irritation and relief.

"I came back to give you a chance to explain this to me."

"I tried to call you about a million times."

"I needed some time to absorb the shock."

"Look, this caught me off guard, too."

I couldn't help but chuckle. "Are you saying you didn't know you had kids?"

"That's not what I meant."

"So, what do you mean, Teddy?"

"I want to talk to you, Chantelle, but you have to be willing to listen."

"Like I said, that's why I'm here."

"I was just about to get them some breakfast."

I shook my head, still in disbelief at the sight of the boys. I followed them into the kitchen. I stared in amazement as he sat them down on the phone books stacked in the chairs and poured juice into their sippy cups. I followed his every movement as he got a box of Cheerios out of the cabinet, filled two bowls, and poured the milk. As much I as was engrossed in watching him, the boys were just as intently watching me. I walked over to the utensil drawer, got two spoons, and handed them to the boys.

"T'ank you," the one with tears and a runny nose said. My heart ached for a second. He reminded me of myself.

"You're welcome," I said, smiling.

Teddy left the room and came back with a radio that the boys could listen to while we talked. I was still leaning against the counter. He stood beside me, but he couldn't look me in the eye.

"First, let me say, I didn't know she was bringing them here," he said in a low voice.

I nodded. "I didn't even know they existed. You should have told me."

"I really liked you when we first met. You had your whole game together. I didn't want to turn you off with baby mama drama before you even got a chance to know me. I was going to tell you. The right time just never came."

"What about before the wedding?" I asked snidely. "That seemed like a good time."

"I tried a couple of times, and I stopped. I couldn't take a chance on losing you."

"But you did, Teddy. Why should I stay with you? This whole relationship is based on lies."

"Don't say that! It's not true. We love each other. That's the most important thing. I thought I had plenty of time to tell you about my kids since Jaycina barely let me see them. She probably did all this to break us up after she heard I got married."

"So, what do you expect me to do?"

"Forgive me," he said, moving closer to me. "Give me another chance. I love you."

I stepped back from him. "It's not that easy."

"We can get through this. I promise," he said, grabbing my hand.

"Everything has changed, Teddy. I keep wondering what other things you haven't told me."

"I might as well tell you everything," he said, biting his lip.

I snatched my hand from his, backed away, and dropped down in the chair next to me with my head in my hands, wondering what more there could be.

"I have another child, a daughter by somebody else. She's thirteen months."

I held up my hand to make him stop talking. "I can't do it, Teddy!"

He kept talking. "I wasn't in a serious relationship with either of them. It just happened."

"It doesn't just happen. You're talking about three kids. Have you ever heard of condoms?" I was totally exasperated. My foot started stamping involuntarily. "I don't understand how you could not tell me this."

"I told you I didn't want to lose you, and I still don't. I love you, and I need you to stick by me. I'll work this out. I'll make it up to you."

"You made a fool out of me. I don't like that feeling."

"I'm the one who's a fool, not you. Give me a little time. If you still want to leave, I can't blame you. We were happy, and we can still be happy. I can work this out. Three months, that's all I ask."

All my instincts told me to leave and run away again. What difference did it make that I had promised for better or worse? It probably didn't even apply in this case. I had been deceived. This situation was in place before I said my vows. I looked over at those little boys sitting at my kitchen table, spilling milk and making a mess. It was Jeremy, the one with the watery eyes and snotty nose, who softened my resolve. We shared a common bond.

"Ninety days is all you have," I said, getting up to leave.

When I got back to Nicklewood Arms, I told Sheree and Aunt Betty everything. Sheree did her best to talk me out of it. Aunt Betty warned me that it might be better to go through the pain now while I was already hurting than to go through even more pain later.

"If you ask me, a man ain't worth having until he's out of his twenties," Aunt Betty told us. "They haven't stopped thinking with the little head yet."

After talking with them, I felt as if I should walk away, except I'd already promised that I would give Teddy ninety days to fix the situation, and I was going to stand by my word. Some people get pregnant on their honeymoon. One month after we got back, I became a mother.

Chapter
Six

For the first ninety days, Teddy treated me like a queen. He avoided asking for any help with the boys. He cooked, did the laundry, and did all the grocery shopping. The whole time, he was calling Jaycina almost every day about taking the boys back to Baltimore. She rarely answered, and when she did, she assured him that it wouldn't be anytime soon.

When the ninety days were up, Teddy asked me for another ninety days to work things out. I agreed, but after a while, he broke down and enrolled the boys in daycare.

During Teddy's granted probation period, I kept the kids a secret from Joanne and everyone else at work. Primarily, because I didn't think they would be living with us that long. And further, I was too embarrassed to tell Joanne what was going on in my life and in my marriage. My behavior was a liability, a critical mistake that would reflect on my judgment. The entire situation made me feel stupid. I should have known better. I should have calculated the risks of marrying a man I had known for only six months. With my persona of being an intelligent young black woman, it would have been a shock to my coworkers. Even I had to shake my head in disbelief. I hadn't done a thorough review or checked for past claims history. I had gotten "mixed up in some ghetto bullshit," as Sheree said.

When the time came for me to make a decision about whether I would stay in my marriage, I needed someone more objective than family to confide in. Joanne had always been a great mentor and had my best interest at heart. I knew I could trust her to keep my situation in confidence, so I decided to tell her the truth. I walked into her office, sat down in the chair across from her, and blurted it out.

"I should have told you about this sooner, but I need your perspective now. A few months ago, I found out that Teddy has twin boys. They're two years old. I came home one day, and they were sitting at the kitchen table. Their mother dropped them off, and it seems like she doesn't want them back. Then Teddy tells me he has a 13-month-old daughter by another woman."

Joanne stared at me for a nearly a minute in disbelief before she said anything.

"Wow, Chantelle! I'm sorry that you didn't feel that you could share that with me when it first happened. I think the world of you, and you can trust me to respect your privacy and keep your personal business just between us."

I breathed a sigh of relief. "Thanks, Joanne. This whole thing makes me feel like a fool, but I want to get your opinion. My family thinks I should have left him the day his kids showed up. Teddy asked me to give the situation some time so he would resolve it. But nothing has changed. I love him, but I don't know what to do."

"I'm a little older than you, Chantelle, so I can tell you that, as women, we all go through different situations with the men in our lives. On the surface, your dilemma is much different from anything I've experienced, but on a deeper level, it has some similarities. My husband was deep in debt when we got married, and it was something he didn't share with me until we tried to purchase a house three years after we were married."

"Did you think about leaving him because of it?"

"No, I didn't, but it's a bit different from your situation. The debt was something we could clear up, and it would be gone for good. Kids are another story entirely. If you decide to stay with him, you are going to have to help him raise those kids. That is a lot to commit to, emotionally and financially."

"He says it's temporary. Hopefully, he will get them back to their mother."

"Being a parent is not temporary; it's lifelong. He won't be able to put these babies back in a box and return them like a pair of shoes that don't fit. You have to think about how this will affect your plans for having kids of your own."

"I hadn't even thought that far ahead."

"Everything we do here at Supreme, what you are the best at, is about curbing and balancing our losses. I know it sounds cold, but it might be wise for you to cut your losses on this marriage. From the outside, I can be more objective. I can't tell you what to decide, but if it were me, I would walk away and allow my broken heart to heal. It's not like you have invested years into this relationship. In my opinion, if you stay, this is going to cause you more and more hurt and never-ending heartbreak."

"How can I walk away from my commitment and say it was all for nothing?"

"You committed to him based on statuses that were based on a lie. You didn't have the benefit of making that choice with all the information in front of you. That wasn't fair to you."

"He didn't trust me enough to be honest."

"No, Chantelle, he simply deceived you."

"Yes, but it's still a hard thing to decide."

"Life teaches us the lessons it wants us to learn. We can't choose them. Just keep in mind that you didn't cause any of this to happen.

Teddy is the one responsible."

I stood up and exhaled. "Thanks, Joanne. Listening to you makes it seem simple. But it's not that easy. I love him."

I walked to my office, doing my best to keep my head held high, knowing the very thing that had earned me so much success in college and at work would probably be my Achilles heel in my personal life: never stepping back from a problem almost impossible to solve.

***

Watching Teddy run himself ragged everyday made it hard not to have some sympathy for him. It reminded me of my mama and watching what she had to go through everyday working so hard and caring for me. After a while, I started pitching in to help out with the boys. Despite warnings from Sheree, Aunt Betty, and Joanne, I gave Teddy another ninety days, then another ninety days, and then another ninety days, until it was ninety days after our second wedding anniversary. By then, instead of feeling like I was sinking deeper into quicksand, I was feeling significant and valued, and I felt like I was an integral part of our marriage.

I had just gotten acclimated to the boys living with us when Teddy's other baby mama dropped his daughter, Terri, off at the house. Again, without warning, I'd come home from work, and Teddy was sitting on the couch with her in his lap. She had those sad puppy dog eyes that make you call up and donate money to the SPCA. And with the dried tears on her eyelashes, she melted my heart.

I explained it to Sheree and Aunt Betty the same way Teddy explained it to me. The boys' mother, Jaycina, had met someone who loved her but not her sons, so she wasn't coming back to pick them up. The deal with Laquinta, Terri's mother, was that she was one of the best clothes boosters in Baltimore—at least she was until she got caught on tape shoplifting in a Burberry store. She's now serving time in the Maryland Correctional Institution for Women. So, not only were Teddy's sons, Julius and Jeremy, still with us, but Terri, his baby girl, would also be living with us for a while.

After Terri came to live with us, the two bedrooms weren't enough. We needed a bigger place. Teddy fussed and cussed about going into debt, but he couldn't blame anybody but himself. We bought a four-bedroom house in Lithonia.

As challenging as it was, I made the best of the situation, and I was proud of the life we were building together. On the other hand, Teddy got stressed and moody when his finances started to tighten up. The once hot housing market in Atlanta was turning cold, and our sex life was moving in tandem with it. The less money he made, the less interested he was in me. It was rough on me because I was carrying most of the load financially and in raising the kids. I needed him to at least hold things down in our bedroom. Aretha Franklin sang it best, I needed some R-E-S-P-E-C-T.

Inching along in traffic on I-285 on the morning of my fifth anniversary, I thought about how quickly the time had flown by. Honestly, it hadn't been an easy five years. I hadn't even made the adjustment to having a husband before I had two children, and then three, to raise. Washing clothes, cooking, combing hair, making lunches, and helping with homework occupied most of my time when I was off from work. It was overwhelming at times, but loving the kids was easy. My mama was a giver, and I guess she raised me to be one, too. It was Teddy who made me want to pack my bags and go.

I had been working my ass off for weeks trying to make sure his kids had a nice Christmas, and he didn't even bother to say Happy Anniversary before he jumped out of bed. I didn't know whether he had forgotten or whether he didn't care.

Even though I complained about Teddy's behavior, Sheree stopped telling me to leave him because she could see I was attached to the kids. Even more than that, she had other things on her mind after meeting this guy named Lawrence a couple of years before. He was in upper management at Bloomingdales, and he was crazy about her. He had proposed to her on her birthday, and they were planning to be married on Valentine's Day.

Since it was Christmas Eve, Sheree and I were meeting at the mall to do some last-minute shopping. There was nothing left on my list, but I needed some time to hang out with my sis.

"What's wrong now?" she asked after I pulled beside her in the parking lot. "It's your anniversary. Where's the afterglow of your morning freak session."

"No such thing," I said, locking my car. "He didn't even mention it."

"Well, excuse the hell out of him!" she said, putting her arm around me. "What is he tripping on now?"

"Money as usual."

Sheree grunted. "That means it's time for some retail therapy. Have you already got your outfit for my New Year's Eve party?"

I shook my head. "I haven't even thought about what to wear."

"All right then, let's get you straight," she said, strutting through the Bloomingdale entrance. "You spend a mint on those kids with Teddy hitting and missing. Don't forget to treat the woman who makes it all possible."

"You're right about that," I said, feeling her spirit lift mine.

I followed Sheree through the store until she traipsed into the cocktail and party dress area of the women's section.

"I see just what you need to bring the new year in right. Sequins and shine, sis." She pulled a gold shimmering dress off the rack and led me to the dressing room. "Put this on," she said with a big smile. "It is straight wicked."

I hung the dress on a hook, staring at it while I undressed. It wasn't like anything I would have picked out for myself. Once I slipped into it, I got a full view of how low-cut the V-neck was and how high the side slit was.

"This is not me," I said stepping out where Sheree could see me. "I don't mind the sequins, but can we look for something darker that doesn't show everything I got?"

"Please stop tripping, Chantelle. This dress is fresh and hot. You will turn every head in the place. You are always toning yourself down. It's time to up your game."

"Can you see if they have this dress in black?"

"No, black is cute, but it is for the background. This dress is going to put you front and center. Go on and get changed," she said, ushering me back into the dressing room. "We don't need to look at anymore dresses. Our next stop is in lingerie, and I promise I won't stop you from choosing black."

Sheree went to the register with the dress and had the woman working there ring it up with her discount. Throwing the hanger over her shoulder, she led me into the lingerie department.

"I don't want anything over the top. Get all that for your honeymoon. I just want something smooth and mellow that will knock him out like brown liquor."

"I hear you, sis. It's time to get your sexy on," she said, looking at a black lace set. "This is it. A teddy for Teddy and a nice little lace robe to match. It won't matter if his money is funny or not, he'll ride you all the way to bankruptcy court and then to the welfare office."

I had to laugh. "You know you're wrong for that. It's not his fault the housing market sucks."

"No comment," she said while another cashier rang us up.

I was grateful that Sheree had held back from running Teddy down in the ground for my sake, but it didn't stop me from knowing how she felt. I wasn't happy about the way things were in my marriage either. I watched the cashier carefully fold up the lingerie in tissue paper, and hoped it would work magic when I got home. Teddy and I definitely needed some fireworks to carry us into the new year.

***

The house was empty when I got home. Teddy had taken the kids to the movies to see *Bad Santa* while I wrapped the last of their gifts. With presents ready and waiting in my closet, the precious time alone was right on time for a relaxing hot bath to get ready for an anniversary night celebration. While the water ran in the tub, I poured myself a glass of wine. Submerged in the aroma of chamomile to relieve anger and irritation and jasmine as an aphrodisiac, I chuckled to myself thinking that Teddy needed this therapy bath more than I did.

In the background of the Quiet Storm playing on the radio, I could hear them come in the house and the kids chattering about wanting to play video games. I was grateful when I heard Teddy tell them that it was too late and that they should straighten up their rooms and get ready for bed. Waiting for them to get tired and go to sleep was not what I had planned for the evening. I started to yell out to Teddy to join me in the bath but thought better of it. He probably needed a few minutes to wind down and decompress from being with the kids all day.

Listening to the Whispers crooning "Make Sweet Love to Me" as I rubbed my body with lotion, sprayed myself with Opium perfume, and slipped into my new lingerie had me in a romantic mood. I unpinned my bun and brushed through my hair before I opened the door to the master bedroom and made a grand entrance. Teddy was lying on the bed with his back to me. Instead of waking him, I put a robe on top of my sexy outfit and went out to the kitchen to make a tray of hors d'oeuvres and a glass of cognac.

I didn't make any effort to be quiet when I closed the bedroom door with the tray in my hand. I wanted to wake Teddy up.

"What's going on?" he asked, turning over with a frown and squinting at me.

"Our anniversary," I said, taking off my robe and revealing my sexy black lace teddy.

He sat up and scooted to the edge of the bed. "My money is crazy, and I know you've spent a lot on the kids, so I didn't think we were celebrating this year."

What in the hell was he talking about? "Celebrating our anniversary doesn't cost anything. It's a special time when we remember why we got married and show the other how much we love and appreciate them." All the while, I was trying not to get angry about him looking at me without any comment on what I was wearing.

"I'm sorry. You know I got a lot of things on me right now."

"We all do," I said, sitting down next to him. "That doesn't mean that we can't take care of our relationship." He didn't say anything. "I've been missing you," I said, moving closer to give him a kiss on the cheek.

"I'm just not in a good head space right now."

"Why don't you take a shower. It'll relax you," I said, refusing to let him dampen my mood. "I poured you a drink. Just mellow out, and enjoy the night. It's our anniversary and Christmas Eve. I know there's something you can give me," I said seductively.

He nodded, got up, and took his drink with him into the bathroom. When I heard the water running, I put in a Luther Vandross CD to warm up the aura in the room. Walking across the floor, grooving to the music, and sipping my wine, I caught my reflection in the dresser mirror, and I surprised myself. I looked pretty damn good. Why was I having such a time getting Teddy's attention? I took off the robe just in case he needed a closer look.

"Feel better?" I asked when he came out of the steamy bathroom with his empty glass.

"Yeah, I do," he said, walking around to his side of the bed and sitting down.

"Lie down. I'll give you a massage," I said, still sensing his resistance to a romantic night. "Clear your head, and focus on us."

I listened to Luther's loving lyrics and rubbed the tight muscles in Teddy's back until I could feel the tension loosen up. Then I started to rub his whole body in between soft kisses. He turned over and finally rewarded my efforts with a passionate kiss. Then we touched and caressed each other for a while. I was ready to take it to the next level, but his body wasn't reacting in the way I needed it to.

"I'm beat. It's been a long day," he said, sensing my sexual frustration. "Why don't we finish this tomorrow?"

"What's the problem, Teddy? This isn't only about tonight. You've been playing me off for a while now. Is there somebody else?"

"Don't be ridiculous," he said, pulling further away. "I've got a lot going on right now with the business. Money is real funny, and I'm under a lot of pressure. It's serious for me. Why can't you understand that and be supportive? Sometimes you don't think about anything else but yourself and what you want."

"I can't believe those words would even come out of your mouth! Look at me! I'm the one who's helping you raise these kids. I'm the one keeping our heads above water, and I never complain to you about it. You're the one who can't see anybody else's struggle."

"I don't need to hear this right now," he said, jumping up and grabbing some pajamas out of the dresser drawer. "I need some space."

I laid back on the bed, totally thrown by the whole scene as I searched my mind for what the problem might be with Teddy. This couldn't be only about money. But he hadn't been hanging out with his partners that much lately either, so it probably wasn't another woman. Maybe we just needed to communicate better. I took off my sexy teddy, found some flannel PJs to put on, and went out to the great room to try to talk.

I could see the light of the TV flashing in the dark, but the volume was turned down low. I was two steps into the room when I saw what he was watching. It was an X-rated porno DVD of two women. He was so into it he didn't even realize I had stepped into the room. My mouth fell open, but I wasn't able to speak. I was more dumbfounded than shocked. This too-tired-to-be-with-his-wife guy was at full attention in more ways than one. I started to turn around and go back to the bedroom without him knowing I saw him, but I asked myself why I should be the only one who couldn't get some satisfaction.

I took four long strides that placed me right in front of the TV. "Really, Teddy? You prefer this to being with your wife?"

It was his turn for his jaw to drop. "Look, I'm just trying to relieve some tension. Don't make a big deal out of it."

"I'm not the one who made a big deal out it. You did that when you put it before me."

I stomped out of the room, shaking my head in disgust. When I got to the bedroom, I slammed the door. There was no need for him to think he was welcome there that night. I turned off the music and climbed into bed. "Happy Anniversary," I said to myself, still shaking my head.

***

The only smiling faces on Christmas morning belonged to the kids. They bounced around opening gifts and expressing their happiness on getting the presents they had written on the list for Santa to bring. I had decided that Teddy didn't deserve any gifts for

Christmas after our lousy anniversary episode. I left the carefully wrapped boxes with his name on them tucked in my closet. I thought things had hit rock bottom, but we still had room to fall.

Terri was so thrilled with her Bratz doll, Yasmin, that she ran over to me shouting.

"Look, Mommy, she's got so many clothes and hats that I can change for her!"

"Yes, sweet pea, she has enough for the whole week," I said, thrilled by her excitement.

All of a sudden, Teddy jumped up and shouted at her. "She's not your mama! Don't call her that."

Terri started to cry, and Julius and Jeremy looked at him with their mouths hanging open. I was stunned, too. His outburst shocked me as much as it did the kids. That's when I realized I had no name to them in my house.

"What should they call me, Teddy?" I asked, shaking my head. "It's been five years. Am I still, Miss Chantelle?"

He took a deep breath and sat back down. "They don't need to be confused. I want them to be respectful." Then he turned toward the kids. "Make sure you answer Miss Chantelle with ma'am. That's how I was raised. Children say yes, sir, and yes, ma'am. Do y' all understand?"

"Yes, sir," Julius said. Terri and Jeremy nodded.

The room got quiet. The kids weren't sure what to do or say.

"Who wants some pancakes?" I asked, hoping to recover the joy of the morning Teddy had put a damper on.

"I do," the boys said in unison.

"All right!" I said, clapping.

Cooking breakfast gave me a reason to leave the room and have a moment to settle my nerves. The way I was feeling, there wouldn't be a sixth anniversary. I put the food on the table and called them in to eat. The kids had relaxed, but they rushed through the meal, anxious to get back to play with their toys. Teddy had seconds, while I nursed a cup of coffee. After breakfast, I cleaned the kitchen and hurried out of the house to spend the rest of the day with Sheree and Aunt Betty.

***

When I got to Nicklewood Arms, Lawrence's car was in the parking lot. That meant that I wouldn't be able to spill my guts to Sheree on how my anniversary night went. I got the shopping bags out of my trunk that I had kept there so Teddy wouldn't see them and climbed the stairs to the apartment. I shook my head again, this time at myself. It seemed as if every time I came to visit, I always had bad news or something was wrong. I pasted a smile on my face and knocked on the door.

"What are you doing knocking?" Aunt Betty said cheerfully, holding the door wide open. "You still have your key, and this is home. Come on in here. They're in the kitchen."

"Merry Christmas!" I said to Sheree and Lawrence at the table as I leaned over to give her a hug. I took a seat and inhaled the familiar smells of bacon and pancakes. "I see folks without children have the luxury of sleeping late and having brunch."

"Not really," Sheree said. "I've been packing all morning. "Lawrence is taking me to Orlando for a long weekend. We going to see Lebron play tonight."

"Wow! Well, I can't top that," I said, giving Lawrence a high-five.

"We're about to head to the airport," Sheree said. "I didn't expect to see you this morning with that anniversary nightie you bought."

"I'll tell you about it when you get back," I said casually, trying not to put a damper on their trip. "Will you be back for your New Year's Eve party?"

"Yes! You know we're going to bring the year in right," Sheree said, waving her hand in the air. "2004 is going to be my year."

"We'd better get going if we don't want to miss our plane," Lawrence said, standing up. "Thanks for the breakfast, Miss Betty." He gave her a kiss on the cheek and went to load their bags in the car.

Sheree gave me a serious look as she got up to leave. "I can tell something is not right. I'll call you when I get a chance."

"I'm cool," I told her, waving my hand. "Have a good time; we'll talk when you get back."

Her smile came back, and she sashayed out of the kitchen. She came back in wearing a blue fox jacket, gave me a kiss on the cheek, hugged her mama, and dashed out the door.

"It makes me feel good to see that girl so happy," Aunt Betty chuckled, sitting down at the table with me. "For a while there, I didn't think she would find anybody to put up with her."

"You didn't have to worry about Sheree; all the guys knew they'd be lucky to get her."

"Well, she refused to settle, and I'm glad about that."

"Do you think I settled, Aunt Betty?"

"I think you sold yourself short, Chantelle, but that's what love will do to you. It takes away your good senses and leaves you with a bunch of feelings. If Teddy had any sense, he would realize how lucky he is to have you. You're beautiful inside and out, and you're smart as a whip. I hope you know that. If a man doesn't appreciate all that, then don't hesitate to give him his walking papers. Life is too short, baby."

I didn't think I could respond without breaking down, so I did a quick half-smile and looked away. "So, what are you doing for the rest of the day?"

"Nothing, except snacking and watching some old movies," she said, getting up.

I followed her into the living room. "That sounds good to me."

"What about Teddy and the kids?" she asked, plopping down and picking up the remote.

I squeezed next to her. "They're playing with their toys; they won't miss me."

***

A week later, Teddy was still playing the victim and bowed out of Sheree's New Year's Eve party at The Stave Room. I took my dress and went over to the apartment to get ready and ride with Sheree. Doreen and Lena were already there when we got there. We squealed and hugged, and I realized it had been a long time since we had hung out together.

"Chantelle, you're looking good, girlfriend!" Lena said, looking me up and down. "I love the dress, and you are glowing."

"Looks like married life is still good to you," Doreen added.

"It has its ups and downs like anything else," I said, thinking about my current hassles.

"I can believe that," Lena said with a sly smile. "Anyway, I'm glad to see you. With Sheree getting married next, the crew is definitely broken.

"So where is the man of the hour?" Doreen asked, looking around the room.

"He wasn't feeling well, so he stayed in."

"That's too bad. He probably caught something from the kids," Lena said, being facetious. "But, hey, that means you get to party with us tonight. Come over to our table. I want you to sit with us. We haven't talked in so long; we need to catch up."

"Let's toast to the evening and the new year," Doreen said, picking up her glass.

Their positive energy was contagious. A smile spread on my face as Lena filled the glass in front of me. I picked it up and toasted theirs with soft clink. The DJ turned up the party with OutKast's "I Love the Way You Move." Lena pulled me onto the dance floor, and Doreen followed. It reminded me of my carefree days. We danced as if we didn't have a worry in the world. Several times, a couple of guys joined us on the floor.

By the time midnight came, Lena and Doreen had made connections with two guys and were still partying. I sat alone at the table watching the couples around the room kiss to bring in the New Year. Sheree and Lawrence looked so happy holding each other. I longed for the few moments Teddy and I had like that before our lives got complicated. I swallowed the lump in my throat before I got choked up. How could a married woman feel so lonely?

I wondered if I would have felt better at the house even with Teddy pouting. At least we would be together. I got up, waved at Sheree on the way out and mouthed, "I'll call you." I stood in the entrance, shivering for an hour until the cab pulled up. In the backseat, I made a resolution that I was going to do everything I could to make 2004 a better year for Teddy and me and our family.

***

The light was on in the office when the cab pulled up in front of the house. I gave the driver a ten-dollar tip. Having to work on New Year's was in stiff competition with spending it alone. Once I was inside, I went straight to the bedroom to change out of my dress and into a pair of sweats. Then I went to the office to talk to Teddy.

It caught me off guard when the door was locked. Why? The kids were already asleep in their rooms. Agitated, I banged on the door with my fist.

"I'll be out in a minute," he yelled through the door.

"What the hell?" I stomped back to the bedroom and dropped down on the foot of the bed. This man was doing his best to make me break my less than one-hour-old resolution.

About five minutes later, Teddy strolled in wearing only his pajama bottoms. "So, how was the party?"

"What difference does it make to you?" I answered, unable to contain my anger. "You didn't want to bring the New Year in with me."

"I was here. You're the one who wanted to spend it with other people."

"Don't play games, Teddy. The party was planned months ago. And don't try to change the subject. I want to know why you needed to lock the office door. What's going on with you?"

"Can't a man have a minute to himself sometime?"

"Sure, you can have some time, but what about that needs to be behind a locked door?"

"It's not that serious," he said, walking around to his side of the bed, pulling the comforter back, and getting into bed. "You're making a whole lot out of nothing."

I stomped out of the room and headed to the office. I looked around the room to find anything out of place, but nothing was out of order. There was a half glass of Hennessey on the desk and candy-cane-colored pipes were running crisscross over the computer screen. I turned out the light and slow walked back to bed.

Chapter
Eight

It was the weekend of Sheree's wedding that things seemed to go from bad to worse. Teddy had an attitude about me staying out late at the bachelorette party, and now he was fussing about something else. I'd bought a digital camcorder for them as a wedding gift, and Teddy was mad about the price.

"I don't think you have your priorities in order, Chantelle," he said, pacing across the floor of our bedroom while I put on my makeup in the bathroom. "Home always comes first."

"I don't have time to get into this with you this morning," I said, tired of his complaining all the time. "I've got a ton of things to do today. You know I'm the maid of honor. I have to pick up Sheree and get her to the church."

He kept on griping. "That's what I'm talking about. Your mind is always somewhere else. This is not the time for us to be making extravagant purchases. Money is tight. I've got four houses on the market with no buyers. They're costing me a grip every month in interest."

"That's not my fault," I said, stepping into a pair of jeans. "I'm holding up my end. That was a business risk you and your partners took. You never consulted me about buying any of them before you made your decision."

"Why would I? Whenever I see an opportunity for us to make some real dollars, you're never onboard. You always want to hold us back. You can't see where I'm trying to take us."

"That's because this is the situation I was afraid of. I didn't want you to take on any new projects that might put a financial strain on us because I'm ready to have a baby of my own. I've been taking care of your kids for five years. The twins are almost eight years old, and Terri is six."

"In the real estate game, you've got to spend money to make money. All I've asked you to do is to give me a chance to get my business to the next level. When I get there, you can do whatever you want, have all the kids you want. Right now, I need you to get behind me instead of Sheree."

"I've already put my life on hold for five years and sacrificed for your kids to have everything they need, and I'm not going to skimp on Sheree. She's my sister, and she's always been there for me. The money I've spent on the wedding and on her gift is not going to make that much difference one way or another."

"What you need to figure out is whether you are going to be worried about Sheree or focused on this family."

That made me angry. "I don't even know how you could form your lips to say that to me. I have always put you and your kids above everything in my life, including me." I pulled on a t-shirt; stuffed my feet into a pair of sneakers; grabbed my makeup bag, my garment bag, the overnight bag with the jewelry for the bridesmaids, and my purse. "I'm not going to let you ruin this day for me or Sheree," I said in a huff as I scooted out of the room with half a face on.

Shaking my head, I gunned the engine when I started it. Teddy had a lot of nerve. He had messed up his money, and now he wanted to tell me how to spend mine. I beat my hand against the steering wheel all the way to Nicklewood Arms because I couldn't tap my feet as I praised the Lord for at least giving me the sense to keep my own bank account with only my name on it.

***

"You look fired up and ready to go," Sheree said, smiling and glowing even without her makeup. "After last night, I thought you were going to stroll in here half sleep since you don't know how to hang out and have fun anymore."

"I probably would have, but Teddy was getting on my nerves so bad I had to leave."

Sheree frowned. "What's his problem?"

"I don't know, and I don't care," I said, following her back into the bedroom. "Today is all about you."

"I know that's right!" Sheree said as she picked up her makeup case. "My beautician is going to meet us at the church, and you know I don't trust anybody to beat my face but me."

"Where's Aunt Betty? Isn't she riding with us?"

"No, she left this morning with some of her friends to help decorate the church. She took my dress, too. So, we don't have to worry about that."

Sheree talked nonstop in the car on the way to the church, reminiscing about when she first met Lawrence Martin and how she had teased him and had kept calling him Martin Lawrence.

"I never thought I would be getting married," she said, laughing. "No offense, Chantelle, but after that game Teddy pulled on you, I was scared to death."

"I don't blame you, girl," I said, sighing. "I can't say I don't have my regrets sometimes."

"That's what you get for marrying the first man that made you holler."

I couldn't help but chuckle at the ironic truth. "I'll let that slide since it's your wedding today."

"No, but seriously, girl, I get on you a lot about the decisions you made, but I really admire you. Not many women can be that forgiving and raise other women's children. That's real love. The Lord is gonna bless you, child."

"I didn't give myself time to find out if it was really love. He rushed it, and I let him. Looking back, I'm pretty sure I was in love with being loved."

"It's been five years though. You are in love with him now aren't you?"

"I guess so. Things are so complicated now, I don't have time to think about it."

"Well, we are definitely going to have to change the subject and talk about something else, or I might end up changing my mind."

"No way. Your relationship is different; Lawrence worships the ground you walk on."

"Yes, he does," she said, looking at herself in the visor mirror. "I love that about him."

***

I stood behind the other bridesmaids waiting to enter the sanctuary and thought about the day I was married in this very church. Seeing Lawrence in his handsome black tuxedo, I remembered how I had gazed so happily at Teddy waiting at the end of the aisle. I had no clue of what I was walking into. I can't blame him for all of it. There were hints and warning signs in the short months we dated. I just ignored them.

One of Aunt Betty's friends touched me on the elbow, bringing me out of my daydream, signaling that I should step forward and proceed down the aisle. Another hope-filled smile crept on my face when I saw Teddy and the kids sitting on the left side halfway to the front. To tell the truth, I hadn't been sure if he was going to show up or not.

Sheree was as radiant as ever as she followed me to the front and took Lawrence's hand. The ceremony was beautiful, and the words *for better, for worse, for richer, for poorer, in sickness and in health, to love and to cherish, 'til death do us part* replayed in my ears. I nodded my head. I had kept my vows, and it hadn't been easy.

Once all the photos were snapped, toasts given, food eaten, and cake sliced, it was time to drink champagne and hit the dance floor. The festivities had lifted my mood, and I was ready to put all the arguments aside and have a good time with my husband, while the kids were being entertained at the children's table. I made my way across the room to where he was sitting.

"Dance with me," I said, extending my hand to him.

"I don't feel like dancing," he said, turning away.

I tried to coax him. "Maybe if you try and enjoy yourself, you'll feel better."

"Maybe if you cared more about us than you do about Sheree, I'd feel better."

I sat down in the chair next to him. "That's ridiculous, and you know it. You're letting the money pressure get to you. Business is up and down. Things will get better; they always do."

He shook his head. "You were the one who wanted the bigger house. That note is killing us."

I swallowed the sarcastic response that rose in the back of my throat. I didn't want to attract attention and spoil the reception. "We needed the extra room for the kids. Besides, I don't mind paying it."

He was quiet for a minute. Long enough for me to say a prayer, hoping he would let it go and decide to dance with me.

"You don't seem like you're dedicated to this marriage," he said, deflecting all my efforts to get him out of his foul mood.

"Why do you keep saying that?" I asked in frustration.

"From the beginning, you've had one foot in and one foot out," he said, avoiding eye contact.

I was totally mystified. "What are you talking about?"

"Why do you have your bank account separate from the house account?"

"You have a separate account, too."

"That's the account I use for my business expenses."

"We don't need to have this argument, Teddy. If you need money, just ask."

"I shouldn't have to ask," he said, still looking away from me.

Time out. I knew there was no reason to keep talking. He wasn't rational. I don't know how many times he had been to the open bar, but he was obviously drunk on something. The only thing I could recommend was for him to sleep it off.

"I'll see you at the house," I said, getting up from the table. It was clear that neither one of us was going to win this battle.

"Everything all right?" Aunt Betty asked when I slid in the seat beside her.

"Not really, but I'm not going to let it upset me."

Aunt Betty sighed. "It ain't easy, child. Most of the time, it ain't fair. Being in a marriage has its pluses and minuses."

"I know. I'm just trying to stay positive."

Watching Sheree on the floor with Lawrence, beaming with the joy of the day, my emotions danced back and forth between reminiscing and regret. When I saw Teddy get the kids and leave the reception without saying goodbye, my senses questioned whether I would ever feel that happy again.

***

"It's about time," Teddy said when I moped into our bedroom still wearing my bridesmaid's dress. "I've got to make a run; I have to meet some possible investors. This might be real important to me."

"This late?" I said, checking the time on my watch. "It's past 9:30."

"I would have been able to go earlier, but you weren't here," he said with a lot of attitude. "I couldn't leave the kids here by themselves."

"Why would you schedule an appointment on the evening of Sheree's wedding anyway?"

"Unlike some other people, I don't have banker's hours. I have to work around the clock."

I threw my hands up in frustration, but he was out of the bedroom and out of the house before I could ask him another question. I sat down on the edge of the bed, took off my strappy sandals to rub my tired feet, and spent the next ten minutes thinking how different the day should have been. Hopefully, he could get the investors he needed into the project, and it would get him out of his funk. I took off my dress, hung it up, took a shower, and went to bed.

***

Too mentally and physically spent after a week of wedding preparations and arguments with Teddy, I laid in bed, skipping church and my much-needed blessing to recover before the new week started. I could hear the kids laughing and playing in the great room. At least somebody in this house was well-rested.

Teddy's side of the bed was empty. I'd slept so hard that I couldn't tell if he hadn't come home or whether he had gotten up early and left again. I put on my robe and went to find out which.

On my way to the kitchen, I got my answer when I saw him lying fully dressed on the couch in the great room.

"You look like I feel," I said, standing over him. He peered at me through squinted eyes and then at his watch. "How did it go last night?"

"Not bad. I got a real good vibe from the meeting," he said, dragging himself off the couch to his feet.

There were brownish smudges all on his shirt, and I got a big whiff of stale liquor and cigar or cigarette smoke as he walked away.

Curious, I followed him into our bedroom. "Where did you all go?"

"We talked for a while at the office, and then we went out for a few drinks."

He took off his shirt and undershirt and tossed them onto the bed. Then he took off his slacks and threw them over the back of the chair before he went into the bathroom and closed the door. I picked up the shirt from the bed, hoping it was one of my visions and that what I thought I saw wasn't really there. No such luck. It was there: foundation and lipstick smudges from the neck to the navel button.

The flow of water in the shower started just as Terri ran into the room with the *Finding Nemo* DVD in one hand and a bag of gummy bears in the other.

With her bottom lip pooched out, she said, "Mommy, Julius and Jeremy won't let me watch my movie."

"That's all right, sweetie. You can watch it on your daddy's computer."

I took her hand and led the way to Teddy's office. I pushed the power button on his computer and then the DVD release button to put the disc in. When the compartment slid out, there was a disc already in it. My hand snapped back as if it had been burned. The title and the picture left no room for doubts.

"What's the matter? Terri asked, puzzled by my reaction.

"Nothing, baby," I answered, removing the disc and putting in *Finding Nemo*. "Sit down, and enjoy your movie."

I closed the door behind me as I hurried back down the hall. Midway, I paused and glanced at the boys for a second in the great room. They were preoccupied with their Nintendo game, so I kept moving. In our bedroom, Teddy was out of the shower, standing in front of the sink with a towel wrapped around his waist, preparing to shave.

"We need to talk," I said, shutting the bathroom door to keep the conversation between us.

"What about?" he asked, being smug, "You did what you wanted for Sheree."

"It's not about Sheree," I said quietly. "It's about you and the makeup on your shirt."

He frowned as the words came together with the picture in his head. "It's not what you think, Chantelle, so don't get started. The business meeting went well, and after that, the clients wanted to go somewhere to relax. I took them over to the Onyx Club."

"Was it their request or your idea?"

"Baby, you wouldn't believe how many deals are closed in strip clubs."

"I can imagine. From the looks of your shirt, you were definitely taking care of some business."

"Don't even trip. Some of the chicks were showing out to make a few dollars. It's not that serious." Then he turned on the electric shaver, probably hoping it would drown me out.

No such luck. I just raised my voice. "Really? It was asking too much for you to dance with your wife at the wedding yesterday, but now you're telling me it's okay for you to be all hugged up with some strippers."

He kept shaving. "You're making more out of it than it was."

"I might have believed you, except things haven't been that great between you and me. You barely give me the time of day anymore, but you have time for strip clubs and your dirty movies."

"You're talking crazy, Chantelle."

"No, I'm not. I just got this out of the computer in the office," I said, reaching in the pocket of my robe and waving it in the air.

He turned off the shaver. "I'm a grown man. I like to look at women. It's a guy thing."

"You must want to be with other women."

"If I wanted to be with other women, I wouldn't be here with you."

"You weren't here last night."

"Me chilling out at a club with the guys doesn't have anything to do with you."

"Oh, yes, it does have a lot to do with me, especially when you choose to spend money you don't have on strippers and looking at other naked women instead of being with me."

"I'm tired of talking about this. You're flipping out over nothing. I haven't been with any other women," he said, storming out of the bathroom.

"I'm getting real tired of you always walking away from me."

I stood in the bathroom doorway as he snatched a pair of jeans and a sweatshirt out of the closet, put them on, and jammed his feet into a pair of high-top Jordan's.

"I'm out of here," he said without looking in my direction as he stomped out of the room. "I'm working my ass to death for you and the kids, and you keep harping on petty shit."

I was mad as hell. Once again, he was trying to turn his dirt around and lay it on me. What made me even madder was that he had run out leaving me with the kids. I wanted to be the one who stormed out and slammed the door.

I checked the time on the clock sitting on my nightstand. I needed to talk to somebody. I needed some peace, but it was too late to go to church. I couldn't tell Aunt Betty about this, and Sheree's plane had already taken off. Then it occurred to me that I wasn't about to have any other woman come before me in my own house, real or facsimile.

Chapter
Nine

I sat in my office, one foot rocking against the other foot in a rhythm that matched my pulse, and I tapped my middle finger against the arm of my chair. I had gotten a small bit of pleasure in taking out his trash, but I still wasn't satisfied. I had searched through every drawer, closet, and shelf in the house. I'd found enough dirty magazines and DVDs to fill a large garbage bag. I tried to burn them in the style of Bernie in the *Waiting to Exhale* movie, but the paper in the magazines must have been inflammable. I hosed the whole mess down, put it all back in the garbage bag, and threw it in a dumpster behind the grocery store. I kept staring at the phone, half expecting Teddy to call me in outrage, but it didn't ring.

"Do you want to have lunch?" Joanne asked, sticking her head inside my office door.

"Yes, that sounds good. I'm starving," I answered, standing up and grabbing my purse from the back of my chair.

"Is the cafeteria okay, or do you want to go out?" Joanne asked as I reached for my coat.

"It's cold and dreary out there," I said, thinking about it for a second. "The cafeteria is fine with me."

I followed Joanne in the line of hot entrees, picking up a tray and a set of utensils that were wrapped up in a thick paper napkin. My eyes scanned across the selections of chicken, meatloaf, glazed ham, mashed potatoes, corn, cabbage, and green beans and the aroma-filled steam that rose above it all. There were so many choices but nothing that appealed to me. As empty as I felt inside, the last thing I wanted was food. I was hungry for attention and affection. It didn't make any sense to me. How could I be married to a man I loved and be so lonely all the time?

"Do you want something from the grill?" Joanne asked, seeing my empty tray.

"Not really. I guess I don't have much of an appetite after all. I'll just get some soup."

I dipped up a bowl of soup, grabbed a few packs of saltines, poured myself a cup of coffee, and headed for the register. There were plenty of places to sit, but I made a beeline for a spot near the windows in the back. I was munching on the crackers when Joanne joined me at the table.

"Do you have something to tell me, because that looks like morning sickness to me," Joanne said with a smile as she sat down across from me.

"I wish," I said with a sigh, thinking about all the times I'd told Teddy that I wanted to have a baby of my own.

"How are things going at home?" Joanne asked, adding more sugar to her sweet tea. "You have that far away look in your eyes again."

"Not the greatest. We're barely speaking."

"Been there, done that, got the t-shirt and the mug for souvenirs. It'll get better."

"Sometimes I'm not sure. I feel like I'm fighting as hard as I can, and I'm still losing."

"How long have you and Teddy been together?"

"Five years."

"Hang in there, girl," Joanne said, rubbing butter over a roll.

"This is just a phase. Marriage is full of peaks and valleys. I've been through them all. After about five years, men get bored and restless with the responsibility of it. It passes and then comes back again in another five years."

"That's not fair. Why does he get to zone out and leave me high and dry? I thought a relationship is supposed to be fifty-fifty. Since we've been together, I feel like I've given seventy-five to his twenty-five."

"Are we talking financially or what?" she asked curiously.

"We're talking emotionally; the financial part doesn't bother me."

Joanne stopped eating. "I can't believe it, Chantelle. That man acted like he was gonna die until he put that ring on your finger. I think both of you need some quality time together without the kids to get back on track."

Joanne had shared some personal things with me over the years: her son's drug addiction, her father dying and leaving her nothing, and when her husband cheated. I wanted to tell her about the magazines, the DVDs, and the smudges on Teddy's shirt, but it seemed so salacious. And even though I trusted her, I couldn't take the chance that my private business might end up all over the company.

"You're probably right," I said, making light of my situation. "Maybe the two of us can get away during the summer when school is out. We haven't been away by ourselves since the honeymoon."

"Oh, yeah, I think that will help. Go someplace warm and sunny, and rediscover what brought you guys together in the first place."

Joanne kept talking, telling me about one of her vacations to Mexico. I was only half-listening when the movement of a bird near the window caught my attention as it poked around in the small puddles on the walkway. It froze for a moment as it listened cautiously to its surroundings. Then out of the bushes, a squirrel dashed over toward it.

"That's exactly what we need," I said, as I watched the bird fly to an escape high into the sky.

***

"What's going on in here?" Sheree said, bursting into my house right after I had gotten home from work. I had been staring into the fridge, wondering what I was going to make for dinner, and the kids were in the great room watching TV.

Seeing her made me feel better. "Welcome back, Mrs. Martin," I said giving her a hug. "I didn't know you were back."

"We got back on Monday night," she said, sitting down at the kitchen table. "Hand me something to drink out of there."

"How was your trip?" I asked, taking out two coolers.

"It was fabulous! I wasn't ready to come back."

I opened both the coolers and handed her one. "I can't wait to see all the pictures."

"I went by Mama's yesterday. She said she hasn't seen you since Lawrence and I left for the honeymoon."

I took a big gulp from my bottle. "Things have been kind of busy around here, and I haven't had time to check on her. Is she doing okay?"

"Yeah, Mama's fine. I guess you been too busy to go to church either," she said, looking at me suspiciously. "Something is up."

"If you have something you want to know, just ask me," I said, sitting down in front of her.

"What I know is that Teddy had some kind of attitude at the wedding. What is his problem? That nigga ain't never happy."

"He's just messed up because his money is tight. The real estate market has slowed down, and nothing is selling."

"He shouldn't be tripping; you carry the load around here anyway. Besides, I'm not worried about him; I'm here to see about you. You know I can read you like a book. You've got those wrinkles in your forehead again."

I was tired of holding it in. "Teddy is still into those dirty magazines and porno flicks. I found a DVD in his computer; and when I looked around, I found more of them and a ton of magazines."

"Uh, so Teddy is a freak," she laughed. "A lot of guys like that kind of stuff. It doesn't mean anything."

"It's not that simple to me, Sheree. The morning after your wedding, he stayed out most of the night and came home with makeup and perfume all over his shirt. He said he was at the Onyx strip club with some clients."

"I know that kind of shit gets on your nerves, but it's not the same thing as cheating."

"It feels like it to me. Why is he doing all this extra stuff?"

Sheree chuckled. "Maybe he's a sex addict like Eric Benet."

"What if I did the same thing to him?"

"Girl, that sounds like a plan to me. I didn't get a throw-down bachelorette party anyway. Let that brother watch his own kids while we get our groove on," she said, standing up and shaking her hips. "I feel like making it rain myself."

I couldn't help but laugh hard, down to my guts, and I needed that laugh. My thoughts had me wound up so tight for days, I was near a breaking point. I thanked the Lord that Sheree was there. It helped me relieve a lot of that tension.

"You're so crazy!" I said, catching my breath.

"I'm serious. Tomorrow is ladies' night. We are going out."

"You just got back from your honeymoon. I know Lawrence isn't going for that."

"He won't mind. We've been together 24/7 for ten days. He probably wants some time to hang out with his fellas. Tell that man you have to work late; don't even come home. Let him take care of his own kids for a change."

***

Chosen as the designated driver for the evening, I parked on the end of the row to lessen my chances of getting dinged on both sides of my car in the narrow spaces. The last one to get out, I still wasn't certain of what I hoped to accomplish as I watched several groups of women scrambling toward the entrance. It was way past ironic that the building we were rushing toward had previously been a church before it was converted into a nightspot. The club was named Revival, but the high-pitched roof and stained-glass windows belied the actions that currently took place inside. We stood in the line of anxious patrons, paid our $20 in the vestibule, and walked through the big double doors.

The bass in the music was thumping so hard I could feel the vibration from the wooden floor through my shoes. Sheree—leading Doreen, Lena, and me—strolled down to the VIP section near the stage. As soon as we sat down at our reserved table, a slim but fit light-skinned man wearing a black t-shirt with the word "Revival" in large letters on it came over and took our order of cocktails and a ginger ale for me.

My eyes panned around the large low-lit room that had once been a sanctuary. It was wall-to wall with women of every size, shape, race, and age, with a few sprinkles of men among them. The excitement and expectations that filled the space reminded me of church members rejoicing with the choir before the pastor begins his message.

"To the first of many," Sheree said, raising her glass for a toast.

"I heard that," Lena added, clicking the rim of her Hennessey-filled glass against Sheree's. "I'm glad you called me; this is just what the doctor ordered."

"I know that's right," Doreen said. "I definitely need some more protein in my diet, and I'm ready for some dark meat tonight."

I shook my head, laughing. "Y 'all are so crazy."

"It's okay to be crazy, girl," Sheree said, standing up and shaking her booty to the music. "Just don't let nobody drive you crazy. Go there all by yourself."

Sheree wasn't looking at me, but I knew her words were directed at me. I had given up so much to make my marriage work. I couldn't understand why Teddy wouldn't give up his fixations on other women, and it was working my last nerve.

"I wouldn't mind somebody driving me crazy," Lena hollered. "I'm not getting it on the regular like you married ladies."

"Hush up, girl," Doreen said to Lena. "That's you fault. There's not a man in the world who can pass all your tests."

"You don't know that, and I'm not settling," Lena responded. "I know what I want and how I deserve to be treated."

That made me take a big swallow of my ginger ale, wishing it was something stronger. Then the DJ put on "Freak Like Me" by Adina Howard, and the room went wild. Most of the women in the club were on their feet, gyrating their hips and swinging their arms, while they sang along. Determined to relax, let go, and have a good time, I stood up and joined the party. The lights dimmed as the emcee, dressed in a cream-colored double-breasted suit, walked onto the stage.

Sheree held up her hand for Doreen to give her a high-five, "Now, that's what I'm talking about, girlfriend!"

"Welcome to the Revival, lovely ladies," the emcee said in a deep voice. "We have a dynamite show for you this evening. Are you ready to get freaky tonight?"

"Hell, yeah!" Lena shouted along with the crowd.

"We have all you can stand and more," he said, taking off his jacket and reaching toward his crotch. "Order another drink. You're going to need it."

A combination of squeals, screams, and shouts engulfed the room. The lights on the stage went out for a few seconds. When they came back on, there was a black guy standing there in Levi jeans and a jacket over a t-shirt. He was giving off straight cockiness, and I had to admit he was sexy with his fade haircut. The DJ pumped up the volume to Snoop Dogg's "Drop It Like It's Hot." The guy turned around and let the jacket fall to the floor, displaying his biceps and well-defined back muscles. He began circling his hips slowly and seductively.

"All right now!" Sheree hollered, pulling some cash out of her wallet. "Check him out, Chantelle. The brother is fine."

The first dancer's routine was a mixture of sexual gestures and a body-builder display as he removed each piece of clothing. The women enjoyed every minute of it and tossed and tucked bills into his black satin G-string. The rest of the male line-up covered a variety of tastes: young and wild, hot Latino, even a white guy. I got more of a kick out of the women's reactions and actions than I did out of seeing the glistening toned bodies of the dancers.

I was finishing my second glass of ginger ale when Sheree ordered me a glass of wine from our waiter.

"You need a drink, sis."

"I'm cool," I said with a smile to show her I was having a good time.

"One glass won't hurt you."

I was sipping on the wine when the emcee brought a chair out onto the stage and introduced Mr. Wonderful. A few women yelled out as if they knew him. Then a man dressed in a stylish suit, carrying a briefcase, walked onto the stage. More than his baldhead, it was his mustache and beard that caught my attention. They were the perfect blend of a sprinkle of salt with the pepper. A jazzy instrumental song was playing as he took off his jacket, his tie, and then his shoes. He seemed oblivious to the audience. It was like watching a man who had come home from work undress. He placed each article of clothing neatly on the chair. All the ladies were having a fit, and I stood on my feet when my view was blocked.

Wearing only a pair of Calvin Klein boxers, he walked down the stairs onto the main floor. He stopped in front of a woman at the edge of the stage and took her hand, and the music changed. The drums were thumping on the Nelly song "It's Getting Hot in Herre." He started dancing with her as if she was the only woman in the room. He was in great shape, and he could move his body. After about 30 seconds, he backed up and moved to another lady waving a handful of money. He worked the room, doing his thing, and the women couldn't give him their money fast enough.

"Over here! Right here!" Sheree yelled, pointing at me.

Mr. Wonderful came over and took off his briefs in front of me. I was relieved to see he had on a G-string. He put my hand on his left butt cheek, grabbed me around the waist, rocked his body against mine, and pulled me down to my chair. The rhythm of the music and his body was hypnotizing as his eyes locked onto mine.

The room was cheering as he straddled me. I was stunned; a total stranger was touching me in the way I so needed to be touched. It wasn't him I wanted; it was the intensity of the touch, the urgency of desire, even though I knew he was acting. I couldn't remember how long it had been since I'd gotten that feeling from Teddy. I slid the moist ten-dollar bill I had been squeezing in my hand under the elastic of his G-string, and he set me free, moving on to another patron waiting with open arms.

"Now that's what I call sweet revenge," Sheree said, holding up her hand for a high-five.

I slapped her hand and smiled. "You're so crazy." I downed my glass of wine in two gulps. I was flushed and starting to perspire as if I was sitting in a sauna.

Doreen fanned me and laughed. "Looks like Teddy is going to have to put out a fire tonight."

"I know that's right," Lena said. "I got heated up just watching. That brother is hot." She pulled out her phone and started texting.

"I don't know about you horny sisters, but I've got a taste for a ghetto burger," Sheree said as the show came to an end.

"That sounds good to me," Doreen added.

"Y 'all can drop me off first," Lena said, standing up. "I'm expecting company."

"Oh, no, you didn't sit there in front of us and make a booty call!" Sheree said, pretending to be indignant. "That is so disrespectful."

"Hell, yeah, I did!" Lena said. "I would have been home minding my own business, but y 'all drug me out here and got me upset."

"Well, let me take you home where your company can calm your nerves," I said, sniggling as I got up from my chair.

"So, what did you think, Chantelle?" Sheree asked on the way to the car. "Are you still pissed about Teddy going to strip clubs? It was all in fun."

"I think it opened her eyes to the fact that there are other men in the world," Lena chuckled.

"Not really," I said, starting the car and turning up the music on the radio.

I didn't feel like talking. The sexy dancer didn't open my mind or create a desire for another man, he only made me want Teddy more. He reminded me of what I was missing at home. I wanted all of Teddy's love and adoration, and I wanted to have his baby. I absentmindedly laughed at my girls as they chattered about their favorite guys at the club. By the time I got home, all I wanted to do was show Teddy how much I loved him.

"Where've you been all night?" Teddy said when I walked in.

"I went out with the girls. What's the problem?"

"You forgot to check your watch," he said with an attitude.

"You didn't think it was such a big deal when you came in at the crack of dawn."

"That was different. I was trying to handle some business. This is just disrespectful. You expect me to believe you were with some chicks all this time."

"Trust goes both ways, Teddy. Besides, I don't want to argue," I said, trying to put my arms around him for a kiss.

He lifted his arms and backed away from me. "I'm not feeling you right now."

I shrugged my shoulders and walked back to our bedroom. I took a shower and changed into one of my short nightgowns, hoping he had calmed down enough to make love. *Doreen was right*, I thought and smiled to myself. I headed into the great room, thinking he was watching TV, but he wasn't in there. He wasn't in the kitchen either. I went to his office, opened the door, and peeped in. He was there, so hypnotized by the images of naked women spreading their legs and private parts that he didn't hear me come in.

"So, you'd rather fantasize about these fake hoes than be with your wife!" I yelled, startling him.

He clicked the computer off. "It's nothing, Chantelle. Don't start tripping."

"It's too late for that. I told you that you can't be with me and keep doing this."

"Look, baby, it's not a big deal. You shouldn't be bothered by it."

"But I am, especially when you choose them over me. You must be hooked on that porn shit."

"I'm not hooked on anything," he said defensively. "I've been looking at what you call porn since I was a teenager."

"You're not a teenager anymore. You have a wife who needs your attention."

"Look, we're not joined at the hip. There's nothing wrong with needing some space every now and then."

"It's not every now and then. It's more often than not."

"I really don't want to talk about it anymore. I've said all I'm going to say."

"Uh uh, that's not going to cut it, Teddy. I think we need to get some kind of counseling about this. This really bothers me."

"I don't need anybody else to tell me how to live my life."

"That's not what it's for. It's someone who can help us communicate better. There are some things that I don't understand about you and things you don't understand about me."

"Then you get yourself some counseling because I don't want any."

"You are so selfish. All you think about is yourself," I said, breaking down into tears. His dismissive attitude was too much for me.

He got up from his desk chair and put his arms around me, but I was past wanting to hug him. I kept crying. There were limits to the amount of rejection that I could take.

"Why don't we take that trip you were talking about when school is out? I'm down for that, but I'm not going to no head-shrinker," he said through a crack in his cold exterior. "My mom can keep the kids, and we can have some time to ourselves."

Holding my breath to stop the release of more tears, I nodded. Maybe in another city he might see me in a different light, and we might be able to find each other again. He followed me back to our bedroom, and we laid beside each other without talking until we both fell asleep.

Ten

It was a four-hour drive to Tybee Island. I had thought about flying out to Vegas, but there would be too many distractions, and we really needed some time to focus on each other. At this point, I didn't feel optimistic about much changing, but I was out of solutions. My mood was still in a bad place, so for most of the drive, I leaned my head back on the headrest facing the window and pretended to be sleep.

I wasn't quite ready to let Teddy off the hook. I hadn't decided how I could move forward from our issues or if I even wanted to. Even while shopping at Victoria Secret with Sheree, I hadn't told her that things were still rocky. I'm pretty sure she sensed it because she told me that, if I wasn't happy, I should leave his ass. It was much more complicated than that for me. The one thing that upset me most was to admit I had failed. It was hard for me to give up on anything. It was something Mama never let me do. That's when I made up my mind to try to forgive him.

We had rented a small cottage not directly on the beach but a short walk across the street.

"This place is really nice," Teddy said after he brought our luggage in. "This is the kind of property I need to bring in some real cash."

I certainly didn't want to start off our long weekend talking about real estate, so I changed the subject. "It feels good to be away from everything for a few days. It's been a long time since we've really been alone together."

"Hopefully, this is what we need to get back on the same page," he said, looking around the cottage as if he wanted to make an offer on it.

I took a deep breath. "I'm going to take a shower, and maybe we can go out and get something to eat."

"Yeah, go ahead," he said, still checking out the cottage like a prospective buyer. "We passed a couple of decent places that we can probably walk to."

I took my bags into the master bedroom and unpacked. I made up my mind to do what Sheree always told me. I was going to set the stage for the evening by dressing the part. I let my hair down literally, put on a full face, a bright yellow sun dress and flowered sandals, and sprayed myself with Romance by Ralph Lauren. I stepped into the living room to make a grand entrance.

"It's about time!" Teddy barked without paying me the compliment I had taken such care to earn. "I thought you said you were hungry."

Obviously, I was in the company of a tough audience, but I wasn't about to let that discourage me. "I am," I said, picking up my purse from the end table. "Let's get this show on the road."

It was a beautiful evening. The sun was setting, and there was a salt-air-filled breeze that cleared my head and lungs. After a few more deep breaths, my shoulders relaxed as the stress eased out of my muscles. My jaw was next, and a small smile crept onto my lips.

"It's really nice out here," I said, trying to break the ice and make conversation.

"They have a lot of tourists out here tonight," Teddy said as we weaved through a large group blocking the sidewalk.

I reached for his hand to keep from getting separated, but he didn't grip my hand. I felt as if I was holding on to him, but he wasn't feeling it. My jaw stiffened with doubt, but I stayed in character and held on to him as we walked about a half block. Then he pulled away to get a piece of gum out of his pocket.

"This place looks good," I said, looking through a fence around one restaurant when we stopped at a traffic light. "It's says "bar and grill." It probably has whatever you want to eat."

"Fine with me," he said, sounding indifferent.

Teddy turned toward the entrance and pulled the door open for me. It was casual, but the food smelled exceptional as we walked in. A smiling hostess met us at the door. "Welcome to North Beach Bar & Grill," she said politely.

Most of the restaurant seating was open to the outside, and there were some younger college kids talking loudly and eating under the umbrellas. The hostess led us to a table inside next to the deck where we could see out onto the street.

"Can I start you off with something to drink?" she asked, still smiling.

"Yeah, a Corona for me and white wine for the lady," Teddy answered, smiling back at her.

She nodded and placed two menus down on the table. "Very good, sir. Your waitress will bring your drinks in a minute and take your order."

Teddy ordered jerk pork, and I ordered the crab cakes. He kept looking around at the walls as if this was the most fascinating place he had ever seen, while I kept looking at him, wondering when we were going to get to the meat of the problem in our marriage.

The crab cakes were delicious, but after eating one, I started the conversation. "Teddy, there are some things that have really been bothering me lately, and I want to see if we can come to an agreement."

"Go ahead. Talk," he said, sounding disinterested.

"The biggest thing for me right now is that I think you're obsessed with other women."

He shook his head as if he was disgusted. "That's what you think, but that's not true. But if you want to believe that, I can't stop you."

"That's not what I want to believe; that's what I see."

"Chantelle, you want me to fit into this perfect mold of a man that you have dreamed up in your mind, but that's not real. I'm not breaking any laws."

"I'm not saying that. I just don't think it's normal for a man to want to spend more time looking at porn or going to a strip club instead of having sex with his wife."

"The problem is you keep putting pressure on me."

"Is this about me wanting to have a baby?"

"Not completely, but that's part of it."

"Well, as far as I'm concerned, it's about you being hooked on porn."

"I'm not hooked on porn. I enjoy it. I'm a man. It's a man thing."

"If something is causing problems for you in your life or your marriage and you can't let it go, then in my opinion, you're addicted."

"I don't have to look at porn, I choose to look at it."

"Well, I'm asking you to stop. I'm asking you to choose me."

"Why is this such a big deal to you?" he asked, exasperated.

I kept a cool tone. "Because it's ruining our relationship."

"All right," he said, throwing up his hands. "I'll stop."

"Just like that."

"Just like that. I promise. When we get back, I'll throw out the tapes and the mags."

"Thank you. That's all I wanted."

There was an awkward lull for a minute before the waitress came back to see if we wanted refills on the drinks.

"Just the check," Teddy told her.

When she walked away, I changed the subject to something less intense. "You know the boys want to play Little League baseball. What do you think?"

"I think it will be another expense we don't need," he snapped.

I wanted to snap back and ask if we needed the expense of his dirty magazines or him making it rain at the Onyx, but I let it go. He had promised to stop. I would pay the fees for the boys myself. It was time to enjoy the rest of the weekend.

We finished eating, paid the check, and walked back to the cottage. I felt better, hopeful even. Now it was time for him to show me some of the love I'd been missing. After we got inside and locked the door, I put my arms around him for a kiss. I was disappointed. It was a cold kiss, void of any tenderness, emotion, or saliva.

"What's the matter?" I asked, stepping back, puzzled.

"Nothing. I'm just tired from the drive. I think I'll watch some TV and try to wind down for a while. You go on and get some rest. We have to hit the beach tomorrow.

"Okay," I murmured, too tired to put up a fuss. I went into the bedroom, changed into a nightgown, and went to sleep.

***

I got up early, dressed quietly, and walked to the beach. I didn't have an appetite, and I didn't feel like sitting across the table from Teddy. I needed some time to think. I took off my sandals and felt the cool damp sand between my toes. The sun was still crouched over the horizon and the water glistened as it came in waves. The vision of it was the definition of tranquility. I couldn't help but throw my head back and stare at the sky. It was the opposite of how my life felt. I was in turmoil, more like a tornado, caught up in a mess of my own making.

I reached into my bag, pulled out my big hat and sunshades, and sat down to the let the waves wash over me. Maybe the water could absorb all my troubles and pull them out to the sea. I wasn't sure how long I had sat out there, but when the sun was high in the sky radiating its heat, I figured it was time for me to look for a cooler spot.

The tourist shops were the perfect place to cool down. I bought t-shirts for Jeremy and Julius, a bracelet with Terri's name on it, a mug for Aunt Betty, and some big earrings for Sheree. I wanted to walk further, but I was beginning to get hungry. I headed back to the cottage to see where we might go for lunch.

"I thought this trip was about us spending some quality time together," Teddy grumbled when I walked in the door. He was sitting in the living room reading the paper that had been on the doorstep when I left.

"You were still sleeping, and I didn't want to wake you, so I took a walk. I did a little shopping for souvenirs, but it's still early. Have you eaten?"

He shrugged his shoulders as if he was totally outdone. "Whatever, Chantelle."

"Do you want to get something to eat or go for a swim?" I asked, wondering why he had an attitude,

"It doesn't matter to me," he said.

I went into the bedroom to change into the two-piece bathing suit that Sheree had gotten for me at Bloomingdales. I put it on and was checking myself out in the mirror. "This should put him in a better mood," I thought.

"Why don't we check out a movie," he said when I came out ready to head back to the beach. "*Lethal Weapon 4* is playing. I've been wanting to see that."

"Okay, no problem," I said, going back in the bedroom to change again.

Teddy relaxed and started to enjoy himself at the movies. We bought burgers and popcorn. I got soda to drink, and he got a beer. It wasn't very romantic, but at least we were having a good time. When the movie was over, we stopped at a bar for happy hour.

"I'm not trying to give you a hard time," Teddy said after we got a couple of drinks. "Things are going to get better, and I'll make it up to you."

"I've heard that before," I said half-heartedly.

"I know, but I mean it."

We ordered hot wings and had a few more drinks before he said, "Let's hit the beach."

We went back to the cottage and changed into our swimsuits and made the short walk to the beach. We rented an umbrella and found a spot among the crowd to set up.

"There are more people out here today," he said, sneaking a peak at some of the girls in the group close to us.

"Yeah, it looked like it might rain yesterday. Today is perfect."

"Come on, let's have some fun," he said taking off his t-shirt.

I unzipped my cover-up and let it fall to the ground. Teddy took my hand and pulled me to the water. It felt good to walk in the waves together holding hands, even if he pulled away after a couple of minutes. It gave me a momentary flashback to the days when there were public displays of affection toward me. We swam close to the shore and splashed in the water until the tide started coming in and the sky began to dim.

"I brought some wine," I said, reaching in my beach bag. "Do you want some?"

"Why not? I'm not driving."

I poured two glasses, and we watched the sunset.

"The sky is beautiful," I said.

"Yeah, it is, but this sand is making me itch. I'm ready for a hot shower," he said, standing up and brushing the sand from his trunks.

"Sounds good to me," I said, stretching to my feet.

"I like your swimsuit," he said as I was folding up the towel.

"I was wondering if you'd noticed," I replied, smiling.

"Oh, yeah, I noticed."

I gave him a sexy look. "I like your trunks."

"You'll like them better when I take them off."

"Is that right?"

"Oh, yeah, that's right."

"In that case, we better get back to the cottage," I said, putting the cover-up around my shoulders.

Our walk back to the cottage was a lot quicker than when we ventured out. And even though we weren't holding hands, I felt as if we had turned a corner, and maybe things could get better.

"I'll start the shower," Teddy said as soon as he closed the door behind us.

I took off my bathing suit and climbed in behind him, and he stepped to the side to share the streams of water. I soaped up a washcloth and began to wash his body. He reached for one and did the same to me. Touching him made me wonder how long it had been since we'd had sex. One thing I know is, if you have to think about it, it's been too long. Things got steamy in more than one way very quickly. We got out of the shower before our love scene turned into an accident.

"I have some massage oil I think you'll like," I told him as he was drying off.

"That's what I'm talking about," he said, turning on the CD player and turning off the lights.

We rubbed each other down with the oil, and I felt as if some of the magic was back. I had missed touching him and him touching me. I wanted to get lost in it and never find my way back to the loneliness I had felt. The passion between us was real, but it was different somehow. I didn't know what was missing. When both of us were satisfied, we laid next to each other, the light of moon shining across the bed. Then it occurred to me. He hadn't kissed me on the lips.

***

I woke up in the morning with mixed emotions. I was glad that we had reconnected intimately, but something was still bothering me. Teddy had abruptly turned hot from being so cold like the water from a faucet. I couldn't tell if his feelings were genuine. I decided to let it go since I have a tendency to overanalyze things.

"You hungry?" he asked, slapping me softly on the behind.

"Very, but I don't think we have anything in the fridge."

"Relax. Don't get up. Get some more rest. I'll go out and get something," he said, getting up and heading toward the bathroom.

Who could argue with that offer? I turned over and closed my eyes. The sound of the front door closing woke me up about an hour later. Teddy was back with breakfast. I hurried into the shower to get cleaned up. Thoughts of last night ran over me like the warm sprays of water as I soaped my body. We weren't where we needed to be, but at least we had taken the first step.

When I got out of the shower, Teddy was on the phone. I grabbed two plates out of the cabinet and put them on the table beside the bags of food and cups of coffee. In one take-out plate, there were scrambled eggs and biscuits. The other container was full of shrimp and grits. I scooped some from each container onto the plates and added cream to my coffee. Teddy ended his call and joined me at the table.

He took a few bites of the eggs. Then he said, "I hate to tell you this, but I need us to leave a day early. There's a client I have to meet. It's important. I have to get back."

"Teddy, I rearranged my schedule to make this trip. I thought you did, too."

"I did, but Warren called, and he's got some important buyers lined up. This could put us back in the black."

"What about us? We're not where we need to be in this relationship."

"What difference does it make whether we're at home or out of town? We can keep working on it when we're back at home."

"Then what was the point of making this trip anyway?"

"You were really stressed. I wanted you to get away and relax."

"So, I really could have made this trip by myself?"

"I'm not saying that, but it's you who feels like we have a big problem. Our money is tight, but I love you, and you love me. The kids are fine. It's not that serious."

Without saying a word, I stood up and went into the bedroom to pack. There wasn't much I could say. On the drive back home, there were a few times I felt as if he was trying to pick a fight, but I wasn't falling for that trick. That way, he could shift any blame on me. I kept my eyes on the road in front of me, even though I wasn't driving. This mini vacation was supposed to be the prescription to get our relationship back on track, but it was a long way from being recovered.

***

"So how was the weekend?" Sheree asked after I got out of the car.

On the spur of the moment I drove over to her house after work instead of going straight home. She was sitting on her porch drinking what looked like sweet tea.

"Not as great as I had hoped," I said, sitting down beside her.

"Do you want something to drink?"

"No, I'm good."

"Well, did you get your groove back or what?"

"It was good to spend some alone-time together, but I could still sense some resistance or resentment between us."

"I don't know, Chantelle. You must really love that man because I would have left his ass a long time ago."

I let out a huge sigh. "I probably should have, but now I've invested over five years in this marriage. It's time for all that hard work to pay off."

"It's still not too late to cut your losses," Sheree said, chuckling.

I smiled. "Stop, it's not just him. I can't walk away from the kids."

She nodded, and then her facial expression turned serious. "I hear you, girl. I've been waiting for the right moment to tell you that I'm pregnant."

My heart jumped, and then my stomach flipped. I was happy for Sheree, but it brought my disappointment about not having a baby of my own to the surface.

"I never thought I would be a mother," she said sincerely. "My plans were to be an aunt to your babies."

"Hopefully, you will be," I said, blinking back the water in my eyes.

Sheree's facial expression quickly changed from softness to indignation. "What do you mean "hopefully"? We know Teddy can make a baby. Is there something wrong medically that you haven't told me?"

"No, that's not it. Teddy wants us to wait until he gets his finances to a certain point."

Sheree rolled her eyes. "If he hasn't gotten his money together in all these years, I don't think it's going to happen any time soon. It's getting even rougher out here. He might need to let that real estate thing go for a while and find a regular j-o-b."

"Who's hiring? You know things are real tight in the job market."

"You've got that right. They're even laying off at the store."

"Maybe he's right. It's not the time for a baby."

"I'm not trying to cause problems for you, Chantelle, but the truth is you don't have to ask a man when to have a baby. Stop using those pills, and let God decide."

"I don't want to be tricky like that. That's what his baby mamas did. This is something we both should agree on."

"There's a big difference between you and his baby mamas. You're married to the man; they weren't. It's not fair for you to have to raise his kids, and you can't have one of your own. You're paying most of the bills anyway. Do what you want."

"We have enough problems without adding another one to the stack."

Sheree threw her arms in the air. "Like what?"

"He's keeping some late hours. I think he's hanging in the strip clubs again."

"So, he doesn't have money for a baby, but he has plenty for some hoes. Don't tell me anymore, Chantelle," she said, shaking her head and raising her hand. "I can't take hearing this bullshit. You can do what you want to do."

"Don't be like that, Sheree. I need your support on this. If my marriage is in trouble, then I don't need to be thinking about bringing a baby into it anyway."

"Well, you're right about that. I don't know what his problem is."

"It's like he's not interested in being with me anymore."

"Don't let him make his issues your issues. He's insecure, and he's making you insecure. You're only 30 years old, and you look as good as you did the day he stepped to you. He probably can't handle the fact that you are the one keeping a roof over his head."

"I don't know. He still won't go to counseling, so I don't know what to do."

"Chantelle, quit worrying about him and what he thinks. You have to make the decisions that are best for you."

"I know," I said, getting up to leave. "I guess it's time for us to have a serious conversation."

"Call me later, or I'm coming over there!" Sheree shouted.

***

I got the kids to help clean up the kitchen after dinner, while Teddy went into the great room to watch the news. When we finished, the boys went to their room to play video games, and I sat across from Terri and watched her practice writing her letters. I searched my head for the right words to begin this conversation, wondering if it made any difference how it started, being that I had some idea of how it would end. Nevertheless, I couldn't avoid it, I had walked around this impasse for long enough.

When Terri finished her homework, I read her a story, made sure she brushed her teeth, and tucked her into bed. I could see that she was hiding the portable DVD player that she got for her birthday under the blanket, but I let it slide. Maybe it would keep her from hearing us talking if things got heated.

I walked into the great room and sat down on the opposite end of the couch where Teddy was sitting.

"I want to talk to you about something," I said, crossing my legs.

"What's up?" he asked without taking his eyes off the TV screen.

"Terri is going to the second grade in the fall. She's not a baby anymore. The years have flown by so quickly."

"I know. I can't believe it," he said, nodding while still looking straight ahead.

"I've been thinking that it's the right time for me to get pregnant."

That finally got his attention. He sat up and scooted to the edge of the couch.

"Slow down, Chantelle," he said, trying to keep his voice down. "Don't you know that it's a recession going on? Nobody's buying houses right now. We've had to rent two properties just to keep from going further in the red. Money is real tight right now. It's definitely not the time for extra expenses."

"Money won't be a problem. I'm in line for a promotion, and I can absorb the cost."

"We already have three other mouths to feed, and clothes ain't cheap. What if you have to be off from work for a while?"

"I have some money saved. We'll get through it."

"In that case, we could use your savings to pay off some bills I'm struggling with."

"I don't think you appreciate the fact that I've worked my ass off. Your kids haven't gone hungry or wanted for anything. I've seen to that. But I want to raise my own flesh and blood."

"When we were on the trip, I thought we reached a compromise for us to move forward. You said you would give me another year to get some things squared away, and then we can have another baby."

"I know that, but Sheree just told me that she and Lawrence are having a baby. We've been together for five years. A few months earlier shouldn't make that much difference."

"So, this is about Sheree. I should have known. That's your problem. What goes on in this house doesn't have anything to do with what goes on in another house across town."

"I'm not concerned about what goes on in any other house but this one, and I don't like what's going on."

"What's that supposed to mean?" he asked, getting defensive.

"I mean, you hanging out in strip clubs and spending most of the night out here on the couch instead of being in bed with me."

"I have to clear my head sometimes, go out for a drink, or just relax. You're always riding me about a baby. That turns me off."

"So, you're saying that everything that has been going on with you is about me wanting to get pregnant? That doesn't make any sense to me. I'm not on your ass every day about having a baby. I'm the patient one who has been raising two other women's kids."

"Now you're going to throw that up in my face again?"

"Excuse me, but it's in my face every day," I said, my voice getting louder. "I've loved your kids like they were my own, but they're not. You've made sure that they don't see me as their mother. I've bent over backwards for you and for them. I want to have a child of my own."

"Look, baby, like I've said before, give me a little time. We need to get some things fixed up around the house, and then it will be no problem."

"I'll let it go for now, but I'm tired of waiting."

The weight of everything going on had me exhausted. I took a hot shower and went to bed early. I woke up around 2:30, and Teddy hadn't come to bed yet. I figured he had fallen asleep on the couch. I got up to tell him to come to bed, but he wasn't there, but I could see a sliver of light under his office door. I tiptoed to the door and slowly turned the knob. He was sitting there staring at his computer. I couldn't see what was on the screen, but from the look in his eyes and the motion of his arm, I could tell what was going on. He was masturbating to some porn.

I turned away quickly. I didn't know how to react. It was pure instinct, like snatching your hand away from a hot stove. I didn't want to be hurt anymore. I faulted myself that, over the past five years, I was still in the same predicament. Our relationship was like a Ferris wheel. It carried me up and down and around in a vicious circle where nothing changed. My biggest regret is that I hadn't gotten all his DVDs and destroyed them myself.

Chapter
Eleven

Six months passed, and I was avoiding Teddy just as much as he was avoiding me. The sight of him sitting there all engrossed in that crap made me sick whenever I thought about it. Teddy and the kids drove up to Baltimore for Christmas. I pretended to be sick with a cold. I knew we would be apart for our anniversary, and I didn't care. The truth was I didn't feel like pretending everything was okay. I was so glad I stayed home because Sheree went into labor on Christmas Eve. She had a baby girl she named Monica. She told me the name meant cheerful and pretty, two things I wasn't feeling at the time.

A couple of days after the holiday, Teddy and the kids weren't back yet. I left home early to stop by Sheree's house for coffee and to see the baby on my way to work.

Aunt Betty answered the door. "Good morning, child, you're up early."

"The kids are still in Baltimore, so I don't have them to slow me down," I said, taking off my coat.

"That's good, sweetie," Aunt Betty said, giving me a hug. "You deserve a break. Sheree's in the kitchen eating breakfast and holding the baby. I've told her she's gonna be sorry later for spoiling her like that."

"I heard that, Mama!" Sheree shouted from the kitchen.

I followed Aunt Betty into the kitchen and gave Sheree a hug from behind her neck. I hung my coat on the back of the chair beside her and sat down.

"You want something to eat, Chantelle?" Aunt Betty asked, going over to the stove.

"No, ma'am, I'm trying not to gain weight with all the sweets everybody brings in to work. Just some coffee, please."

"I wish I could drink a cup so bad," Sheree said, throwing her head back. "I was up half the night, but the pediatrician advised that I can't have caffeine in the breast milk."

"Is Lawrence still sleeping?" I asked, sipping from the mug Aunt Betty gave me.

"Yeah, he was up with me. He changed her, and I fed her. I don't know what I'm going to do when he goes back to work and Mama goes home."

"You'll be fine," Aunt Betty said. "You know I'm just a phone call away."

"Me, too. You know I'll be here in a heartbeat," I said. "She's a doll, so pretty. I'm so happy for you and Lawrence."

"She is my heart. I can't believe that I actually have a baby, a new life for me to love and take care of. I used to think that I didn't want kids."

"I didn't think you did either," Aunt Betty said. "You were always a little on the selfish side."

"Stop, Mama, I was only trying to focus on doing me for a while. Now, all that has changed."

"I always wanted a family," I said, gazing over at Monica. "I still want to have a baby of my own though."

"We have been through this a hundred times," Sheree fussed. "Stop letting that man dictate to you. You are more than an equal partner in that relationship."

I nodded. "I'm definitely going to make some changes for 2005."

Sheree shifted the baby to her other arm. "Well, I'm glad to hear that. Monica wants a cousin to play with."

"I wish I could take her with me," I said, checking my watch and putting on my coat. "I've got to get out in that traffic."

"It might not be too bad," Aunt Betty said. "A lot of people are taking off until New Year's."

"I thought about it, but nobody's home. I might as well go to work."

"Okay, sweetie," Aunt Betty said, walking me to the door. "Don't work too hard."

"I won't," I said as I waved back.

The sight of Sheree and her baby lingered in my mind as I drove. Neither of our lives had turned out the way we thought they would. Sheree was going to be a model and then a top buyer for Bloomingdales. I was supposed to have a successful husband who adored me, two children, and maybe a dog. Instead, even though she didn't have to work, Sheree still worked at Bloomingdales; and I was the major breadwinner with a husband who ignored me, stepmother to three children, and no dog. I envied Sheree.

Joanne was getting out of her car when I pulled into my parking space. She paused and waited for me to catch up with her.

"Happy Holidays!" she said, pushing the elevator button when I joined her.

"Happy Holidays to you, too," I answered as cheerfully as I could.

"Did you have a nice Christmas?"

"It was quiet. Teddy took the kids to Baltimore to visit his mother."

"You didn't want to go?"

"No, I needed some time by myself to think about our relationship. It can't keep going the way things are now."

"Are you all having problems again?"

"It's the same old thing. I can't even tell Sheree about it," I whispered as we walked down the hall toward our offices. "She'd have a fit."

"Come on in my office," Joanne whispered back. She hung up her coat, took my bag out of my hand, and guided me into one of the chairs in front of her desk. "Now, what happened?"

"It's what's *not* happening," I told her. "We barely have sex anymore, and when we do, it's like he's doing any other job he has to do around the house like cutting the grass or washing the car. He'd rather go to the strip club."

"Men get bored from time to time. Get yourself some rated-X lingerie, and do some role playing," Joanne said. "That worked for me and my husband when things slowed down. Sometimes you have to spice things up."

"Why do I have to be the one who spices it up? He's the one with the problem. I think he needs to get some counseling or something."

"It's not that serious, Chantelle," she said, lifting one hip onto her desk. "Try something different. Maybe you should go to the strip club with him. I hate to say it, but sometimes you have to get out of your comfort zone and get freaky. Trust me, I know what I'm talking about."

"I'll think about it," I said, grabbing my purse to leave. "I thought marriage was supposed to be a fifty-fifty proposition, not eighty-twenty."

"I hate to tell you, it could be worse. And if you were by yourself, it would be on you 100 percent all the time."

"I hear you," I said, closing her door behind me.

***

If people would have told me that I would be shopping in an XXX store to save my marriage, I would have called them crazy and laughed in their faces. I remember the days when Teddy wanted to sop me up like a biscuit in gravy. Now it's like he doesn't even see me. His preoccupation with naked women in magazines progressed to DVDs and then to the steady stream of porn from the internet. They say the only way to stifle a raging blaze is to fight fire with fire. So, I had decided to take Joanne's advice and surprise Teddy when he got back home.

"Do you need any help finding anything?" the man behind the counter asked with a smile.

I gave him a scowl. "No, thanks. I'm just looking."

And I was getting more than an eyeful. There were men parts and women parts for sale in all shapes, sizes, and colors. There were games, chains, handcuffs, and stimulating oils of all types. I reached for one of the strawberry massaging oils and moved to the lingerie. They had the usual French maid costume and countless happy hooker outfits. I decided on a baby doll ensemble with crotch-less panties.

There was one more thing I wanted to buy. The thing that I thought would intrigue him the most: a DVD. Perusing the aisle of never-ending selections of sex of all kinds, I could see a man on the other side of the aisle trying to make eye contact. There was no way I was going to do that. I bowed my head and looked down, and that's when I saw it. It was an X-rated version of the comedy movie *Barbershop*. My curiosity was piqued. I snatched it up and headed toward the checkout. Maybe it would be funny and hot at the same time.

"Did you find everything you need?" the guy at the counter asked, taking my baby doll outfit off the hanger and folding it up.

"Yes, thank you," I said in a low voice. I watched in embarrassment as he glanced over my choice of DVD.

"Your total comes to $83.10. Will that be cash, credit, or debit?"

"Cash," I answered, not wanting any record of this sale.

"Enjoy," he said, handing me my bag with a smile.

"Thanks." I grabbed the bag, and with three large strides, I was out of the store.

***

Teddy had some late appointments and a meeting with his partners afterward, so that gave me extra time to take a relaxing bubble bath before he got home. The boys were going to a sleepover with friends, and Sheree was glad to have Terri come over and spend the night and help with Monica. The DVD was already loaded up in the player, the ice bucket was filled, and I had a bottle of Courvoisier to take the edge off.

I heard his car door close just as I was slipping into my crotchless panties. Quickly, I ran the comb through my hair and laid down in a seductive pose on the bed and waited.

"Where are the kids?" he asked, coming through the bedroom door.

"The boys are at a sleepover, and Terri is at Sheree's house," I answered, waiting for him to comment on my outfit.

"What's going on?" he asked, looking puzzled.

"An evening with your wife," I replied, giving him a sexy stare. He kept standing there, looking confused. I tossed my head toward the dresser. "Why don't you pour us a drink?"

He finally moved and went over to the dresser and opened the bottle. "What brought this on?" he asked as he added ice to the glasses and filled them halfway with the brown liquor.

"I wanted some private time with my husband," I said, sliding off the bed and standing near him. "I think we both have been taking our relationship for granted. I don't want to do that anymore. I want us to have a new start."

"I don't have a problem with that," he said, smiling.

"I was thinking we might do something different," I said, picking up the TV remote. "Since you like to watch sex videos, I thought we might watch one together."

His eyes squinted for a second. "Why would you think that?"

"I want to see why you like them so much. Maybe I might like them, too." Then I pushed play on the remote.

"Where did you get it?" he asked suspiciously as the movie started.

I took a sip of the drink. "I bought it."

"Where?" he asked edgily, pulling his sweater over his head.

"What difference does it make?" I said, sitting down on the bed.

He sat down on the foot of the bed to watch the TV screen. The first scene was hilarious, not because of any comedy, but because the acting was so bad. The truth was, I was more interested in Teddy's reaction than I was in the movie. Then the script flipped when the female in the first scene took off her clothes.

"She's a bad lady," he said, not once, but every 15 seconds.

"Your comments are killing me," I said.

But he kept talking like I wasn't in the room. "She's good. She's all shaved. I like her fingernails."

I was speechless. Why couldn't he see the baddest lady in this whole scene was sitting in the room with him? Maybe he was trying to make me feel bad about myself. I was totally confused and insulted by his non-stop compliments about the so-called actresses. One by one, he praised all the women as they performed. Was he saying it to hurt me for some reason? Now, if I would have commented on how well the men were hung, that would have been out of order.

Then the insults morphed into humiliation. "These girls remind me of some chicks I've dealt with in the past," he said, staring at the screen. "Now that I think about it, I should have treated them better."

"Are you serious?" I asked, dumbfounded. Was he for real, or was he trying to mess with my head? In what level of his consciousness did he not realize that I was one of them? The low-budget trash movie ended, and I turned the TV off and turned on some music.

"Not a bad movie," he said, draining his glass. "Why don't you play it again?"

"No way," I told him. I couldn't believe it. I had already compromised by letting it play to the end with all his inappropriate remarks. I put my arms around his neck. "I'd rather we do our own show."

"Turn it back on. I want to see it again," he demanded, pushing me away.

Rejection was the worst when he decided that he would rather watch the whole DVD again instead of jumping in bed with me. I couldn't believe he asked me to play it again. It was all so disrespectful to me.

Now I was mad. "Hell, no! You have gone way too far. You're acting like a drug fiend jonesing for another hit."

That's when he turned on me and pitched a fit. "You're the one who brought the shit in here!" he shouted, standing to his feet. "What the fuck did you think you were doing? You've been bitching about me indulging in porn for years, and now you expect me to sit here and not enjoy it! Next time, check yourself. I'm getting tired of the bullshit. If you can't deal with it, then leave!" He grabbed his sweater off the bed and walked out of the room.

He had said those words to me before, ignored my feeling and belittled my pain, but I never saw how cruel it was. Maybe I did, but then I still had hope. Now I didn't. Granted, it was my fault for bringing that porno DVD in the house, but how was I supposed to know it would blow up in my face? I should have picked up on the warning signs when I asked him if he wanted to watch it. Like a fool, I thought us watching it together would spice things up, but he got caught up, and I disappeared again.

Who does that to his wife? Acting an ass on me over some fucking video hoes. If it wasn't so outrageous, it might be funny. He didn't come back. Sleeping in the bed with me was not on his list of priorities. I took off my sexy lace ensemble and put on an oversized t-shirt and crawled under the covers.

No apology came minutes later, not after an hour, and not the next morning. It was as if I wasn't there; my presence went unacknowledged. Honestly, I couldn't imagine that there was anything he could say to repair the damage that had been done. How could I have known that a damn porn tape would be the catalyst for the ending of my marriage? I promised him the last time we had an argument that, if he told me I could just leave again, I was out. I was going to keep my word to him and to myself.

***

Over the next few days, we walked around as if the other wasn't there. He slept on the couch in the great room and stayed there until I left. He stayed out late or made himself scarce when I came home from work. He didn't eat at the table with us. After I fed the kids and combed Terri's hair, I spent the evenings in the bedroom.

The hurt I was feeling was not attended to, and the wound festered, growing larger and moving deeper. Memories flooded back, and I began to relive all the pain and suffering I had endured over the years in the marriage. On the fifth morning, I called Joanne and told her I would be in late. I put on some sweats and took the kids to school and then went back to the house. I was so stressed out that I needed to do something to burn it off so I could function. I was riding my stationary bike in the garage when Teddy showed up.

"We need to talk," he said, holding a greasy bag with a bacon and egg sandwich inside.

I shook my head in disgust. Did he think I was a hungry dog he could buy off with a bag of food? I stopped pedaling and got off the bike.

"I'm listening," I said, curious to hear what he had to say.

"You were wrong for bringing that porno tape in the house," he said in a low voice.

"Excuse me?" I said, completely taken aback.

"Don't bring anymore porno tapes in the house."

"You have got to be kidding, Teddy. This isn't about the tapes; it's about you losing your damn mind."

"I'm not the one at fault here. You orchestrated that whole thing. I wasn't feeling it, and now you want to play the victim again."

I almost choked on the insanity of it. I could feel my body temperature rise and sweat break out all over me, even though I hadn't been exercising that long. I took a breath to calm myself before I spoke.

"First of all, you most certainly were the one who was wrong. When I asked you if you wanted to watch it, you should have said no if you were so-called uncomfortable. But that's not what happened. You started in talking about how good those women were, calling them ladies. I tried to be cool and let it slide, but you kept on. Even when I told you I didn't like it, you kept on. They were hoes, prostitutes, fucking on camera for money."

"It was all fake, Chantelle."

"What do you mean it was all fake? They were screwing on camera, and you couldn't stop saying how wonderful they were in front of your wife. What kind of sense does that make? After all your praises, I want to hear what they really are, Teddy—video hoes and prostitutes."

He refused to say it, talking around it. "That's not the point."

"I can't take listening to this," I said, staring up at the ceiling. Defending them to me was more degrading than him being obsessed with them. He could tell me how wrong I was, but he couldn't say anything derogatory about the working girls on the DVD. My ranting had left my mouth so dry, I walked away to the kitchen to get some water.

He followed me. "I mean it. Don't bring anymore porno tapes in the house."

In the kitchen, I gulped down a half glass of water before I said anything. "You don't tell me what to do. I'm a grown-ass woman. What you need to do is take responsibility for your actions and stop trying to blame me. This is nothing but a mind game, and I'm too old for that."

Teddy kept repeating himself, trying to blame me. He should have known that trick was not going to work. It was only pushing me to the edge. Then I lost it and kicked the chair closest to me, and it flipped over onto the floor. "Look, Teddy, at no time did you ask me to turn it off or express that it bothered you. You got mad because I refused to play it again. You should be apologizing, telling me how sorry you are and asking me to forgive you."

"That's exactly what you should be doing for bringing that porno tape into the house in the first place," he said angrily, staring me down.

"I'll bring whatever I want into my house. I'm grown!" I yelled. "You're not my boss. It's a shame that you call yourself a man, but you can't be accountable for your own behavior. You disrespected me. Now you have the nerve to stand here indignant after all the pornographic magazines that you brought into this house over the years, all the tapes you bought and hours you spent watching hoes on the internet, instead of spending time with a real live woman."

I thanked God that the kids were gone because I refused to pull any punches. Why did he make me bring up the past? He definitely wasn't an angel.

"Why don't you leave?" he hollered angrily.

"Why don't you?" I screamed back at him. "You can't deal with a real woman anyway."

Finally, I stopped. I didn't want to get so far out there emotionally that I couldn't get myself together to go to work. I stomped out of the room and up the stairs. I was so full of anger and hurt that I started clapping. I felt like I wanted to shout. I felt like it was inappropriate under the circumstances, but I couldn't stop calling Jesus as I undressed. "Draw me nearer, Lord!" I yelled to the ceiling. I shouted and danced my way into the bathroom as if I was in church. It was out of my control. I was overcome.

In the shower, I stomped my right foot over and over, splashing against the water. "My, my, my!" was all I could say. I hummed like the old sisters in Aunt Betty's church. All the emotions inside me were too much. I had to release them or explode. I turned off the water and continued to shout. Drying off, lotioning up, I continued to praise the Lord. I got dressed, all the while venting my overflowing emotions.

Teddy was still in the kitchen when I went down to eat breakfast. I poured myself a bowl of Rice Chex, but the sight of him there reading the paper was too much to bear. I took my bowl into the bedroom to eat in peace. I brushed my teeth, and when I finished, I went back into the kitchen. I walked past him, put my bowl in the sink, grabbed my bags, snatched a coat out of the closet, and rushed out to go to work.

In the car, I was still full of emotion. I banged my hand against the steering wheel to help release some of the tension. I hit the change button on the CD player until I found the album I wanted, *War*. I pushed the play button on the dash. I had been listening to it for days now. I pushed the forward arrow up to song number five, "Deliver the Word," because misery was my best friend and it had gotten so I couldn't pretend.

Chapter Twelve

You get busy with the hustle of everyday living, and the next thing you know, another four years have passed. Tempers continued to flair. Teddy offered half-assed apologies, but mostly, it was the fear of giving up too soon that made me reluctant to walk away from nearly eleven years of marriage. There were intermittent episodes of what felt like happiness in between the steady drama of heartbreak. The occasions when we did have sex, it was in the dark without kissing. I was like a drug addict, knowing I should leave this thing cold turkey; but I was hooked, searching for that same high I felt when we met at the Cosmopolitan Club.

The Isley Brothers' tune "Here We Go Again" became my theme song. The sexy lingerie I spent a small fortune on was a waste of money, so I bought cookbooks and tried cooking gourmet meals to get his attention. Then I tried exercising and dieting. I changed my hair. I even dyed it blonde to have more fun. I had a dozen facials, added more eyelashes, waxed and bejeweled my pubic area. I even considered plastic surgery while watching an episode of *Atlanta Plastic*. I had done a lot of things, but there was no way I was going under the knife. Then I thought, *This is ridiculous. It shouldn't take all of this to get love from the person you're married to.*

"Forget him," Sheree said. "Get yourself some toys, and handle your own business."

"Why should I have to get toys when I have a husband?"

"I could never figure out your relationship from jump street," she said, shaking her head. "At least he's finally getting his finances together."

"Thank God for that," I said, raising one hand in the air. "At least now I can get pregnant without him stressing about money."

"You should have had a baby years ago, two by now. I don't see how you let him dictate everything to you."

"I really don't have an answer for that. I still love him, and I guess I feel like I have invested a lot into our family. When the kids were babies, I thought they had already been shifted around enough. It's hard to believe the boys are going on fourteen and Terri is almost twelve."

Sheree shook her head. "I just want you to be happy, Chantelle."

"I think my time has finally come. I've waited long enough."

***

"We closed on a commercial property today," Teddy said that night, coming into the bedroom and waving a bottle of champagne. "And we have offers on the two foreclosures we remodeled to flip."

I looked at the clock. It was after midnight. "Congratulations. That's good news. Maybe you won't have to work so hard and so late."

"Come on, Chantelle, don't bring me down. I'm on top of the world."

"I'm ready to celebrate, too, Teddy. Celebrate me having a baby."

He froze. "What are you saying?"

"I'm saying I'm not taking the pill anymore."

"Here you go with this again. We agreed we'd do that when the time is right. Things are finally turning around for me. We can really get our game on solid ground."

"Me having a baby won't change that. We did all right with a lot less money and many more bills. It won't happen tomorrow. There's still time for us to get even more solid."

"I was hoping that we could fix up the house first. This crew we're working with is topnotch. Once we pay this mortgage off, then I can go out on my own and make some real money. Property is dirt-cheap in Atlanta right now."

"I've already waited long enough. If I wait for you to do all that, I'll be going through menopause. You keep asking me to sacrifice; now it's your turn to sacrifice."

"I'm sorry," he said, putting the bottle of champagne down on the dresser. "I'm not sure I want any more children. The kids are up on their feet. I can't think about starting all over with a baby."

My mouth opened, but I had no words. My eyes filled up, and the streams of tears ran over my lips and dripped onto my chest. I screamed.

I saw the look of disgust on his face. "Here you go with this again."

My shock and anger to his reaction to my pain steeled the wavering emotions inside of me. With one iota less of self-control, I would have thrown something at him from across the room because the very thought crossed my mind. I bawled up my fingers lest they have a mind of their own and grab something. Luther Vandross said, "Anyone who had a heart would surely take me in his arms and love me." This man had no heart, just a cold lump of flesh that pumped the ice through his veins.

***

I called in sick for the rest of the week. I didn't have the wherewithal to get out of bed. I had given all I had to my marriage, the children, my job, and I didn't have anything left. I didn't even have the strength to talk to Sheree or Aunt Betty.

On Friday, I showered and made my way into the kitchen to get breakfast. I would have given my last dime to smell and hear bacon sizzling. There was barely anything in the fridge; I hadn't been to the grocery store in over a week. I poured myself a bowl of Cheerios and sat down to eat. I heard a car in the driveway. Teddy had taken the kids to school earlier. He must have forgotten something.

Teddy walked into the kitchen and dropped an envelope on the table. "It's a loan application for the house," he said brusquely.

"For what house?"

"This house. I need to refinance it."

"Why is that?" I asked, clueless.

"I can't afford the note as it is; it doesn't leave me enough to live on."

"What are you talking about? I've been paying this mortgage for years. What's the problem?"

"We're not going to make it, Chantelle. We don't want the same things. I went to an attorney, and she suggested that we redo the mortgage."

I couldn't believe the words that were coming out of his mouth as they jammed into my ears. As much as this man had put me through, he had the nerve to go to an attorney.

I pushed the bowl of cereal to the side and propped my elbows on the table. "You went to see an attorney about a divorce. You should have gone somewhere to get some counseling. I'm not going to allow you to upset me any further. If you want to throw away your family over the way you behaved with your porno addiction, then go ahead and do it. But believe me, I will tell the kids why you did it. I'm not keeping any more of your secrets."

"It wasn't an attorney; it was more like a mediator," he said, a little less arrogant.

"I don't care which one it was because if you want to get a divorce, you are going to need an attorney. I'm not giving you any breaks. You have put me through too much. You should have been trying to mediate with me for years now."

"I tried to talk to you a couple of days ago. You weren't receptive."

"That's because you came to me all wrong. You weren't apologizing for your behavior. You were trying to flip it and blame me for what went down, and I wasn't accepting that. I know what kind of woman I am and what I deserve."

Teddy stood there looking blank. I pulled the bowl back in front of me and stuffed my mouth with several spoons of the Cheerios. They tasted like wet cardboard. My appetite was gone.

"I've done the best I can," he said., looking me in the face.

"If that was your best, then that's pretty sad. In the past, I put up with a lot of bullshit because of the children. I saw that you were a good father to them. I stood by you, and we worked hard and provided for all their needs. It was because of them that I swallowed so much hurt. Now, after all these years of asking me to wait to get pregnant, you tell me you don't want to have any more babies. After all the sacrifices I've made. It's obvious that you have never cared how I feel."

"That's not true, Chantelle. I cared about how you felt."

"If you honestly cared about how I felt, you would have never let the sun go down without trying to fix whatever the problem was. If the problem came in the night hours, you shouldn't have let the sun come up with trying to talk to me."

He dropped his head, and then he said it. "I'm sorry. I was wrong."

It was too little and much too late. I got up and poured the rest of the bowl of cereal down the garbage disposal and walked out of the kitchen. I was blown away that he would have taken steps to divorce me after all that he had put me through. There was food residue still in my mouth because I couldn't swallow. I needed to brush my teeth so badly. I walked by the bed and thought that I would've loved to lie down and have a big ugly cry, but I needed to get to work. A few tears escaped, and my eyes were red. So after brushing my teeth, I put a drop of Visine in each eye to hide the redness.

***

I don't know how I even managed to get through the workday without screaming at the top of my lungs. How I smiled on cue and carried on small talk with Joanne about her new grandbaby boggles my own mind even now. It's probably because I'd spent twelve long years holding in my feelings.

I left work a few minutes early to pick Terri up from her ballet class. She usually looked out for my car and came right out; but after ten minutes, I went inside the dance school to see what the delay was. I didn't see Terri in the changing room, so I peeked through the window of the class in session.

The teacher walked over to the door. "Hi, Mrs. Griffin. Terri's dad picked her up early today. I thought it was some kind of emergency. He must have forgotten to call you."

"I guess he did," I told her. She went back to her class, and I hurried back to the car.

That was weird. Teddy never picked Terri up from her class. He was always too busy. I wondered what could possibly be wrong. Back on the interstate, I pulled into the high-occupancy lane to bypass some of the rush-hour traffic.

When I got home, I expected to see Teddy's car in the driveway, but it wasn't there. I rushed inside, wondering what was up, but no one was home. That was strange. Usually, the boys were already playing video games. Maybe Teddy decided to take them out for dinner.

I went into our bedroom to change. I took off my shoes and walked to the closet. That's when my jaw dropped. All of Teddy's clothes were gone. I ran down the hall to Terri's room. Most of her clothes were gone, too, and some of her things were missing from the walls and the dresser. With my mouth still hanging open, I went to the boys' room. It was the same thing in there. What in the hell was going on?

I ran back to the bedroom to get my phone to call Sheree. My foot tapped nervously as I waited for her to pick up.

"What's up, girl?" Sheree answered.

"I just got home, and nobody's here. Teddy's clothes are gone and so are the kids' stuff."

"Are your things still there?" she asked, flustered.

"Yeah, they are."

"At least you know you didn't get robbed. I'm on my way over there right now."

"I think he left me, Sheree. This morning, he told me he went to see an attorney."

"Don't do anything. I'm going to get off this phone so I can drop Monica off at Mama's house. Lawrence isn't home yet. Just sit down, and wait for me."

"All right," I said, sitting down on the edge of the bed. I was stunned. For all the bullshit that I dealt with and had stood by him, he's the one who left me. I would have left him a long time ago if I had known it was going to come to this.

It didn't seem like much time had passed before I heard Sheree banging on the door. I was stuck in a daze, similar to that vivid dream you have when you're lightly sleeping. I stood up like a zombie in a horror flick and dragged my feet to the door.

"I was one second from busting this door down!" Sheree said, pushing her way in. "Now tell me what the hell is going on in this crazy house!" I stood there looking blank, and she grabbed my hand and dragged me back to the bedroom. She stopped in front of the open closet and shook her head. "This is some bullshit!" We stood there for a minute, looking at the empty side where Teddy's clothes used to be. "Are you going to tell me the story?"

I sat down and tried to gather my thoughts. "We had an argument about me getting pregnant, and then he said he didn't want any more children," I said slowly.

"That low-down no-good mothafucka has played you all these years!" Sheree shrieked. "He was just looking for somebody to support him and his snotty-nosed kids. Now that you did that, he bounces. He better be glad I know Jesus, or I would buy a gun, hunt his sorry ass down, and pump him full of holes."

"The worst part is he never stopped watching internet porn and fantasizing about other women while he pretended I wasn't even here."

"I never wanted to hurt your feeling, sis, but you have been a complete fool for that man. That's okay though because there is a silver lining to this mess. The shit is over!"

"I'm so tired," I said, falling back on the bed and crying out.

"You can be tired, and you can cry," Sheree said, scooping me up in her arms. "Hell, we'll all cry with you. But when we get done crying, you got to leave this house. There's nothing left here for you."

I cried like a baby with colic, and Sheree held me tight and rocked me until I fell asleep. When I woke up, daylight was breaking, with a ray of sunlight shining through the window. I peeled off the dress I had worn for 24 hours and made my way into the bathroom. I was shocked by my own reflection. My face was puffy, and my eyes were almost swollen shut. My makeup was smeared, and my hair was matted. I looked as if I had gone the distance with Muhammad Ali. I climbed into the shower to wash away the evidence of my heartbreak.

Sheree was waiting with a mug of hot coffee in her hand when I came out of the bathroom. I drank half of it before I put the cup down. I felt better. The water had refreshed me, and the coffee had reinvigorated me. I was beaten, but I felt as if I could fight one more round.

"Let's get out of here," Sheree said, throwing my empty luggage on the bed.

"I might as well," I said with resignation.

It was a slow process at first. I was painstakingly arranging each piece ever so neatly. I must have been numb. When the pain came rushing back like a runner on my heels, I began to move faster and faster until I was packing my suitcases feverishly and breaking a sweat. I didn't let up. I could feel my dignity slowly seeping back into my open pores.

Chapter
Thirteen

It wasn't by choice, or maybe it was, but a lot of my time was spent alone. Teddy was now my ex-husband. I dropped his name and recovered my own. As divorces go, ours was among the nastiest. He reclaimed the children, Jeremy, Julius, and Terri, whom I had thanklessly raised for his two baby mamas. The real ass-kicker was that I didn't have any parental rights after almost 13 years of mothering. Not only that, he wanted half of everything, including the house, everything in it, and alimony. We were all lucky that the judge didn't give it to him, or Sheree would definitely be doing jail time.

The house is still on the market, but I've moved to a two-bedroom townhouse in Buckhead. I thought about getting three bedrooms for when the kids come to visit me, but they rarely call.

It took a while for me to learn how to cook for just myself. I gained ten pounds trying not to waste the extra food until I started carrying the leftovers to work. For the first few months, I supplied a hefty lunch for Joanne and my administrative assistant, Mindy. When their clothes also began to fit tighter, they told me I had to stop. I started shopping at the Friendly Foods Organic Grocery store near my apartment to train myself how to buy less food. After a few months of going there three times a week, I was familiar with everybody who worked there on the afternoon shift.

There was Arlene, the short, chubby manager with dark brown hair and gray roots that she tried to cover with a black baseball cap with the letter "A" on it. There was Iris, the young, slim black cashier with braids who never made eye contact or conversation. There was Miss Trudy, the tall widow who wore her thin blue hair in a tight bun. And there was Jimmy, the Latino college kid who never stopped dancing.

I pushed my cart through the aisles and the maze of shoppers going in opposite directions. It confounded me how we could weave around one another without exchanging any pleasantries. Having already collected my self-directed maximum of items, I moved toward the front of the store. I paused for a moment between the two checkout lines to judge which line was moving the fastest. A usual, Iris was working at twice the speed of Miss Trudy, but it wasn't just her youth that made her move faster. My guess was that Iris's hands paced themselves to the speed at which she chewed and popped her gum.

Not feeling patient, I chose the line Iris was working. I guided my cart through the narrow aisle and placed my items on the counter. I stood and watched as she absentmindedly scanned my items, while Jimmy, the bag boy, energetically packed oatmeal and milk into the plastic bags, bouncing to the salsa music in his headphones. Iris was making good progress until, all of a sudden, a lanky white kid rushed up to the counter. My first thought was that he was rudely breaking line.

Then he shouted at us. "Put your hands up in the air, and move back!" His voice cracked as he tried to disguise his tenor register as a baritone. The torn leg of nude-colored pantyhose did little to conceal his acne-covered face.

He pointed his gun at Iris, who had been sleep-working behind the register. She was instantly shocked into attention. She raised her arms and backed up, her eyes stretched wide and her speechless mouth poised to scream.

"Just my luck," I muttered under my breath as I stood there as frozen as the bag of broccoli and cauliflower still in my hand. That was the moment when I realized that I didn't value my life.

The whole scene was like watching an episode of *Law and Order* on TV. The skinny teenager nimbly jumped on top of the counter, then over it. He punched the top of the register with his hand—the same hand holding a small revolver—until the cash drawer opened.

In the background I could hear Mariah Carey singing "A Vision of Love" as the boy feverishly snatched the bills from each compartment in the register's drawer. Looking like an adrenaline-filled animal that had finally captured his prey, he nearly fell to floor after he hopped back over the counter and fled the store through the automatic doors. Iris, still trembling at the bagging area beside Jimmy, caught her breath and finally released the scream from the back of her throat.

Arlene, in her black pants and crisp white shirt bearing the Organic Foods emblem, came jogging out from behind the customer service booth toward us. "What's going on out here?" she hollered. "What's all the noise about?"

"We just got robbed," Iris yelled, her hands now tangled in her long braids.

"Oh, my God!" Arlene said, pulling her cell phone from her pocket and dialing 911. "What happened? What did they look like?"

Iris closed her eyes to concentrate. "It was one guy. He was white with light brown hair; kind of tall, but not that tall. He had on low-rider skinny jeans and a black fake leather jacket with a lot of zippers over a white t-shirt."

Arlene then shifted her attention to the dispatcher on the phone. With her hands still shaking, Iris called someone on her phone.

Two other customers, a man dressed in biker gear and an older woman wearing a long bohemian looking dress splotched with paint, walked up to the checkout line behind me. They were asking each other what happened. Neither of them asked me anything. It was as if I wasn't even there. I dropped the bag of frozen vegetables I had been holding onto the motionless conveyor belt next to the organic farmed salmon and the wild rice I had placed there earlier and walked out of the store.

There was no reason to stand around and wait for the police or the cashier to get back to business. After all, Iris hadn't swiped my card. The fact was the most certainly amateur robber, who had never looked in my direction, had stolen my appetite along with his meager take of cash. Walking to my car, I could hear the sirens growing louder. This was another episode in the story of my life. I'm always in the midst of some swirling drama like the air in the center of a powerful tornado.

Aunt Betty was worried about me and suggested I move in with her for a while, but I was sure that seeing me mope around would only have worried her more. I told her I would think about it when my lease was up. Sheree thought I was spending too much time by myself and convinced me to go back to school to keep my mind occupied.

The night classes worked like a tonic, slowly bringing me back to my former self before I met Teddy. On weekends, I entertained myself with the television remote, channel surfing, watching mostly news, talk shows, and individual sports like track and field, and tennis.

In my self-induced seclusion, I became opinionated, having passion-filled conversations about politics, religion, and relationships quite often. But they were only in my head. There was no one around to hear them. I became a kindred spirit to the solitary jaguar in the forest whose spots keep it camouflaged while living life in its established territory. Similarly, I became strong but not aggressive; I did what I had to do to survive.

***

It had been a year and a half since the divorce, but I hadn't completely healed yet. Count me among the other soldiers of love who suffer from post-traumatic syndrome disease. On a happier note, Sheree had another baby, Lawrence Jr. She suggested we join a gym to workout. I think it was more about getting me out of the house.

"It's hard, but it's fair, sis," she said slightly out of breath. "We've got to get our summer bodies back."

"I have a treadmill in my apartment. Why do we have to come here just to get some exercise?"

"You need to get out and breathe some fresh air, be around other people. There are some nice specimens walking around in here."

"I hadn't noticed."

"You've got to get that booty tight to meet somebody new," Sheree laughed, watching me sweat as I jogged.

"Please don't curse me like that," I told her. "I'm doing fine by myself."

"Trust me. I know Teddy took you down through some shit, but that doesn't mean that you won't find the right guy who'll give you the love you deserve."

"My stomach is growling, and my muscles are aching and trembling they're in so much shock. This is ridiculous. Does it take all of this to get some love?"

"It's not only about the exercise, sis; it's about getting in the right frame of mind. I don't want to see you cut yourself off. You're a great lady with a lot of love left to share."

"That's what I thought when I met Teddy. Giving of myself only got me used up."

"Stop with the negativity," Sheree said, slowing down to a walk. "Don't let him make you the victim. Let him be the loser. You're still on your feet, Chantelle. You look good, you're still young, you have a great job, and you have a family that loves you."

"I'm almost 39 years old. What hurts me so bad is that I wasted so many years of my life, my youth, with somebody who didn't give a damn about me."

"You took a chance, sis. That's what life is all about."

"I gambled and lost."

"So what? You're not broke. You're still in the game."

"I hear you, sis. I just need a little more time to steady my nerves before I place another bet."

Sheree shook her head. "Uh, uh. No, you don't. Waiting just gives more time for your fears to build up."

"I can't argue with that. Thinking about being in another relationship scares me to death."

"Well, I was trying to work this into the conversation, but you aren't cooperating, so here it is, point blank. One of Lawrence's frat brothers is in town, and I want you to come over and have dinner with us. It'll be fun."

"Come on, Sheree," I said, coming to a halt. "You know I'm not in the mood for that."

"You've haven't been in the mood for any fun, even before you and Teddy broke up. Now it's time to fake it. Tomorrow, we are going to buy you a new dress, go to Shear Beauty to get our hair and nails done, and then sit down and have a nice meal.

***

"You look fabulous, sis!" Sheree said, opening the door and grabbing my arm. "Come on in. Mama is watching the kids tonight, so it's strictly a grown folks evening." She led me to the living room where the guys were talking. They stood up when we walked in.

"What's up, sister-in-law?" Lawrence said, giving me a hug. "You're looking good."

"Thank you," I answered, stepping back.

"This is my frat brother, Alex Bivins, from Nashville. He drove down for some business and is spending the weekend in the ATL." Then he introduced me. "Alex, this is Chantelle. She's Sheree's cousin/sister. They grew up together."

"I can see the resemblance," Alex said, extending his hand toward me. "It's a pleasure to meet you, Chantelle."

"Thank you, Alex," I said in my formal working tone.

"Let's eat," Sheree chimed in. "My dinner is getting cold, and I worked too hard for that."

"Don't worry. It won't have time to get cold," Lawrence said, his arms around Sheree's waist. "I've been smelling that roast cooking all day. I'll help you bring the food to the table."

I stopped at the dining room table while Sheree and Lawrence went into the kitchen. I sat down in my usual seat, the one next to Sheree, and Alex took the seat across from me.

"So, what do you do, Chantelle?" Alex asked politely.

"I'm an actuary."

"She's a senior actuarial analyst at Supreme Life Insurance downtown," Sheree said, setting a serving platter on the table before she sat down. "She's also working on her master's degree at Emory University."

"That's pretty impressive," Alex said, nodding in approval. "Beauty and brains, too."

"It runs in the family," Sheree said, smiling.

Lawrence came in carrying a steaming dish of scalloped potatoes and a bottle of wine under one arm. "Let me bless this food real quick, and then you all can chow down." He put the bottle of wine down on the table and said, "Bless this food, Lord. Amen."

"You're right, baby, that was real quick," Sheree said, teasing him.

"Like you said, I don't want your meal to get cold." Lawrence opened the wine and filled the glasses that were elegantly placed on the table.

"What brings you in town, Alex?" Sheree asked.

"I own a couple of Meineke franchises, one in Nashville, and one in Chattanooga," Alex answered. "I'm thinking about opening one in Atlanta. I'm here to check out the market." Then he turned toward me. "Maybe you could give me the benefit of your expertise, Chantelle."

I put a forkful of the prime rib in my mouth before I answered. "That's really not my area."

Sheree rolled her eyes at me. "With all the cars on the road here, you should not have a problem finding a good spot. Buckhead is nice or maybe someplace on the Perimeter."

"I'll get my brother hooked up. Believe that," Lawrence said, giving Alex a fist bump.

"I appreciate that, my brother," Alex said. "It helps to have connections in a new market."

"So, how do you like Nashville?" Sheree asked, changing the subject. "It seems kind of slow to me. I cannot do the country music scene."

Alex smiled. "It's not bad. It's a great place to raise a family."

Sheree perked up. "Do you have any children?"

"No, I don't. I've never been married. After college, I spent most of my time and energy trying to get my businesses off the ground. That took a lot of focus. It's something I'm thinking more about lately."

"I can understand that," Sheree said, smiling. "Chantelle is divorced, but she has that in common with you. She focused on her career, too, and has moved up the ladder at her company. I believe she's thinking about getting back out there in the game, too."

I rolled my eyes at Sheree, and I didn't care who saw it. She was being real extra. I didn't need to be talked up and sold to a casual buyer just to get me off the market. I had already sold myself cheap once, and I wouldn't do it again.

I pushed my chair back and picked up my plate. "I can't eat another bite. The dinner was delicious, sis. Can I get anybody anything from the kitchen?"

"No, thank you. I'm good," Alex said, rubbing his stomach. "Thanks for inviting me; I haven't had a home-cooked meal in a long time."

I stood up and reached for the serving dish.

"I can clean up later, Chantelle. Sit down, and relax."

"No, that's fine. I got this. You cooked, so I'll help with the dishes."

Lawrence sensed the building tension in the air. "I'm going to take Alex out on the patio for a smoke. I can't wait to sample the prime cigars he brought from Miami."

"Okay, baby," Sheree said. "We'll join you guys in a little bit."

Once Sheree heard the door slide closed, she started in on me. "What's your problem, Chantelle? You're acting like you don't want to have a good time."

"I'm here, and I had a nice time. What more do you want?"

"Alex is a good guy. He's fine. He's doing his thing, and he doesn't have a boatload of baggage to deal with."

"I don't have anything to say against him. He's cool."

"Well, you only gave him one-word answers all night. He probably thought you weren't interested."

"You were trying too hard, Sheree, and it was getting on my nerves. If I want a man, I can find him by myself. I don't need you to play matchmaker for me."

"Maybe you do. Maybe if you had listened to me for one minute, you wouldn't have had to go through all that bullshit with Teddy in the first place."

"You're probably right, but I can't do anything about that now, can I?" Sheree's shoulders dropped. "I'm sorry, sis. I didn't mean to push. I only want you to be happy. You deserve to have somebody who cares about you."

"You're right. I do. But I don't want you to find a man for me or feel sorry for me. I don't want a man who will date me out of convenience or just because he's tight with my brother-in-law. He probably wouldn't even have approached me if we had met on the street."

"It's not that serious, Chantelle. You're saying he wouldn't have noticed you, except that's not true. You are gorgeous, but you shut people out. You won't let anybody get close to you. It's like there is a wall around you."

"That's not true. If that was true, how did I get so hurt?"

Sheree put her arms around me and hugged me. I felt warm and safe, safe enough to cry the tears that had been held back by the virtual dam in my head. Then we heard the guys talking as they came back inside.

"It's getting ready to pour down raining out there," Lawrence said, sliding the patio door shut.

"I guess I should hit the road before it gets bad out there," I said, firming up the dam behind my eyes. I picked up my clutch from the table and gave Sheree and Lawrence a quick hug. "It was very nice to meet you, Alex."

"Same here," he said politely.

It was already drizzling when I dashed out to my car. Through the raindrops on my window, I could see Sheree waving to me from the open front door. I pressed the horn lightly to signal another goodbye as I backed out of the driveway.

I replayed some of the dinner conversation in my mind as I drove. Could Sheree have a point about me shutting myself off from contact with other people? Then there was a loud crack of thunder and lightning in the sky above me. It was as if the heavens had shattered and water was pouring through the break. I turned my high beams on and the window wipers up as high as they would go, hoping for more visibility in the darkness.

That's when I saw a huge truck, probably an eighteen-wheeler, running close on my back in the storm. I was already in the right lane for slower traffic, but his lights were so close that they illuminated the whole inside of my car. I considered changing lanes to get him off my back, except I didn't have room to change lanes. Then another car sped up beside me. Water splashed up on my windshield, and I was blinded for a second.

The truck behind me changed lanes and passed me, speeding up as he went. As he pulled ahead, I could feel my car hydroplaning as the draft from the truck sent me into a tailspin. I felt as if I was moving in slow motion inside the fast-spinning car. I heard tires screeching as other cars dodged around me. My hands were shaking so much that I took them off the steering wheel. I wondered how this moment would end. Would I be hurt? Would I be killed? I thought I saw a shadow in the road. I thought it might have been a deer.

Suddenly, the car slid across the road, and I stopped spinning. The front of the car was pointing toward the sky, and my rear tires were deep in a ditch. I took a few minutes to thank God that I was alive and okay. After I stopped shaking, I turned on the emergency blinkers. I waited for about ten minutes. More cars sped by me as the storm continued. I climbed out of the car to assess the damage and to see if there was a way for me to get the car out.

There I was on the side of the interstate, a woman wearing a silk magenta party dress and strappy heels. I was drenched from head to toe and standing beside a car that was obviously disabled, but no one stopped. Instead, cars sped by and splashed me with water. I released the dam behind my eyes again and let it mix with the rain. When that flood was over, I got back in the car, dug my cell phone out of my purse, and pushed the number on the top of my contacts for AAA.

***

The car accident was another entry in my series of unfortunate incidents. I was on a roll of bad luck. My beautician of fifteen years over-processed my hair; and despite spending a small fortune on multiple deep conditioners, more of my hair was falling around my feet every morning. It's hard enough to be knocked down, but whittling me down piece by piece was shear torture. I finally surrendered and went with Sheree to her beautician and got a weave.

"I can't win for losing right now," I told Sheree as Roger, her stylist, braided my hair.

"You have to do something wild to flip the script," Sheree said sympathetically. "Maybe you need to take a cruise or a long vacation to push your reset button."

"That would surely push mine," Roger shouted. "If you need a partner in crime, a security guard, or a photographer, I'm your man, honey."

"Step back, Roger," Sheree said, pretending to be in a huff. "That position is already filled."

Roger laughed. "I hear you, girl. I'm just saying, I'm available, will travel."

"You are both silly. With my luck, I'll get caught in a tsunami or kidnapped by a terrorist."

"As long as he's fine, honey, lock me up," Roger said.

"I'm not listening to y'all anymore," I said, giggling.

"By the way," Sheree said, "I meant to tell you that you should have gotten with Lawrence's frat brother. He's talking to the chick he met at the real estate office. She doesn't have anything on you, Chantelle."

"Did he ask you for my number after I left?"

"No, but that's because you dissed and dismissed him."

"It wasn't like that, and if he was interested, he would have asked for my number."

"That's true, Sheree," Roger interjected. "If he was really feeling her, he would have asked."

"Excuse me, Roger, while you are all in the conversation. If you put up a fence, most people won't take the time to climb over it. They'll walk around it."

Roger snapped his fingers. "That's gospel, Sheree. Preach in here today."

"It didn't work out. My bad," I said, throwing up my hands. "Can we please change the subject?"

While Roger installed my weave over the next hour, we talked about music, TV shows, and Sheree entering the Mrs. Georgia pageant.

"You would blow all those heifers away, Miss Thang," Roger told her.

"I don't have any doubts about that," Sheree said, checking herself out in the mirror.

"Okay, born-again diva," Roger said, swiveling my chair around to face the mirror. "How do you like it?"

I frowned. "This is entirely too much hair. I need you to thin it out some and cut it."

Roger took a step back. "Perish the thought, honey. This is some of my best work."

"It looks good, Chantelle, and that's the truth," Sheree said, looking in the mirror at me.

"I'm not saying it doesn't look good. It's just a little over the top for my taste."

"Then you must not have any taste," Roger protested. "This is how it's done in the ATL. You go big, baby, or you go home. I'm telling you, that's how we do it. I worked my magic today."

"You all don't know how I've been struggling with the thought that I'm not enough being who I am. It seems like wearing all this hair is buying into that."

"You're just not used to seeing yourself in full fabulousity," Sheree said, trying to reassure me. "That is you. Don't be afraid to embrace it."

"How can I embrace it?" I said to both of them. "When I left work on Friday my hair looked like rats had been chewing on it. Now I'm supposed to stroll in there Monday looking like Chaka Khan."

"Look here, chile," Roger said, waving his hands. "I do hair all day long every day, so believe me when I quote my girl, Indie Arie, "You are not your hair." It's like a crown you wear. It can be short, long, straight, or curly. You can even shave it off or put on a hat. It's still a crown."

Sheree nodded in agreement. "You have to start thinking differently about your style and your hair. The truth is hair is an accessory just like your jewelry and your shoes. It completes the look. Stop putting yourself in a box."

Roger started clapping. "That's right, sugar. Go back in time and ask Nefertiti, Cleopatra, and Miss Ross."

"Who can argue with that?" I said, laughing.

Fourteen

When I debuted my new look at work, it didn't take long for all the raised eyebrows to settle down. I stopped worrying so much about what people thought of me and if they even noticed me. It was my time to focus on what I thought about me. I was on a new kick to come out of my comfort zone and live my life to the fullest. On my thirty-ninth birthday, I treated myself to a red Corvette. If I couldn't make an impression, the car could do it for me.

I was cruising home from work, enjoying the Bose sound system, when I noticed a light flash on the dashboard. It was my gas light; the car was practically on empty. I got off the interstate and pulled into the first gas station I saw. With the luck I was having, I couldn't risk trying to make it to the Shell station where I usually bought gas.

For some reason, standing there pumping my gas made me thirsty. It was probably all the ads and pictures of soft drinks on the market's windows. Why not get a little fuel for myself for the ride home since I was still in the "treating myself mode"?

I walked along the cooler's wall of glass doors, eyeing all the selections, waiting for that random choice of caffeine to jump out at me. One bottle had me curious. It was an opaque white flavor of Mountain Dew. It looked refreshing enough and peaked my interest on what it tasted like. I grabbed a bottle and made my way to the shortest of the three cashier lines at the front of the store. In the line next to me, I saw a guy talking into his Bluetooth and motioning to somebody in my direction. I turned around to see who he was motioning to, but there was no one there.

"You," he said, pointing at me. I pointed at my chest, puzzled. He nodded. "Yes, you, Miss Lady, over there looking all good."

"I didn't know you were speaking to me," I said, a bit put off as he approached me. "I thought you were talking to somebody on your phone."

He came too close, ignoring the three-feet rule of invading someone's personal space.

"I was talking to you. I'm Samuel," he said, grinning. "I'd like to meet you."

I didn't know how to react to the unexpected attention. What did he want? Was it a ploy, a ruse to take advantage of me in some way? The store was bustling with customers, or witnesses, so that wouldn't make sense.

"What's your name, Miss Lady? I know you have one."

"Chantelle," I answered, wishing the cashier would pick up her pace so I could get out of there and back to my car.

"That's a beautiful name. It sounds like royalty. You look like a queen."

"Thank you," I said, taking a step forward. At least I was next in line.

"I wish you would be my queen."

I ignored his remark and put my drink on the counter for the cashier.

"That's $1.67," the cashier said. "Do you want a bag?"

"I've got hers," Samuel told the cashier, putting his bottle of sweet tea and pork rinds on the counter. "We're together."

I looked at him indignantly. "We are *not* together."

"We will be," he said matter-of-factly.

I stared at his profile as he paid the cashier, wondering where he got all his nerve from. That's when I discovered he wasn't bad looking. Truthfully, he was handsome in a rough kind of way: dark-skinned with curly hair, small eyes, and a thin mustache.

"Are you going to keep the drink?" I asked once we were out of line. It was in his bag, and giving it to me seemed like the last thing on his mind.

"No, Miss Chantelle, I want to carry it for you to your car."

"That's not necessary. I can manage."

"I'm sure you can. That's not the point."

Arguing would take more time. The quickest way to end this was to get to the car. I led the way, thinking this could be another episode that might go left. Even so, I found Samuel to be amusing in a good way. I kept a straight face though. I wasn't sure why he was checking for somebody he met in a gas station market.

"Nice car," he said when I stopped beside my Corvette.

"Thank you, I said, holding my hand out for the cold drink. He gave it to me grudgingly.

"Can I see you tomorrow?" he asked after I unlocked my car door.

"Are you serious?" I asked doubtfully.

"Yes, ma'am. I'm serious as two heart attacks."

I almost laughed. He was so country. "You want me to meet you back here again?"

"No, I want to take you on a date. Let's go see a movie."

"I don't even know your last name."

"It's Goodman, Samuel Goodman. What else do you want to know?"

"Are you married?"

"I was once. I'm divorced. What else you want to know?"

"That's enough for now," I said, feeling comfortable enough to laugh.

"So, can I see you tomorrow?"

I got in the car and closed the door. Thoughts of my commitment to coming out of my comfort zone ran through my head. I rolled the window down. "All right, Samuel. Why not? Let's see a movie."

He reached his hand through the window. "Give me your cell phone."

"Why?" I asked. This guy had no boundaries.

"I'm going to call my phone, and that way, I'll have your number, and you'll have mine." I handed him my phone, and he dialed his number. "I might call you tonight. That way we can get to know each other better before tomorrow."

All I could do was laugh again. He was being a bit presumptuous, but he wasn't arrogant. I hoped he would call. It would be something else to entertain me after *Scandal* went off.

***

A smile crept to my lips when I saw Samuel's number flash on my phone. I let it ring two more times before I answered.

"Hello," I said, pretending to yawn as if I had been sleeping.

"Hey there, Miss Lady. Don't tell me you're in bed already."

"Yes, I am. I was very tired. I had a long day at work today."

"I can help you relax. I do great neck and back massages," he said, being facetious. "Do you want me to come over?"

"Stop your madness. I just met you. Besides, you don't even know if I'm married."

"I checked the finger on your left hand, and you weren't wearing a ring."

"Oh, so you're a smart one. That doesn't mean I don't have a man."

"But you don't," he said matter-of-factly.

I was slightly insulted by his comment. That he would assume I didn't have anybody put me on the defensive, probably because there was truth in it.

"And how do you know that? Are you psychic?" I asked, feeling somewhat offended.

"If you had a man, he'd be with you right now. When you become my woman, I'll never leave you alone."

I laughed, partly because he squashed the attitude I was about to have, partly because I was flattered, and partly because he was so full of himself.

"You know you're crazy, don't you?" I said after I caught my breath.

He responded as serious as a judge. "Miss Lady, I'm keeping it real with you."

I chuckled again. "That's too deep for me right now, Samuel, I'm exhausted."

"I won't keep you up, Chantelle. Go on back to sleep. I want you rested when we go out tomorrow."

"Good night, Mister Man," I said, hanging up.

I turned over with a smile still on my face. Samuel did not disappoint me. I knew he would be fun to talk to. I was sure to disappoint him, because that's all I wanted, somebody to talk to when the lonely hours came.

***

Samuel wanted to pick me up for our movie date, but I wasn't sure I wanted him to know where I lived. He finally agreed to meet me outside the movie theater at Phipps Plaza. I changed clothes after work into a black jumpsuit. Something in me had clicked back on. If I had to guess, I would say it was my ego, and I wanted to wow Samuel when he saw me.

I circled the parking lot until I saw his car. I found a space in the row next to his. It's kind of hard not to notice a red Corvette, so he was already coming toward me when I got out of the car.

"You look amazing!" he said, eyeing me up and down. "I like a woman with a lot of style."

"Thank you, but I'm not really the fashionista type."

"Obviously, you are, and you don't know it. So, what movie do you want to see?" he asked, taking my hand and putting it through the crook of his elbow as we walked.

My eyes panned across the marquee. "Umm, I don't care much for horror flicks or superheroes. What about *Great Gatsby*."

"It doesn't make any difference to me. I'm happy to have your company. You can see whatever you want."

"You're easy to get along with, sir. How long will it last?"

"Always and forever, baby. I don't ask for much."

I laughed. I didn't know why everything he said amused me.

Samuel got the tickets, and we went inside. "What do you want?" he asked, his arms opened wide. "I'll buy you whatever you want to eat, sweetheart, money is no object."

"Would you stop with the 'Big Willy' routine. You know this is a cheap date."

"I told you I'd take you anywhere you wanted to go. We don't have to see this movie. I'm flexible. My schedule is wide open."

"Look, buy me some popcorn, peanut M&Ms, and a Dr. Pepper, please. We're here, and I want to see this movie."

Samuel never ceased to amaze me. For most of the movie, he kept his arm around the back of my seat as if I was his woman and had been for some time. There wasn't any of the usual awkwardness of two people who just met yesterday. He talked during the movie, sometimes too loud, and that was a little embarrassing. But he was comfortable with who he was, and he was so comfortable with me that I began to feel comfortable with him, too.

"Do you want something else to eat?" he asked as we left the theater.

"No way. I'm full of popcorn."

"I'm not ready to let you go, Miss Lady. I want to spend some more time with you."

"I wish I could, but it's late, and I have to get up early in the morning."

"Can I see you again tomorrow?" he asked, looking intently into my eyes.

"I don't know, Samuel. That's kind of soon. Shouldn't we let this marinate for a few days."

He shrugged his shoulders. "Why should we? I'm not a kid. I know that I like you, and I want to spend some more time with you."

"You are too much. I don't know how to take you."

"You think too much, Chantelle. Just do what you feel. There are no rules to this."

I threw up my hands in surrender. "All right, we can go out tomorrow."

"There you go. That's what I needed to here. I want to take you out to dinner for a real meal."

"Well, you can call me and let me know where to meet you."

"There you go with that again. I'm a gentleman. I don't like having a woman meet me anywhere. I'll pick you up and take you home."

"What if I'm not ready to tell you where I live?"

"I already know where you live," he answered casually.

"How do you know that?" I asked, taken aback.

"Sweetheart, it's 2013. There are no secrets on the world wide web."

All I could do was shake my head and laugh. "I still might like to have my own car. I don't know you like that."

"So, what do you want to know? Ask me anything."

"You said you were married before. How long have you been single, and why did you get divorced?"

"I was married for seven years. I've been divorced for eight years. We broke up because I was in the military and gone out of the country a lot. We didn't have any children of our own. She had a daughter from a previously relationship. We were not that close because I wasn't there most of the time."

"Where do they live?" I asked, wondering if there would be family drama.

"They live in Chicago. What about your ex?"

"He lives in Baltimore; we've been divorced for two years. He had three children by two previous relationships that I helped him raise. They really aren't in contact with me that much."

"Sorry to hear that," he said sympathetically.

"Well, are you still in the military?"

"No, ma'am. I retired with 20 years in. I'm in a training program to learn how to repair computers. All I want to do is pick you up and take you out to dinner. I'm not a criminal. If you don't believe me, I'll give you my driver's license, and you can do a background check on me."

"Okay," I said, giving in. "You can come and pick me up at my house. Let me know what time so I'll be ready."

"No problem," he said, opening my car door.

***

Samuel and I went out together three days in a row. He probably would have insisted that we go out again on the following Thursday, but I told him I had plans with my family. He did push the issue, saying he wanted to meet them. The only way I got him to back down was to promise him that we would go out on Friday. I needed a day to catch my breath and catch up on things with Sheree. Aunt Betty was going on a trip to Florida with some of her friends and wanted to have a cookout for us before she left.

"Child, where have you been?" Aunt Betty asked when she saw me coming around the back. She eyed me for a moment before she said, "You look okay. I was just about to come and hunt you down."

"I know that's right," Sheree chimed in, getting up from her chair to hug me. "Sister girl hasn't been returning my calls, only responding with short text messages like she's being held hostage. I thought I was going to have to call the cops and put out an APB on her. If it wasn't for these kids keeping me tied up with play dates and dance classes, I would have been at your apartment days ago."

"Both of you are being sensational as ever. I was a little out of pocket for a few days. It wasn't that serious."

"The last time you disappeared like that it was about a man," Aunt Betty said. "So, there must be something going on that we need to know about."

I sat down, straining my brain to think of what I could say to stall this conversation. I had planned to tell them about Samuel, I just thought we would finish eating first. Now they were making more out of it than it was. I had rushed into things with Teddy, and I definitely wasn't going that route again.

Sheree pulled her chair closer to mine. "Sit back, and spill the tea, sister."

"It's not that much to tell," I said with a sigh, knowing we were going to get down to it before I got to eat a bite. "So don't get hyped. I met this guy when I stopped to buy some gas. He asked me out, and we went to a movie. We've gone out a couple more times. It's not that big of a deal."

"Oh, yeah, it is a big deal because you haven't gone out with anybody since you and Teddy split up," Sheree said, sitting at attention. "What does this guy look like?"

"Please don't tell me you're falling for another one of those pretty boys," Aunt Betty added, "You know they ain't worth a dime."

"He looks okay, really built from being in the military, but he's kind of country. He's nothing like Teddy."

"Thank God for that!" Aunt Betty said, clapping. "You should have brought him over here with you so we could check him out."

"He wanted to come, but he's just a friend," I said, trying to calm them down. "We're not a couple like that. He's just somebody to get out of the house with sometimes."

"I still need to lay eyes on him," Aunt Betty said, fixing me a plate. "You can't trust everybody out here, even to be a friend."

"It took me a while, but I learned that the hard way, Aunt Betty."

"At least she's going out with somebody," Sheree snickered. "She wouldn't give Lawrence's friend the time of day, and he was all that. You're too young to give up on loving someone."

"Relationships are not for everybody," I said in my defense. "I'm beginning to think I might stay by myself. I'm getting used to it, and it's not that bad. I can do what I want when I want, eat what I want, and buy what I want. Being married wasn't all it's cracked up to be."

"That's because you were married to the wrong man," Sheree said. "You should have gotten out of that mess years ago. Now you're scared to give a decent man the time of day."

"Y' all don't understand, and I can't explain it to you. I just know I can't put myself out there to be taken advantage of again."

"You don't have to explain it to me," Aunt Betty said. "I know about no-good men. I ran into a few of them myself. They're smooth talkers. They can sell wet to water. It ain't nothing wrong with taking things slow."

"Mama, she can't be suspicious of every guy who tries to talk to her," Sheree said, disagreeing. "There are some good brothers out there looking for sisters who have their act together. Chantelle has always been kind of standoffish."

"What are talking about?" I said, surprised by her comment. "That's not true."

"Yes, it is," Sheree said sternly. "A lot of guys in high school wanted to step to you, but you acted like you didn't want to be bothered."

"I don't even know how you could say that. You were the one who was popular in school. If it wasn't for you, none of them would have known I was there. I was just Sheree's cousin."

"You're the one who has it wrong," Sheree said, offended. "Most of them figured you thought you were too smart to deal with them."

"Come on, I've always been friendly to people."

"Yeah, that's true, but you've kept a wall around yourself. The only person you let in was Teddy, and you should have left him locked out."

I had to acknowledge that truth. "Maybe so. Maybe that's why I got involved with him. He broke through that wall."

Aunt Betty smirked. "Hell, yeah, he did. He needed somebody to help pay them bills and raise them kids."

I blinked back hot tears that were burning my eyes. "I know I was a fool for him, young and dumb, but you don't have to rub it in," I said, trying to hide the emotion in my voice. There was no way for them to know how much I had lost. It wasn't only my marriage; I lost the kids. I had invested a lot of love in them. I sniffed the tears that tried to sneak out through my nose. "That's why I'm happy to be alone and at peace. I'll never be that vulnerable again."

"I'm sorry, sis," Sheree said, reaching over to pat me on the arm. "I'm not trying to make you feel bad. You're a beautiful person inside and out, and I want you to find someone who appreciates that."

"Right now, I'm focused on finishing my MBA. Trying to hook up with anybody is the last thing on my mind. Can we just eat this food that is smelling so good and change the subject to what swimsuit Aunt Betty is going to wear on the beach?"

"Oh, my goodness!" Aunt Betty said, giggling. "I'm going to keep a sundress over those things Sheree bought me. I'm only going to wade close to the shore. I guarantee you those waves won't touch my knees."

Even though her words reminded me of Mama, we all laughed, and the tension I felt evaporated in the heat of the day.

***

My guard was up on Friday when Samuel came to pick me up from work at noon. We were going to have lunch, and then he was taking me to see the Atlanta Braves play the Los Angeles Dodgers. He was a huge baseball fan. The only problem was sitting in the stands reminded me of the years when I took Jeremy and Julius to their Little League games.

I was in a funky mood after the game and didn't say much on the ride back to pick up my car from the parking garage at work.

"I'll trail you back to your house," Samuel said as I got out of the car.

"You don't have to. I'm fine," I said with a smile, hoping to end the date.

"No problem. I'll trail you," he replied.

Evidently, he didn't catch the hint that I needed some space. We had spent four out of the last five days with each other. I decided to make it clear once we got back to my apartment. As far as I was concerned, he was pushing things way too fast. I glanced at him in the rearview mirror. He was staying close to the tail of my car during the whole drive. I felt as if I was the mouse and he was the cat in a Tom and Jerry cartoon.

It was my intention to say our goodbye without him getting out of his car, but he was opening my car door before I could speak.

"It has been a nice afternoon," I told him, pausing in front of the door of my townhouse. "I'm glad your team won the game."

"Are you trying to kick me to curb out here?"

"Stop it," I said with a forced laugh. "It has been a long day. I'm kind of tired and want to put my feet up and relax."

"I'm not going to stop you from doing that. If you want, I can give you a foot rub."

"You never like to accept no as an answer."

"Why would I want to do that? I want to sit and relax with you. We can watch the news, the Lifetime Channel, TV One reruns, whatever you want."

I couldn't help but laugh for real. He always made me laugh, and that made me feel better. I figured it wouldn't do any harm for him to come in and stay for a while.

"All right. Come on in, but if you're hungry, you might have to order something. I'm not cooking anything."

"Woman, I don't need you to cook for me. I know how to cook," he said, following me in the house. "I've been taking care of myself since I was ten years old. I might even make something for you to snack on."

"Help yourself," I said, going up to my bedroom to change into shorts and a t-shirt.

When I came back down, Samuel had made a tray of cheese, turkey, olives, grapes, and crackers and had placed it, along with a couple of wine coolers, on the coffee table in front of the TV.

"You do know how to put together a snack," I said, admiring the spread.

"That's only one of my many talents," he said, giving me one of those sexy looks that LL Cool J did in his videos.

"I'm sure," I said, moving toward the sofa.

"I want to kiss you," he said, stopping me in my tracks.

"Can't we keep this on the friend level," I said, not wanting to cross that line.

He took a step toward me. "We can be friends and lovers."

"That's complicating things," I said, still frozen in my tracks.

He took another step. "Come on, and give me a kiss," he said softly. "One kiss and you'll be mine forever."

"No, that's not what I'm looking for," I said, resisting temptation.

"Come over here," he said, pulling on my arm.

I moved closer to him, and he started feeling on my neck.

"What are you doing?" I said, wondering what was wrong with him.

"I'm feeling for your Adam's apple."

"What do you mean? What are you talking about?"

"You must be a man because no woman has ever resisted me."

I laughed so hard I fell down on the sofa. "I told you, you're crazy!" I said, still laughing.

Then he sat next to me and wrapped his arm around my neck and made love to my mouth. First, a long kiss, then short kisses around my lips, then another long kiss where his tongue touched every centimeter in my mouth. He rubbed his lips against mine; then he stopped and smiled at me.

I picked up the TV remote and started surfing the channels. I pretended I didn't feel anything, that I was unfazed, that my panties weren't moist. Why shouldn't he believe that was an everyday occurrence for me?

Chapter
Fifteen

I thought about that kiss long after Samuel had gone home and for most of the night. When he called the next day, I convinced him that I wouldn't be able to see him for a week because I had to study for an exam and finish a business project due for my graduation in a month. He was skeptical, but he gave me the benefit of the doubt because he was in school himself. I did have a ton of work to complete, but more than that, I needed some distance to let things cool down between us. He was ready to charge full-speed ahead and I needed to put things in reverse.

Supreme Insurance was considering a merger with another company, and there were countless meetings for long hours late into the evenings with a team of consultants from Chicago. The conferences were draining, but they were a valid excuse for why I didn't have time to see Samuel for a couple of weeks. We talked on the phone at least once a day, and that was fine with me. The only problem was that one of the consultants was flirting with me constantly. His name was Evan, and he seemed a few years younger than me. I wasn't sure why he was trying so hard. He was waiting outside my office every morning.

"Good morning, Chantelle, you look very nice today," he said, greeting me as usual. "Can I get you some coffee, tea, a bagel, a donut, anything?"

"No, I'm fine, Evan, thanks for asking."

Joanne waited until he was gone before she came charging into my office.

"Chantelle, it looks like you have a handsome admirer. Evan has been hanging around your door all week."

"I am not interested in being his substitute lady while he's in town," I said, shuffling folders on my desk.

"Come on, I think he really likes you."

"It's funny how men don't notice you for years until somebody else does."

"Does that mean you've met somebody?" Joanne said, sitting down and getting comfortable.

I sat down and took a deep breath. "I met this guy on my way home from work a few weeks ago. We've gone out about five times, and he calls me every day; but I don't think I'm interested in a serious relationship. I know it's been over two years, but I'm not completely over that drama with Teddy. My trust level is way below normal."

"Well, give me the details. How old is he, how does he look, and what does he do?"

"His name is Samuel. He's 45, not a pretty boy type, but he looks good. His hair is cut close, and he has a nice mustache. He was in the military, he's now retired, and he's going to school to repair computers."

"So, what's the problem?"

"There is no problem. I just think we were seeing too much of each other."

"How is that a bad thing?"

"That's the same thing I did with Teddy. Before I got to know him, I was married to him, with three step-kids to take care of."

"I'm sure this guy is totally different from Teddy."

"I'm not so sure. He told me he wanted me to be his woman the first day he met me."

"That was a line. He probably didn't mean it like that."

"I don't know, but he's coming on so strong that I know he'll be expecting me to sleep with him soon."

"I know that I've been with the same man for thirty years," Joanne said, shifting in her chair, "but if I was single, I doubt that I'd be saving it. Go for it, Chantelle. Live a little. You've done the marriage thing. Now is the time to get out there and enjoy yourself."

I sat back and looked out my window. "I don't know, Joanne. I think I've forgotten how."

"Give Samuel a chance; I'm sure he can refresh your memory."

"That's not what I'm worried about. He's been single a long time. He might have a disease. I need him to get tested and give me the doctor's report."

"Would you stop? He's going to be wrapped up anyway."

That raised my eyebrows. "Joanne, I'm surprised at you. You sound like Sheree."

"We both just want you to be happy," she said, blushing. "You deserve it."

"That's one thing I can't argue with," I said with a sigh.

***

"I was beginning to wonder when you were going to invite me to your place again," Samuel said, coming through the door of my townhouse on Friday evening.

"I had to take some time to get you to pump your brakes, sir. You were moving a little too fast for my speed."

"That's okay. You'll catch up," he said, putting his arm around my waist.

"See, that's what I'm talking about. You're so physical. I'm slow to let anybody get in my personal space."

"We have taken it slow, baby, but we're not teenagers," he said, pulling me close for a kiss.

"I don't know you like that," I said, pushing him back.

"Stop tripping, Chantelle, you are not a virgin. I'm not trying to get you to do anything you haven't done before. I just want to make you feel good."

"Before we go there, I have to get a doctor's note or something. I can't trust you like that."

"That's cool with me, but I don't mind wrapping up until then."

My eyes rolled back in my head. This man never gave up. "Can we just sit down and talk?" I asked, sighing.

"Sure, Miss Lady, let's talk."

"What are you looking for, Samuel? Do you want something casual, a steady lady, or what?"

"I'm not looking anymore," he said straightforwardly. "I've already found what I want."

"Would you stop talking crazy? I'm trying to have an intelligent conversation with you."

"We can talk some more later," he said, moving closer and kissing me on the mouth. It was so passionate, I felt slightly dizzy.

I pulled away. "We're not going there."

"Yes, we are," he said, softly kissing me again.

Joanne's words filled my head, "Live a little. Enjoy yourself." Samuel was right. I wasn't a teenager, and here I was, damn near forty, acting like one. Then I decided to take the risk, something that I consciously avoided every day in my profession.

"You're not going to mess up my new sofa," I said, putting the pillows back in place. "If you want to do this, then we need to take it to the bedroom."

He stood up and reached out his hand to help me up. "You make the rules, Miss Lady."

"Do you need to take a shower?" I asked.

He laughed. "No, ma'am. I scrubbed down before I came over here, but if you want me to take another one, I will."

"I'm not that neurotic. So, where's the condom?"

"You're going to have to relax, Chantelle. I've got that under control. You're messing with my romantic flow. Come over here, and sit down," he said, patting a spot next to him on the bed.

Samuel bent over and lifted my feet up into his lap and took off my shoes. "I like your feet," he said.

Thank God Sheree had insisted that I went with her to get a pedicure. Samuel massaged my feet, and if he had stopped there, I wouldn't have complained. He massaged my entire body as he removed each piece of clothing. It was almost more therapeutic than it was sensual. Once I was undressed, he took off his clothes in front of me so I could watch. He was taking his time, as if we had all night to get this done.

Sex with Samuel was totally different than with Teddy. He touched and examined me more thoroughly than my primary care physician, except he used his tongue. Before the night was over, Samuel had turned me every which way but loose. When day began to break, I saw him staring at me. His gaze was intense, like the glare and the heat of the sun. It made me want to shield myself.

"I want to see you without your weave. I know your hair is not that long," he said, studying me like a picture on the wall.

"Excuse me?" I said, indignant.

"I want to see every part of you. If you have false teeth, take them out. If you have one leg, I don't care. I want to see you inside and out. I want to know you."

"You are crazy," I said, covering myself with the sheet.

"No, I'm not. I want to see what you really look like. I'm totally serious. I'll pay to put your weave back in if you want."

"It's much too early to talk about this. I need a couple more hours of sleep before I can deal with you."

He laughed. "Go on and get your rest, my lady. You deserve it. I'm glad you relaxed and let me love you. I really enjoyed being with you."

"I don't think any of that was about love, Samuel."

"Speak for yourself," he said with confidence.

"Like I said, it's too early for me to talk to you."

He laughed again and got up from the bed. "I'm going to take a shower, so you won't have to direct me to."

"There are towels and washcloths in the cabinet under the sink."

"I know my way around in a bathroom," he said, teasing me.

I pulled the sheet over my head and giggled under my breath. Samuel was always making me laugh, and I was thankful for it. Still, this was definitely an awkward situation for me. I would have preferred to have said our goodbyes last night without him staying over, but I was too tired to usher him to the door. Besides, after all the good loving he gave me, I didn't want to seem ungrateful. In comparison, he put Teddy square in the lazy lover column.

I must have dozed off because, when I woke up, I could smell coffee. Then I smelled bacon sizzling, and it gave me a flashback to Nicklewood Arms and mornings with my mother. I could almost hear her saying, "Get up, there's no time to be late." I tiptoed into the bathroom, and it was still neat with Samuel's wet towel hanging on the rack. This man continued to amaze me with the fact I hadn't found anything to complain about him yet.

After my shower, I put on a robe and followed the aroma of the coffee and the bacon.

"I see you know your way around in a kitchen, too," I said, pouring myself a mug of coffee.

"I told you, I'm a military man. I do it all."

"I'm not going to argue that point," I said, smiling.

He grinned back at me. "That's what I like to hear. I want my woman satisfied. If you want, I can take care of you again before I leave."

"I'm good," I said, avoiding his gaze. "I've got some things to do this morning."

"Me, too. So, if you don't need anything, I'm going to let you have your space."

"This breakfast is all I need," I said, walking him to the door.

"I'll call you," he said before he kissed me.

I rushed back to the kitchen and called Sheree. "What are you plans for today, sis? I need to talk with you."

"In about an hour, I'm going over to Mama's to pick her up and take her shopping. What's up?"

"I need to get a new dress for my graduation, so I'll meet you over there."

I was searching in the closet for something cute and comfortable to put on when my cell phone rang. I chuckled and shook my head. Samuel hadn't even waited a half hour before he called. I got a head rush when I picked up my phone and saw Teddy's number. I threw the phone down on the bed as if it was a spider that had crawled on me.

***

"Hey, Aunt Betty, are you ready to spend that money?" I said, catching up with her and Sheree at the mall.

"I don't know about all that," she answered with a laugh. "Whatever you girls are willing to throw my way, I'll take it."

"The way you're holding that purse under your arm, it must be loaded," Sheree joked.

"Don't you even worry about my purse. I'm not like you two. I'm not about to spend my last dime on that name brand stuff y'all like to sport around in."

"I have got to have quality, and I never sacrifice style," Sheree said.

Aunt Betty grunted. "Well, maybe we need to split up and meet back at the food court later."

"No, Mama, we're going to do this together," Sheree told her. "Then we're going to help Chantelle get a chic new dress or a power suit. Getting that MBA next Saturday, she's got to be on point."

"Well, give me a little space. I don't need you all up in my business."

"Okay, we'll be over there sitting in the shoe section," Sheree told her, determined to keep an eye on her.

"Take your time, Aunt Betty, we have all day," I hollered back over my shoulder.

"So, what's up with you?" Sheree asked, looking in her bag for something to munch on.

I glanced around us to see if anyone was standing in earshot. "You won't believe it. I don't even know where to start."

"Uh-oh, this sounds juicy," Sheree said, finding a pack of cheese and peanut butter crackers.

"You know that guy, Samuel, that I told you I met?"

"Oh yeah, y'all have been out a couple of times."

"He came over to my place last night, things got heated, and he spent the night."

"Hot damn, sis, I need a drink!" she said, patting her chest. "I'm about to choke on these dry crackers. And you're right, I can't believe it. You've had that stuff on lockdown ever since Teddy left."

"I know you think I'm half robot, but I'm not. I get lonely sometimes."

"I hear you, sis. I'm not mad at you. Now let's get down to the details."

"I didn't intend for things to go that far. We haven't known each other that long, but he never takes no for an answer. He started rubbing my feet, and I got weak. This brother gave me the treatment for two hours. I was so tired, I fell asleep. When I woke up it was practically daylight."

"Now that's what I'm talking about," she said, digging in her purse. "What's his address? I need to send him some flowers."

"Girl, you are so silly. The thing that got me was he was staring at me when I woke up. It freaked me out a little bit. He kept saying he wants to see me without my weave. The whole thing was deep."

She clapped her hands and said, "I like it. The deeper the better."

"I'm serious, Sheree. I don't know where I want this to go. He's looking for a relationship, and I don't know what I'm looking for."

"Just relax, and stop trying to control everything. Let it do what it do."

"Anyway, that's not the real kicker. I thought Samuel was calling me this morning after he left, but it was Teddy."

Sheree started coughing. "See, you're trying to kill me," she said between coughs. "I've got to get something to drink. We need to find Mama quick."

We weaved through the older ladies' section in Macy's until we found Aunt Betty.

"We'll be in the food court when you get through, Mama," Sheree said, attempting to clear her throat. "Take my bank card, and get whatever you want."

"What's going on with you two now?" Aunt Betty asked, suspicious. "I didn't say anything earlier to you, Chantelle, but I know something is up. It is written all over your face."

"We'll tell you later, Mama," Sheree said, trying not to cough. "Go on and shop till you drop."

Once we were out of Macy's, I started to speak, but Sheree waved her hand for me to stop. She bought a Coke out of a vending machine in the center of the mall, and we sat down nearby. She took a few swigs and then a deep breath.

"Now I can listen. That last bomb you dropped almost took me out. What the hell was Teddy calling you for after the foul shit that he pulled?"

"I don't know. I didn't answer. It was too much of a coincidence. Right after I get busy with a new guy, then all of sudden, he calls me."

"Call him back right now. I've got to hear what this is about."

I reached in my bag and got my cellphone, pushed redial, and put it on speaker.

"Hello," he said like he didn't know who it was.

"It's Chantelle. I'm returning your call."

"Oh, yeah. I wanted to talk to you about Terri."

"Okay," I said, refusing to make it easy for him.

"She wants to come back to Atlanta for a while." He paused for me to comment, and when I didn't say anything, he continued. "She's having a rough time with her moms, and she would like to stay with you for a while."

Sheree started coughing again. She took another swig of the Coke and covered her mouth. My mouth was so dry, I grabbed the bottle from her and took several gulps.

"Teddy, I haven't talked to any of the kids for months. It took me a while to get used to that. I don't think it would be a good idea for me to get involved. If she's having problems with her mom, maybe she should come and stay with you."

"I'm not really in a stable place for her to come to right now. You were more of a mother to her than her own mama."

"You're right, I was, but you didn't think about that when you packed all of their bags and refused to let me see them."

"The way I handled that was wrong, Chantelle. I apologize for that. I wish we could get together and talk about this over dinner. I've had to learn a lot of things about myself, and now I can see that most of the problems we had were because of me."

Sheree started motioning for me to hang up.

"This isn't a good time to talk. I'll have to get back with you."

"No problem. I'll talk to you later."

I hung up the phone just before Sheree hollered. "That negro has a lot of nerve! You know what that's about, don't you?"

"I have no idea. I'm still shocked."

"He's trying to get back in, and he's using his daughter to open the door."

"He knows better than that!" I said, shaking my head in disbelief.

"Evidently he doesn't. I bet his ass is back in another financial hole and is looking for you to dig him out again. I can't believe this. I have been doing so good with my temper, and this rotten mofo is trying to get me in jail."

"Calm down, sis. I'm not going to be that fool again. I'm just stunned that he would think that all he had to do was pick up a phone and I would fall for his nonsense again. All I can say is thank God the love is gone."

"Here comes, Mama, loaded down with her bags," Sheree said after Aunt Betty spotted us. "We might as well go on to the car. I'm through. There's no way I could get my mind right to shop. We'll have to get something for you to wear next week."

I nodded. I didn't feel like shopping anymore either.

"What's the next stop?" Aunt Betty said, smiling with satisfaction.

"Home," Sheree blurted out. "You won't believe that no good Teddy called Chantelle trying to get back with her."

"He didn't say that," I said, coming to his defense. "He asked if Terri could come back to Atlanta and stay with me for a while."

Aunt Betty sat her bags down on the floor looking confused. "What did you tell him?"

"I didn't tell him anything. I'm still shocked that he called."

"I'm sure you know better than to get involved with him or his kids again."

"I practically raised them, Aunt Betty."

She bent over to look me in the face. "Did they appreciate it? No, they didn't. All of them ran off without so much as a 'thank you' or a 'kiss my ass.' "

"I'm going to leave it alone. He may not even call me back."

That's when my cell phone rang. It was Samuel. "What's up, lover?" he said, sounding upbeat.

"Hey, what's going on?" I said, taking the anxiety out of my voice.

"I want to take you to dinner tonight."

"That's sounds nice," I said with Sheree and Aunt Betty looking down my throat.

"Cool, I'll be by your place around 7:00."

"All right, I'll be there."

"Who was that?" Aunt Betty asked, totally befuddled.

"That was Samuel. He's the guy I met recently."

Aunt Betty shook her head. "Y'all come on. Let's get these bags to the car. This is too much drama for me. I'm tired."

Sheree and I picked up her bags, and we walked to the car in silence.

***

"I've been thinking about you all day," Samuel said, kissing me on the cheek when I opened the door. "You might need to keep those thoughts in your head," I said, closing the door. "Let me get my bag, and we can go."

I took another quick look in the mirror. Samuel was always staring at me as if I had something in my teeth or a smudge on my face, so I wanted to make sure nothing was out of place.

"By the way, Happy Anniversary," he said as we stepped out of the door.

"What are you talking about?" I asked, confused.

"We've been together for a month," he said casually, opening the car door for me.

I couldn't help but giggle. "I thought men never remembered anniversaries."

"I do, and I will after we get married."

Then I had to laugh. "You need to stop talking crazy."

"Get to know me, and you might change your mind."

"It has taken me this long to get my head halfway straight. I can't even think about going down that road again."

He took a cup of coffee out of the cupholder and took a sip. "Once we're together for a year, would that be something you can think about?"

"You're always so deep. Can we cross that bridge when we get to it?"

"Sure, we can. I'll be there waiting for you," he said, starting the car.

"You're so hyped this evening, what have you been drinking in your coffee, cream or alcohol?"

"None of that, Chantelle. I'm drinking in the sight of you."

"Okay, good line," I said with a laugh. "But I set that up for you."

He smiled at me when we stopped at a traffic light. "What do you have a taste for tonight?"

"How about Italian?"

"Whatever my baby wants, my baby gets."

"What am I going to do with you?" I said, amused.

"I'll tell you later," he said in a totally serious voice.

I couldn't do anything except shake my head.

Samuel drove to Maggiano's, which wasn't too far from my house. Not long after we were seated at a table and ordered our food and a bottle of wine, my phone rang again. It was Teddy.

"Who's that?" Samuel asked, curious. "Your pretty smile turned into a frown."

"My ex. He called me earlier about my stepdaughter—or his daughter. I don't even know what to call her anymore. He says she wants to stay with me for a while."

"Is that a problem for you?"

"You don't understand how things went down. It's a long story."

He looked at his watch. "The restaurant doesn't close for another three hours."

I took a deep breath and exhaled. "Let's see if I can shorten this long story. So, I'd only known Teddy for about six months before we were married. That's one of the reasons you freak me out with the marriage talk after one month."

"I get that. But remember, I'm not him."

"Anyway, right after our honeymoon, he surprised me with three-year-old twin boys he forgot to tell me he had; and before the year was out, he surprised me again with his 18-month-old daughter, Terri."

"Damn, that's tough."

"I'm not even going to lie. It wasn't easy." I paused as the server placed our food on the table and poured the wine. "I was in love with him and really wanted to give our marriage a chance. I didn't see any reason to punish the kids for what their trifling parents did."

"That's amazing. Most women would have walked away."

"Looking back, I probably should have. Things just got worse after that. I think he was addicted to porn, although he always swore up and down that he wasn't."

"Hold up. I don't know any guy who doesn't enjoy a little porn every now and then."

"It wasn't just a little; it was all the time. He would rather look at porn than be with me."

"I was trying to cover for a brother, but that's crazy. An imitation can never take the place of the real thing."

"I'm glad to hear you say that."

"So, that was enough to break you up after you sweated through the kids thing."

"It was more to it. We had money problems, or at least he did, and he claimed that was the reason that he didn't want us to have a baby together."

"I can see why you left him."

"That's what killed me. I didn't leave him. He left me and took the kids I had raised for him and went back to Baltimore. I barely heard from them. Now, after two years, he calls me up out of the blue and says Terri wants to stay with me."

"He's got balls. That's all I can say to that."

"The timing is unbelievable."

Samuel nodded. "Well, where is your head at?"

"What do you mean?"

"Are you going to let her come?"

"No way. I don't want to get sucked back into that drama again so they can use me and throw me away when they're done."

"I thought you said you weren't going to punish the kids for the trifling things their parents have done."

"She's not a baby anymore. She's sixteen years old. I'm sure she has a cellphone, but she hasn't called me."

"It's possible that she doesn't know if you want to hear from her."

"I won't accept that. I changed her diapers; dressed her; fed her; combed her hair; and took her to school, the doctor, and church, but she doesn't feel like she can call me? I can't understand that. I know blood is thicker than water, but where was her mama and her people fifteen years ago?"

"Family situations are complicated. Don't make a quick decision. Give yourself some time to think about it."

"What if it's Teddy trying to use her to get to me."

"Then he's wasting his time. You're my lady now."

"There you go again."

"I'm not playing with you, Chantelle. I'm too old for games. I want a serious relationship with you, and I'm not going anywhere."

***

Adjusting my graduation cap, I noticed a wrinkle that I had missed on my gown. I shook my head. I knew that if Mama were here, she would have insisted on ironing it for me, and it would have been pristine. She would have been bursting with pride to see me walk across the stage and get my master's degree. I prayed that she wouldn't have been disappointed with the mistakes and the misjudgments I had made in marrying Teddy.

Going back to school had been a lifesaver for me. Instead of looking at the broken dreams behind me, it had helped me to make new goals and to focus on what I had to look forward to. Taking classes again and managing my workload had been a challenge, and now that I had finished, I was thrilled. I had come through so much and had somehow managed to get my MBA in spite of it. It was the boost my self-confidence needed after the divorce.

Seeing Sheree, Lawrence, Aunt Betty, Monica, and Junior waving and cheering for me as I walked back to my seat made me happy and melancholy at the same time. I was grateful for their love and support, but it reminded of what I didn't have. Samuel would probably be offended that I didn't invite him to come. But I hadn't introduced him to my family, and he was already talking about marriage. In my heart, this day was for me and Mama.

I had just gotten home from the beauty salon after sitting for three hours to get my hair done. Fridays were always booked tight, so I had left work early to make sure I would be finished on time. Samuel wanted to cook dinner for me at his place, and I was looking forward to being pampered. It had been a long week, and I was ready to take Samuel up on his offer to stay with him for the whole weekend to celebrate my graduation.

I was staring in the closet, trying to decide what clothes to pack, when I heard the doorbell. I figured it was him, early as usual to pick me up. I was stunned when I opened the door. Terri, my stepdaughter, was standing there. She looked more grown-up than when I last saw her, but she still had the lost puppy dog eyes.

"Terri, how did you get here?" I asked, noticing the small suitcase in her left hand that she was attempting to conceal behind her.

"I took the bus," she said nonchalantly.

"You took the bus? Come in," I said, ushering her through the door. "Does your mom or Teddy know where you are?"

"I told them I was coming here. They don't care. I can't take it there anymore?"

"What's going on?" I asked, still standing in the hallway. "Why didn't you call me first?"

"I would have, but they told me that you didn't want to be bothered. I didn't know what to do. I just knew I wanted to come back home to Atlanta. I don't have any friends in Baltimore. It's like I'm invisible to everybody or something."

I had been strong and unmovable until she said that. All the barriers that I had securely built up came tumbling down. I hadn't given birth to this child standing before me, but she was mine in every other sense of the word. All I could do was take her in my arms and hold her. She began to cry, and I recognized every tear that rolled down her cheeks. I let her pour out her hurt, and my blouse soaked it up. She gathered herself after a few minutes.

"There's a guest room up the stairs and down the hall on the left. You can put your things in there for the time being. I have to call your daddy and let him know where you are."

I sat down on the sofa with my cellphone in my hand and waited until I couldn't hear her footsteps. This call wouldn't be an easy one. I had promised myself that I would never dial his number again, and now I had no choice. When I spoke with him a week ago, I realized that I was still pissed off by the way things had gone down between us. I scrolled through the phone log, took a deep breath, and pressed the line with his name on it.

"Chantelle, thanks for calling me back," Teddy said, answering on the first ring.

"I wouldn't have called, but Terri just showed up on my doorstep."

"Whew, that's a relief!" he said. "Her mom has been blowing up my phone."

"So, what do you want me to do?" I asked urgently. "Do you want me to put her back on the bus tomorrow?"

"I was hoping we could talk more about it before she got there, but she hasn't been happy staying with her mom. They don't get along that well, and the house is a little crowded right now."

"So, what is her mom saying? I'm sure she wants her home."

"It's kind of complicated. She has a lot on her plate, and it's more about money being tight than anything else. If it's all right with you, she doesn't have a problem with Terri staying with you."

"Well, why don't you have her stay with you for a while?"

"I would, but I'm in a tough spot right now. I'm not settled. I'm in the process of moving back to Atlanta myself."

My stomach flipped. I was right back at the top of the rollercoaster again, speeding down from a high peak. I was just getting my life halfway back to normal. The last thing I needed was more drama from Teddy, not even for Terri's sake.

I swallowed the knot in my throat. "You were very determined to leave Atlanta. Why would you come back?"

"Like I said before, I wish we could have talked about this earlier. In person would have been much better. I have been through some crazy situations since we broke up."

"We didn't break up, Teddy. You left. We got divorced."

"I just left before things got really bad; we were headed in that direction."

"You're right about that. I should have left you."

"What I'm trying to tell you, Chantelle, is that I was wrong. I apologize from the bottom of my heart. You were good to me and my kids, and you didn't deserve to be hurt like that."

"All of that is true, but what does it have to do with you coming back to Atlanta?"

"You probably won't believe me, but I feel like I need to make amends with you."

"Please don't move back here for me. I'm fine. You don't owe me anything. You could only do to me what I allowed you to do. I should have put a stop to it way before you did, but I've gotten over it now."

"I want to see you and talk to you. I miss you. You were a good lady, a good wife, and I didn't appreciate you at the time. That was the biggest mistake of my life." "We all make mistakes, Teddy. But thank God, it's in the past, and that's where it needs to stay. The only thing we need to discuss is what you're going to do about Terri."

"Terri feels closer to you than anybody else. She misses you. The bond is not there with her mom. She was so young when we got her that you were the only mother she knew."

"First, you brought her into our home without asking me how I felt about it. Then you took her away without any thought of how I felt. You told me I didn't have any parental rights, that I wasn't her mother. Now you want to run a guilt trip on me."

"She wants to come back where she can be around you, and I want to make that possible. All I'm asking is for you to consider letting her stay for a while until I get on my feet."

"I don't know if I can do that. It might be asking too much."

"Don't answer right now. Give it a day or two. Think about it over the weekend."

I took a deep breath and exhaled. "Since she's already here, she can stay the weekend. But I'm not promising you anything."

"I understand," he said gratefully. And I could hear the relief in his voice.

I ended the call and tapped Samuel's number in my contacts.

"Hey there. What's up? I was about to leave in a few," Samuel said, sounding upbeat. I hated to bring him down, but what could I do?

"Can I get a rain check?" I asked without having to fake the strain in my voice. "I got a bad migraine all of a sudden."

"Sorry to hear that. Do you want me to bring you anything?"

"No, I'll probably just get some rest."

"I'll be there in a half hour."

"No, you don't have to come over."

"I want to come. If you don't feel well, I want to be there for you. I can rub you head and make the pain go away. We were supposed to spend the weekend together."

"I'm sorry. I'll call you in the morning."

"Okay, cool," he said, hanging up.

"Damn." I could hear the irritation in his voice. I had never heard it before. He was always so tolerant of my moods and craziness. He was the reason I could laugh again. I didn't want to jeopardize that, but I needed some space to think. This had been a super crazy day, and I was exhausted, too tired to stand up.

I kicked off my shoes and laid back, my feet propped up on the arm of the sofa. Staring at my toes as I stretched and wiggled them to help myself relax, it occurred to me how peculiar each one was shaped. They were all individuals designed with a specific purpose that was unknown to me. The best thing was to focus on something I did know. It was decision-making time. Things were about to get out of control. I had to decide what I wanted in my life and how to achieve those things going forward.

Using an approach similar to taking a math exam, I started with the easiest problem first. I was pretty sure that Teddy had dug deep into his trick bag and had plans to mesmerize me: to show me that up was down, black was white, and left was right. There was no way I was going for that feat. My eyes were wide open, and I trusted them. There was no way he could convince me that my eyes were deceiving me and that he was more truthful than they were. Atlanta was a big city, and there was room enough for both of us to live without crossing paths.

The second easiest was Samuel. I loved the way he made me feel like the most beautiful woman in the room, the way he teased me, his sense of humor, and the sensual way he made love to me. I needed all of that in my life. The drawback was that I was uncertain about a long-term commitment. I'd been there and done that, and I could testify that it wasn't all it was cracked up to be.

Then there was Terri. I had loved her as if she was my own, changed her diapers, wiped her snotty nose, and combed the tangles out of her hair. I kept her clothed and fed for thirteen years, helped her write her name, count up to 100, and tie her shoes. I took her to daycare, to elementary school, and then middle school. I couldn't have been more of a mother if I'd given birth to her. She was almost seventeen years old, and most of those years had been with me. That said, my door would always be open as far as she was concerned.

***

The ray of sunshine slipping between the drapes hanging on my front window woke me up. I was obviously more worn out than I had thought. My sofa, bought more for its good looks than for comfort, was not where I had planned to spend the night. I grunted and limped up the steps, my back muscles aching and leg bones cracking in reaction to the mistreatment they had been subjected to. Thankfully, the hot shower coaxed them into forgiveness and cooperation.

I found some soft knit pants and a t-shirt and hurried back down the stairs to the kitchen. My stomach was reminding me that I hadn't eaten dinner. I found some potatoes in the cabinet and pulled eggs, bacon, cheese, milk, apples, oranges, and pineapple and honeydew chunks out of the refrigerator. I couldn't remember the last time I had cooked a big breakfast, but there was one on the menu for us that morning.

The sound and smell of the bacon sizzling took me back to when I was seventeen and my mama was cooking breakfast for me.

When I realized what was different, I turned the radio on.

"Good morning, Mom," Terri said, dragging her bare feet into the kitchen, wearing an oversized t-shirt. "I'm starving."

"Pour yourself some milk or juice and have a seat. There's a fruit salad on the table, and the fried potatoes are almost done. I was hungry myself, so I have a big breakfast for us."

"I missed this," Terri said, pouring a glass of milk. "They don't cook much in Baltimore."

"Who were you living with?" I asked out of curiosity.

"I lived with my mama, her boyfriend, my grandmama, two younger sisters, and a baby brother. It was kind of crowded."

"Sounds like it," I said, nodding. "I talked with your daddy last night. He says that your mother doesn't mind if you want to stay here for a while. He's planning on moving here himself; and when he gets on his feet, you can stay with him."

"All I want is to stay here with you for my senior year. I'll get a job and help out, and when I graduate, I can go to college and be on my own."

I sat down next to her. "I don't have a problem with you living here, Terri. I love you very much and want you to be happy."

She kept her head down, and I saw a tear roll down her cheek. "I love you, too, and I'm sorry for what Daddy did."

"You're not responsible for what he did or what your mama did. After we finish eating, we can go out to the mall and pick up whatever you need."

She reached over and gave me a hug, and I had to make it a short one so I wouldn't cry. I was happy that Terri was there. What Sheree and Aunt Betty might feel was a different story. I was enjoying the moment when the doorbell rang. For a minute, I started not to answer it. I looked through the peephole and saw it was Samuel.

"I was going to call you later," I said, opening the door.

"Now you don't have to," he said, walking in. "This is supposed to be our weekend, remember?"

"Yeah, I remember, and I'm sorry for flaking out on you. I had something unexpected happen. Yesterday, Terri, my stepdaughter, showed up just like you did. I answered the door, and she was standing there."

His narrow eyes widened. "Wow. That was unexpected."

"She's still here. She's having breakfast in the kitchen."

"I guess you should introduce us then," he said, stepping through the doorway.

"We've talked, but I haven't mentioned that I was seeing anybody yet."

"Come on, Chantelle. You and her daddy have been divorced for almost two years. She's not a kid. I'm sure she won't be surprised to meet your man."

I threw my head back. "There you go with that again."

His eyes narrowed. "Are you saying that I'm not your man?" he asked.

"No, I'm not saying that."

"That's good to hear, but what are you saying?"

"Nothing. I'm sure she can hear every word that we're saying anyway."

"All right then. Let's do this," he said, walking past me. "The food is in the kitchen, and I'm hungry, too."

I shook my head and trailed him to the kitchen. Terri was sitting at the table looking wide-eyed when we came through door.

"Terri, this is Samuel. He's a very close friend of mine."

"It's nice to meet you, young lady," Samuel said, reaching out his hand to shake. "You don't mind if I join you for breakfast, do you?"

"It's okay with me," Terri said, shrugging her shoulders and shaking Samuel's hand.

Samuel sat in the seat across from her.

"Terri is going to be staying with me for a while," I said, fixing him a plate.

"That's a change," he said, looking over at me.

"I'm so full," Terri said, pushing her chair back from the table. "I guess I'll go take a shower and get dressed."

"All right. Towels and things are in the bathroom closet."

Terri put her plate in the sink and nodded toward Samuel. "Nice to meet you."

I rewarmed my plate and Samuel's in the microwave and sat down next to him. We ate in silence, glancing at each other between bites.

"You're going to have to catch me up," Samuel said after he heard the shower start. "It was only yesterday that you told me you weren't going to get drawn back into the drama."

"I know, but I didn't know how I would feel when I saw her. I love that child."

"I hear you, but that child is practically grown. If you want a baby, I can give you one. Just let me know. You don't have to settle."

"Being a mother doesn't end when the child leaves, and her age doesn't make any difference to me."

"But it did end for you, didn't it? What's to stop her from walking out and leaving again whenever she feels like it?"

"Nothing. Nothing stops anybody from leaving whenever they feel like it."

"I'm not going anywhere, Chantelle. I told you that, and I meant it."

"I don't understand you," I said, shaking my head.

"That's fine. I understand you."

"We just met," I snapped, venting my frustration. "I didn't take the time to get to know Teddy, and look where that got me."

Samuel answered calmly. "You were young and dumb then, and you had time to wait. We're twice grown now. We should know what we want."

"You want some coffee?" I asked, changing the subject.

"I'll take a cup, but what I really want is what you promised me."

"What's that?"

"This was supposed to be our weekend."

"What can I do? Terri is here."

"Figure it out because she's going to be here for a while."

"You're welcome to spend the day with us. We're going shopping."

"No, thank you. You two go ahead and rebond," he said, getting up to leave. "I'll be at the house when you get done. I don't think she needs a babysitter."

***

While sitting in the car in the parking lot outside of Nordstrom's, I texted Sheree. I told her what had happened so she wouldn't have a hissy fit if Terri and I ran into her at the mall. She texted me back, asking if I had lost my mind. I responded that I would call her when we got back home from shopping.

Being in the mall with Terri brought back a lot of memories. But even so, the two years that she had been in Baltimore had changed both of us. She was less talkative than she used to be and more guarded with the words she did speak. I must confess that I was still caught up in my feelings about her not calling or keeping in touch with me. She hadn't been so obedient during the last years we were all living together for her to obey any orders not to contact me. I realized it would probably take some time before we were comfortable around each other again.

Aside from that, we were out for most of the day. She schooled me on all the stores that teens prefer and that she didn't need help picking the things she liked. We bought clothes and shoes, everything from underwear to socks, shirts, pants, skirts, and sundresses. I guess opening your heart and your home means opening your wallet as well. We stopped for Chinese takeout on the way home.

"I'm going to take a nap," I told Terri after we brought all the bags inside. My feet were tired, and my body was beat after the night on the sofa. "We shopped, and I'm about to drop."

"Thank you for buying all the stuff for me today," she said, giving me a loose hug.

"I can't have you wearing those torn jeans every day."

She smiled. "These were my favorite, but now I've got some I like better."

"Good," I said, heading up to my bedroom.

It took me a few minutes to relax and to fall asleep. I was so wound up, and so much in my life had changed in 24 hours. I woke up an hour and a half later feeling much better. I took a shower and put on a casual but sexy orange dress and some strappy gold heels. I decided I was going over to Samuel's place, and I wanted to wear something that would keep the conversation about Terri to a minimum.

Taking my phone off the charger, I saw that Sheree had texted me again with all caps, telling me to call her ASAP. I responded with one word: "Tomorrow." I didn't want to spare the energy to talk to her tonight. This night was for Samuel and me.

Terri was kicked back on the sofa, watching TV and eating her sweet and sour chicken. I grabbed the remote and pushed the mute button. "I'm going out with Samuel tonight, and I'll probably be out very late. Can I trust you here by yourself?"

"Definitely. I don't even know anybody here anymore."

"Okay, you have my number in your phone if you need anything. I'm going to set the alarm, so don't open the door, or the police will be here in fifteen minutes."

She nodded, and I turned the volume on the TV back on. I locked the door behind me as I left. As I backed out of the driveway, it felt strange to see the light on, realizing that I wasn't living alone anymore and that I was a mother again.

*****

"I'm glad to see you," Samuel said, answering the door. "I wasn't sure if your plans were going to include me."

I unbuttoned his shirt and put my arms around him. "I don't want to talk," I whispered in his ear. "Can we pretend that there's nobody else in the world but you and me for one night?"

"Yeah, we can do that," he said, making love to my lips again.

It was a night to remember, and that's what I needed. I was usually the one who got tired first and wanted to go to sleep. But this night, I kept him up. I didn't want it to end because it might be our last.

Samuel said I should figure it out, but I couldn't. Things weren't adding up as they should have. I needed and wanted to concentrate on Terri during her senior year without feeling as if I was being pulled in opposite directions. Not to mention, I suspected that it wouldn't be long before Teddy was going to try to hang around. The few months I'd spent with Samuel were lovely and carefree. It was great, but now my life had gotten complicated.

*****

The romantic night with Samuel bought me some time. After serving him breakfast in bed, he grudgingly said he would give me some space for a couple of weeks to get Terri settled. I knew

Sheree was going to be another story all together.

Terri was still in the guest room when I got home. It was too late to make it to church, so I turned on the TV to wait until Sheree got home. Aunt Betty would probably be there, and I could tell them both at the same time.

I nodded out for a while, and when I checked the time, it was 1:00. I brushed my teeth and stuck my head in the door of the guest room to let Terri know I would be going out. She was wearing headphones, bobbing her head to the music, and she waved bye without taking them off.

Traffic was light, and I got to Sheree's house before I had prepared a sufficient defense to the arguments that I was sure she and Aunt Betty would raise. They were all sitting in the backyard when I pulled into the driveway. Aunt Betty was holding Lawrence Jr.'s hands while he hopped up and down, thrilled with the feel of his feet under him. Monica jumped up and came running to greet me.

"Hey, Aunt Chantelle," she said happily, wrapping her arms around my waist.

"Sweetie, you are getting so tall," I told her as I pulled one of her long ponytails.

Then Lawrence stood up, wearing the familiar look on his face that said he knew the conversation was about to get deep. "Hey, lady," he said, giving me a quick hug. "How's it going?"

"I'm making it," I answered.

"I'm about to take the kids to the movies," he said, reaching his arms out for Lawrence Jr. to walk toward him. "You can join us if you want."

"I probably should," I said, glancing over at Sheree, who was practically swollen with anger. "What are you all going to see?"

"*Despicable 2*," Monica shouted.

"She's already seen it," Sheree chimed in.

"Are you gonna be here when we get back?" Monica asked, looking at me.

"I don't know, sweetie. If I'm not here, call me up so you can tell me about it."

"I will," she said, looking like a miniature Sheree as she followed her daddy to the garage.

As soon as Lawrence and the kids left in his SUV, Sheree started in on me. "Please tell me I had a nightmare and none of this foolishness is real," she said, her fingers pressing the sides of her head.

"It's not a nightmare," I said, sitting across from her. "Terri showed up out of the blue. She's been having problems with her mama, and she says she's not happy in Baltimore."

"What has any of that got to do with you, sis? That is a closed book," Sheree fussed.

"You know I raised that girl. I love her, and I can't just turn my back on her because of what Teddy did."

"Why hasn't she tried to keep in touch with you all this time?" Aunt Betty asked, siding with Sheree.

"Teddy told the kids I didn't want to be bothered with them."

Sheree shook her head in disgust. "I don't buy it, Chantelle. They just want to use you some more."

"It'll probably only be for the summer," I said, recognizing this was not the time to tell them she wanted to stay and do her senior year here and then go off to college. It would buy me some time to get them used to the idea of her being around again.

Sheree grunted, showing her disapproval of that idea. "If you know what I know, you won't let your feelings get in the way, and you'll send Terri back home to Baltimore."

"You are just getting your life back together, Chantelle," Aunt

Betty said. "Sometimes you have to be selfish. The child has other family, including her sorry-ass daddy. You're the one always sacrificing."

"I know things didn't go down well after the divorce, but I need y'all to understand. She's like my daughter."

Sheree shook her head again, looking aggravated. "Okay, sis, do what you want. When this blows up in your face, you know we got your back."

I pushed the toe of my sneakers against her sandals. "Thank you, girl. You know I love you."

"Uh huh," Sheree said, handing me a wine cooler.

Chapter

Seventeen

I tapped my foot impatiently as the elevator climbed to the nineteenth floor. I was running late. It wasn't a big deal, but it was a source of pride for me. I had never been late for work in all my years at Supreme Life. I guess it was a habit from Mama waking me up shouting, "Get a move on. You don't have time to be late," when I was growing up.

Now, all of sudden, with Terri back in the house, my timing was out of whack. Forty-eight hours wasn't long enough to make the adjustment. I rushed down the hall to my office, the only steady place in my life. I had barely sat down at my desk when Joanne walked in with two cups of coffee.

"Well, how was your weekend?" Joanne asked, smiling, knowing something was up. "I can usually set my clock by you. Did this new guy keep you up late last night?"

"No, he's not the reason. I'm off track," I answered, reaching for one of the cups of coffee. "You probably need to sit down before you drop that cup."

"Uh-oh," Joanne said, taking a seat across from me. "This isn't something to do with you finishing up with school, is it?"

"No. You won't believe it; I almost don't believe it myself. I was getting ready to spend the weekend with Samuel when the doorbell rang. I thought it was him, but when I opened the door, it was Terri."

Joanne fell back in the chair. "You're right, I can't believe it. When was the last time you heard from the kids?"

"It's been over a year."

Joanne shook her head in confusion. "What did she say? What did she want?"

"She said that she wasn't happy in Baltimore and that she wants to move back to Atlanta for her senior year."

"How do you feel about that? What did you tell her?"

"Sheree and Aunt Betty are upset about it, but I told Terri she could stay. They don't want to see me get involved in the old drama, but they don't understand that I still see Terri as my stepdaughter. I took care of her for 13 years. I couldn't just turn her away."

"I can see your point of view. My sister adopted a baby girl, and we all considered her to be family as much as a blood relative. It was hard for my sister when her daughter wanted to search for her birth mother, but it didn't change her feelings for her. I think you're doing the right thing. Besides, it's only for one year."

"It's good to hear that I'm not entirely crazy," I said, sipping on the coffee.

Joanne scooted to the front of the chair. "Now, back to the new guy. Do you think this is going to cause problems between you?"

"I don't know. We're just getting to know each other. I hope I don't have to choose."

"You have a lot going on, Chantelle," Joanne said, getting up to leave. "It still amazes me how you hold it all together."

"It's not as easy as it looks," I told her.

I got up and walked over to the window, sipping the coffee. It was times like this that I missed my mama. I looked out at the buildings and down at the street below, wondering what she would think about my life and the decisions I had made.

***

Things settled down, and by the end of the week, I felt as if I had my rhythm back. Terri had called earlier and said she was going to hang out with some friends. I drove home, thankful that it was Friday and I could have a few hours to relax by myself. I was winding down with a glass of wine, about to get into my lavender-scented bath, when the doorbell rang again. My mellow mood was shaken.

I thought it might be Samuel going back on his word to give me some space. When I opened the door, I knew all hell had broken loose. Teddy was standing there. The shock gave me a flashback of another day I came home from work sixteen years ago. The day he was sitting at the kitchen table with Julius and Jeremy.

"What are you doing here?" I asked, feeling the heat of angry engulf me. "I don't believe you're actually standing at my door! You have a lot of nerve! Anyway, Terri isn't here. She's out with friends. You should have called."

"I know. I talked with her earlier."

"Then why are you here?" I asked, totally confused.

"I want to talk to you," he said, trying to look humble.

"Teddy, that's ridiculous. If I recall correctly, you said everything that needed to be said when you left."

He looked puzzled for a moment. "We didn't talk before I left."

"Exactly. There was nothing left to say," I said, slowly closing the door.

"Wait, Chantelle," he urged, pushing his hand against the door. "Hear me out for a minute."

I shook my head. "You want me to listen to you? That's so rich."

"Please, can I come in? I just need a few minutes."

"No, you can't come in. Wait here. I'll put on some shoes, and we can talk out there."

223

I closed the door and locked it. I didn't want him inside my home, disturbing my place of peace. It had taken me so long to find it. Disgusted with him and myself, I stomped up the stairs to my bedroom, still shaking my head. Why was I even going to talk to him? I should have slammed the door in his face.

Teddy was leaning against a car parked on the street when I came outside. It was after 7:00 in the evening, but the temperature hadn't dropped one degree. The uncomfortable heat only added to my irritation.

"So why are you here?" I asked impatiently.

"I know I messed things up between us, and I want to apologize."

I nodded at the sheer insult of his attempt to make amends. "I can't believe you. Apologizing for what you did is like running down somebody in a car and then saying you're sorry like you just stepped on their toes. It falls short. You might as well save your breath."

"I know I was wrong, Chantelle, and I want to make it up to you. I owe you that."

"You're a little late to come back to the rescue. I'm way past needing anything from you."

"I know you think I played you, but I played myself. You were the best thing that ever happened to me. I couldn't see that when we were together."

"Well, I'm sorry for you then."

"I'm hoping you can find it in your heart to forgive me."

I threw my head back and rolled my eyes. "That's asking too much. You took everything away from me. You cut me so deep, I thought I was going to die. It wasn't easy to get over that."

Teddy took a step closer to me. "If you think that it has been easy for me, you're wrong. Nothing has worked out for me since the day I left Atlanta. I've lost my business and every dime I had. I'm starting all over again, and I want to do that with you."

"Are you out of your damn mind!" I yelled, backing away from him.

He reached out his hands. "I was, but I've got my head on straight now. You, me, and Terri can be a family again," he said, having the nerve to force a few tears from his eyes.

"I don't want what we had! Why would you think I would? You made me miserable. At this point in my life, I want something better."

"I can be that person that you want, baby. I've changed."

"It's too late, Teddy. It's best we leave the past in the past. There's nothing left to build on."

"I'm broke, Chantelle. I'm here with my heart in my hands."

Then Terri's friend pulled up. I was hoping Teddy would have been long gone by the time she got home. I saw her face light up when she saw him.

"If you need some money," I said hurriedly. "I'll give you something to get you by, but that's all I can do."

"I don't have anywhere to go," he urged. "Can I just crash here for a few days until I find a job?"

Terri rushed out of the car and ran up to Teddy. "Daddy, I didn't' know you were coming to see me."

"Yeah, baby, I missed you."

"Where are you staying?" she asked, happy to see him.

"I was hoping to stay here with you guys for a few days but—"

"Mom," she said, begging me with sad puppy dog eyes. "Please, can Daddy stay here for just a couple of days. I'll do all the cooking and cleaning and everything. I just want us to be a family again for a little while."

"I don't think that's a good idea," I said, frowning.

Teddy interjected before I could finish my sentence. "I promise I won't be in your way. I just want to spend some quality time with Terri. Her mama was pissed at me and wouldn't let me see her."

"I wonder why?" I asked, knowing he wasn't as innocent as he pretended to be.

"I just want a chance to catch up," he said, sounding pitiful.

Terri kept looking at me, her eyes pleading as she held her breath.

"Only for a couple of days. We can blow up the air mattress and put it in the living room. I'm not about to let him ruin my couch."

"Thank you! Thank you!" Terri said, bouncing in her shoes as she opened the door and held it for us to come in.

"Let me get my bag," Teddy said, dashing to his car. He got a duffel bag out of the trunk and hurried back to the door. "I really appreciate this," he said, following me in.

"It's only for Terri," I assured him.

"Come on, Daddy, you can put your stuff in my room," Terri said, grabbing his elbow.

"This is total bullshit," I said under my breath. This man had somehow finagled his way back under my roof. I knew Sheree was going to make me an appointment with a psychiatrist. She had already thought I was crazy for letting Terri move in. After she heard the latest, there would be no doubt in her mind that I had gone off the deep end.

***

My eyes were closed, but I didn't get much sleep last night. I couldn't get over how much drama had filled my otherwise boring life in the last few weeks. There was a new man in my life, a man who had blown my mind with his disposition and the most satisfying sex that I had ever experienced. Then there was my stepdaughter, who had some back out of the blue, asking to live with me after not seeing me for almost two years. The clincher was my ex-husband, who had put me through a hundred changes and was now camped out in my living room.

My phone beeped, and it was a text from Samuel saying he missed me. I wanted to call him. I needed a level head to talk to, but this situation would probably throw him for a loop. I texted him back, saying that I missed him, too, and would call him later. More tired than I was the night before, I dragged my body into the shower and stood under the water for five minutes before I reached for the soap, praying the water would give me some clarity on how to be a decent human being without being a damn fool.

I put on a blue jean skirt and a t-shirt and called Sheree. She answered on the first ring.

"What's up, sis?" she asked, sounding like a bundle of energy.

"A lot. What do you have planned for the day?"

"Nothing but trying to stay cool. Mama is taking the kids to a picnic at her church, and Lawrence is going to be golfing all day with his boys."

"I need to get out of the house for a while."

"Come on by. I've got free tickets to the Aquarium. I haven't been there in a long time."

"I'll be there in a half hour."

Not only did I need to give Sheree the latest update, but I also needed to get out of my own house. I hadn't gotten used to Terri being there yet, and spending the day with Teddy definitely wasn't on my agenda. I left my hair wrapped and threw on a Braves baseball cap. I could hear them in the kitchen talking when I walked into the hallway.

"Good morning," Teddy said when I walked in, grinning and sounding as if he was in a flashback from fifteen years ago.

Terri, who was stirring scrambled eggs, turned around, wearing a big smile on her face.

"Good morning," I answered.

"I'm making a big breakfast this morning," Terri said. "Do you want pancakes?"

"No, I've got a few things to take care of this morning. You two help yourselves."

"What time will you be back?" Teddy asked.

I frowned at him like he smelled and directed my answer to Terri. "Call me if you need anything."

***

I was so anxious to get away from Teddy that I beat Sheree to the aquarium. I found a shady spot near the entrance to wait for her.

"You look cute," she said, waking me out of a daydream twenty minutes later.

"Thanks," I said. "You look fabulous, as usual."

"Girl, you know how I do it," she said, pulling the tickets from her purse and moving to the line. "You never know who you might run into."

"That's a fact," I said, following her and shaking my head.

Once we were inside, she said, "I need something cold to drink."

We went to the café, and that's when I realized I hadn't eaten. I was starving. I wanted the carrot cake, but I got the fruit tart instead, which I practically inhaled. If I started eating my troubles, I was bound to gain thirty pounds.

We were sipping on sweet tea when Sheree stopped and put her hand on her hip. "I've tried to be patient, but you need to go on and tell me what the deal is. Anytime you call me before 9:00 on a Saturday morning, I know something is up."

"I can't even front. Teddy showed up at my door last night."

Her mouth fell open. "What the fuck? You have got to be bullshitting!"

"No," I said, shaking my head. "I'm dead serious."

"What in the hell did he want?" she shrieked.

"He's moving back to Atlanta. He's damn near broke, and he needs a place to stay."

"Oh, hell no! You know what this is about, don't you? That buster is back to try to ride on your ass again to get back on his feet. I hope you told him where he can dump that load of bullshit."

"I was about to when Terri came home, looking at him like her long-lost dog had found his way back. I let it go and told him he could stay the night. I didn't want to kick him to the curb in front of her."

"I don't know why not! They saw how he treated you. It's not my thing to throw a black man under the bus, but he's the one who crawled under it. Run his ass over immediately!"

"That's her daddy. She's not going to stop loving him because of me."

"I'll be damned. This is unbelievable," Sheree said, looking around and throwing up her hands. "It doesn't make no kind of sense. First, the child, and now the good-for-nothing baby daddy. Chantelle, you're going to have to give both of them their walking papers. As long as Terri stays with you, he's going to use her as an excuse to be in your face. He's not going to stop until he's back in your wallet. I hate to say it, but that was all he wanted from jump street."

"You don't have to worry about that happening. There's no way I would get involved with him again. That's not even an option. He broke me down, betrayed me in every way possible, and then left me. I can't forgive him for that."

"He's slick, Chantelle. He's like oil on glass. I don't put anything past him. He had enough nerve to come and knock on your door after all he did. If I didn't love my family and my freedom, I would go gangster over there and bust a cap in his ass."

As mad as I was, I couldn't help but burst into laughter at the visual of Sheree going after Teddy. She started laughing, too, and we carried on until there were tears in our eyes. That was a much-needed stress releaser.

"That was a good one, Sheree," I said, wiping my eyes. "I was blown away for a minute from seeing him, but I'm over it. I told him that I would lend him some money to get situated. That's all I can do."

"I wouldn't give him a thin dime. He's a grown-ass man."

"It's worth it to keep him off my doorstep. I'm sure Atlanta is big enough for us to live here without you having to go to jail."

"Okay, I'll leave it alone. You handle it. I don't need the drama in my life."

"More than anything, it's the timing that has me messed up. Just when I got my head on straight and was moving forward with Samuel, he comes around to complicate things."

"I'm telling you, sis, that's how it works. When life gets good, up jumps the devil. Don't let him cause problems for you with Samuel. That man loves you, Chantelle. You've tried to hold back, but your heart won't let you. He's a good guy. Don't let Teddy screw it up."

"I know that. Samuel has been understanding so far with Terri coming to stay with me. I don't know how he would react about Teddy hanging around."

"Teddy is lucky you have a kind heart. I would have told him to call Tyrone before I call the police."

We laughed some more as we wandered around the aquarium, looking at all the different kinds of fish and other creatures that live in the sea. I felt better after talking to Sheree, but I couldn't stop wondering about something she said. It was about Teddy only being with me for the money. Surely, I couldn't have been that gullible. The notion that he saw me when most guys didn't was the reason I fell in love with him. He made me feel so special back them. Now, to think that all he saw was an opportunity would be devastating. It would mean that my marriage was meaningless from jump street, and—just like Sheree said—that all I had done and gone through was for naught.

***

It was late in the afternoon when I got back home. Sheree and I had gone by the mall, and she treated me to a manicure and a pedicure. Before I pulled into my parking space, I could see Samuel's car parked out front.

I took a deep breath as I parked my car. Now, it was my turn to throw up my hands. When did people stop calling before they showed up at other people's houses uninvited? I had definitely entered into the Twilight Zone. For a second, I thought about pulling off and going to a hotel where I could find some peace. But technically, I was the only one who belonged here. Maybe the answer was to point them all to the door.

I slammed the car door and stomped up to the door. It was unlocked, so I walked right in to see Teddy on one end of the couch and Samuel on the other. Terri was sitting on the floor, watching an episode of *Bad Girls*.

"I was just about to call you," I said to Samuel, ignoring the other four eyes looking at me.

"Now you don't have to," he said without the continuous smile he usually wore.

"How long have you been waiting?" I asked, wondering if they had had time to talk.

"Not long," he answered.

"I guess you've met Teddy, my ex."

"Yeah, I did. He was the last person I expected to see camped out at my woman's place."

"I didn't know I was stepping on any toes," Teddy said, interjecting himself into the conversation. "Chantelle didn't mention you."

I had seen this movie before. Teddy wanted to start an argument between me and Samuel. I wasn't about to let that happen or let this scene escalate in front of Terri.

"Why don't you wait for me outside while I pack a bag?" I said to Samuel. "Teddy got in town last night to see Terri. He wants to spend some quality time with her, so this will give them some space to visit."

Samuel nodded, got up from the couch, and walked past me out the door without saying a word.

"I didn't know you were seeing somebody," Teddy said sarcastically, turning his eyes toward the TV screen.

"That's probably because what I do and who I see is none of your business!" I said angrily. "Here's a couple of hundred in cash, and I'll write you a check for a grand. But I want you out of here before I get back tomorrow."

Terri was sitting on the floor pouting, but I had done all I could do, and I wasn't going to make any excuses. She was grown enough to know what went down between Teddy and me and how he left. She was born a female, so she needed to learn what she was up against out there.

I went into my bedroom, packed an overnight bag, and wrote Teddy a check. He hadn't been here for twenty-four hours, and he was already causing me trouble and costing me money. Hopefully, he would be gone before I had to go to work Monday morning.

I stopped in the doorway outside the living room. "Terri, I'll be at Samuel's place. If you need anything call me." Then I threw the check at Teddy and slammed the door behind me as I left.

Samuel was sitting in his car. "Do you want to ride or trail me?"

"I'll ride with you," I said.

He got out of the car and put my bag in the trunk. "So, what's going on with you?" he asked, starting the car.

"I was about to call you when I got home. Teddy showed up at my door last night. I hadn't talked to him in almost two years until Terri came. I don't know what he has on his mind."

"If you don't know, I'll tell you," Samuel said, pulling out into traffic. "He wants to get back in with you."

"That's not going to happen," I said, looking over at him.

He kept looking straight ahead. "It already has. He's sleeping in your house."

"Come on, Sam. He's Terri's father. She wanted to see him. What was I supposed to do?"

"Nothing. He can see his daughter whenever he wants to. It doesn't have to be at your place. He's a player, and he's playing you."

"Give me some credit. I've moved on with my life. There's no way I would get involved with him again."

"You probably shouldn't have gotten involved with him the first time, but you did. He's got your number, Chantelle."

I turned to look out the passenger-side window. "You sound like Sheree. He'll be gone tomorrow, and everything will be back to normal."

"I'm telling you from a man's point of view, he has no intentions of going anywhere, and he's going to use your feelings for Terri to manipulate you."

"I'm not stupid, and I'm not weak."

"That's not what concerns me. I need to know if you still care about him."

"No, I don't. I got over that a long time ago. I wasn't even in love with him during the last few years that we were still married. He had put me through so much. I was only trying to hold the family together. I love those kids. I raised them."

"I'm crazy about you, lady, and your ex doesn't bother me. I know what kind of man I am. What I don't know is how you feel about me."

"I really like you, Samuel. You changed my whole perspective on being with someone again. I enjoy your company, and I don't want to lose that."

"When I met you, I told you what I wanted. I'm not interested in dating. I want someone to spend my life with. I don't want to waste my time."

"I hear you, but I've made some bad choices, so I want to take things slow."

"Then we aren't on the same page," he said, stopping at a red light.

"Don't say that," I said, reaching over to rub the back of his head.

"That's not what I said. That's what I heard."

Damn. The bright spot in my day was going dark on me. We stopped and picked up some Chinese before we got to his house, but neither of us wanted much to eat. I took a shower and put on one of his t-shirts, but the evening didn't go as I had hoped it would. I wanted all the closeness he always offered, but he was distant.

Instead of the passion that turned me on, Samuel was polite. He slept on one side of the bed without touching me. It reminded me of the many nights I had spent lying as far away from Teddy as I could after he finished gaping at other women on his computer. What had I done to bring this on?

Eighteen

The next morning, I got something from Samuel that he had never given me before: the silent treatment. That added to my stress level, which was already overflowing. I needed some release, a place where I could let my guard down, a place where I could find peace of mind. I put on the sundress that I had packed, combed my hair, called myself a cab, and went to church.

When the choir sang "Trouble in My Way," the lyrics touched nerves, hearts, and minds throughout the large congregation. When my tears began to fall, I was inconspicuous among all the others who were crying and calling on the Lord. During the altar call, I saw a woman walk up to the front. From the back, she looked like Mama, and the dress looked like the one she wore to my high school graduation. For a moment, I couldn't move. Then I practically ran down the aisle. A crowd had gathered around the altar, and I couldn't get to the woman before the pastor began to pray.

I bowed my head, but I didn't close my eyes. I needed to look in her direction. When the prayer ended, I looked for the woman among those going back to their seats, but I couldn't find her. She had vanished as she always did. I went back to my seat. I knew it was Mama. Whenever I needed her encouragement, she would appear and then disappear.

After the service, I took a cab over to Aunt Betty's apartment. She wasn't home, probably spending the day at Sheree's house. I used my key to get in and sat down on the sofa that held so many memories. The house was quiet, but I could hear the voices of Sheree, Aunt Betty, and Joanne in my head, telling me what I should do. It took a few minutes until I could block out the noise and listen to my own voice.

I sat there for hours contemplating the circumstance in which I had found myself, and after a while, I felt calm. I was finally comfortable with doing what made me happy instead of trying to please anyone else. By the time I stood up to leave, there were three things I was certain of: First, Teddy was the past I didn't want to relive. Second, Terri was almost grown and ready to live her own life. Third, I didn't want to lose Samuel.

***

When I saw Teddy's car still parked in front of my townhouse, I was determined not to lose the joy I had reclaimed at church. I took a deep breath and whispered, "Give me strength, Jesus."

"I fried some chicken," Terri said as soon as I walked through the door, trying to appease the situation. "Are you hungry?"

I was starving, but the sight of Teddy lounging on my sofa with a full belly made me want to gag. "I'll get some later, thank you," I said, forcing a smile. "Your daddy and I need to have a talk first."

"Okay," she said, taking the cue and heading for the door. "I was going to hang out for a while anyway."

"Don't stay out too late," Teddy hollered after her, as if this whole arrangement was normal.

I walked into the living room to confront to him. "Why are you still here, Teddy?" I asked, keeping my cool. "You have enough cash to get a room in a hotel. Why are you here disrupting my home?"

He sat up straight. Then he said, "There are some things in our marriage that I need to be honest about, things I think you have a right to know."

"What difference does that make now?" I asked, exasperated with his presence. "You left. We are divorced."

"I want you to know that it wasn't because I didn't love you. There were other reasons I should have told you about."

"I think you were very clear for a long time that you didn't want to be with me, that you'd rather be with fake women rather than with me."

"It didn't have anything to do with you. I promise."

"Excuse me?"

"What I should have told you was that after looking at porn for so many years, my body stopped reacting the way I wanted to when I was with you. I was too embarrassed to talk about it."

"Is this supposed to make me feel better?" I asked, wondering if he realized what he had just said.

"Hold up. You're taking it wrong. I was attracted to you, but—"

"But jacking off to unknown women on the computer screen really turned you on."

"It wasn't that simple, Chantelle. I didn't feel like I deserved you. You were so together, and it made me feel bad leaning on you for so long. I wanted to be the man and take care of my family on my own."

"You're copping out on me. We were supposed to be a family, working together. I never put you down for anything."

"I didn't see that. I thought you were better than me."

"So, you treated me like shit to put me in my place."

"That wasn't my intention. Let me make it up to you. Give me a chance to prove my love for you. We can be a family again. Terri needs you, and I need you."

"Cut the crap, Teddy, I can't deal with the bullshit. Yeah, you need me, but you don't love me. You never did."

"Believe me, I did. It's just that things were working out for you, and I couldn't do anything right. You made me feel like a failure. It pissed me off. That's why I was tripping on you. That's why I thought I wanted to get away from you. I needed to get my pride back."

"Stop! You lied to me from the beginning. You took advantage of me. You disrespected me. And you're the one who made me feel like a failure."

"You're right. I didn't respect you. How could I? I didn't have any respect for myself."

"There's nothing we can do about that now. You go on with your life, and I'll go on with mine. Terri is not a baby. She'll be fine."

"You don't owe me anything. None of what happened was your fault. But I'm at rock bottom. I wouldn't have come here if I wasn't. Can you give me a few more days to find a job and get a place? I won't get in your way. I did you wrong, but I'm trying to be a better man, a better father for Terri."

I didn't have any more to say. I just looked at him. That's when he pulled out all the stops, broke down, and started crying real tears. I had never seen him this humbled. I didn't know if it was fake drama or if was actual remorse. It really didn't matter, but the performance bought him a little more time. I walked out of the room and came back with my laptop.

"Use this, and find yourself a job and someplace to stay. You have until the end of the week."

***

Samuel and I had only spoken on the phone twice during the week. I had avoided talking too long because I hadn't gotten my house in order yet. Teddy was still sleeping on the air mattress in the living room, and I was exhausted from going to work early and coming home late to avoid any contact with him.

The house was dark and quiet when I got home. I figured Terri and Teddy were out somewhere together, preferably moving him into his new place. I put some deli meat between a slice of bread, poured myself a cup of juice, and sat down at the table.

I saw the laptop and remembered that I hadn't registered Terri for high school yet. I turned it on, googled "high school registration in Atlanta," and clicked on the link. Before I could even create an account, naked pop-ups of porn sites started flashing on the screen, asking me to click on their sites. I cursed out loud. That no-good asshole had been going to porn sites on my laptop when he was supposed to be looking for a job. I couldn't even swallow the mouthful of dry bread and meat. I got up and spit it in the trash.

Seething mad, I paced around the room, trying to calm down, telling myself that he was either gone and out of my house or would be in a matter of hours. I should not have even let him back in my house. I had been a fool again, and I was ashamed to tell anyone that I had been that stupid. I was so mad; I couldn't regain my composure. I had always made it a rule not to drink when I was upset, simply because I would have probably turned into an alcoholic. But I needed a drink, and I needed to get out of the house.

***

After drinking two prickly pear mules at the Whiskey Blue Bar, I mellowed out. I sat there for nearly two hours, but I wasn't ready to go home. I wanted to see Samuel—no, correction—I needed to see Samuel. Why was I avoiding the person who made me feel good and feel good about myself? I paid my tab and headed to his place.

Samuel opened the door and stood there with a strange look on his face. He didn't hug me or greet me with a kiss. I figured he was mad at me for being distant during the week.

"Can I come in?" I asked. He stepped to the side, and I walked in. He was watching a baseball game on TV. "How was your week?"

"It was okay," he said, walking back to his seat on the couch.

I sat down beside him. "I missed you."

"I missed you, too. I stopped by your place about an hour ago."

"Sorry, I wasn't there. I went out for a drink."

"Your ex answered the door," he said with an edge in his tone.

All the wind dropped out of my sails. I was tired of making excuses. "Yeah, I've asked him to leave several times. He claims he needs more time to find a job and a place."

"Didn't you say you were divorced?"

"Yes. We are divorced."

"Then explain to me why it's your responsibility to help him get a roof over his head."

"It's not my responsibility. I was helping him more out of consideration for Terri than for him."

"That's a switch. You took his kids in out of your love for him; now you're taking him in out of consideration of the kid. It's crazy, Chantelle." He wouldn't look at me. He kept staring at his folded hands.

"It's temporary, Sam. Don't let his problems be a problem for us."

"As much as I hate to do this, I'm going to have to back away."

"Come on, you went through a lot to get me to give you a chance, and now you walk away. I trusted you. You said this wouldn't happen."

"This is not what I want. The bottom line is that I'm not trying to be with you and your ex and his daughter."

"Teddy can't come between us unless you allow him to. And as far as I'm concerned, Terri is my daughter. I raised her."

"I'm not gonna argue with you about that, but the fact is he's going to use her to manipulate you. With Terri back in your life, he's back in your life."

"Give me a little more credit than that."

"One thing I've learned in my life is that the heart impairs our judgment."

Samuel still wouldn't look me in the eye. And looking at him, I could only feel as if I was being betrayed again. He had convinced me to let my guard down, and then he landed a knockout punch. I jerked myself up off the couch and snatched up my purse.

He stood up and finally looked me in the eye. "Now, before you go and crawl back in your shell, I want you to think about what I said."

"I heard you loud and clear. You don't want to be with me."

"No, that's not what I said. What I said to you is that I can't deal with your current situation. I'm giving you the space to make the decision that's best for you. I've already said I wanted you. If you decide you want to be with me, clean up your house."

I stormed out of his place angry and disappointed. I had come there for understanding and support, and instead I got the cold shoulder and criticism. I pressed harder on the gas, driving like a bat out of hell, wishing I could outrun the issues that dogged me, but I had nowhere to escape.

I breathed a sigh of relief when I didn't see Teddy's car parked out front. At least I didn't have to deal with him. I stomped into the house and went straight to the kitchen. I opened the fridge that was always damned near empty since Terri and Teddy had moved in. Starving, I slammed the door, grabbed the phone, and dialed the number to order a pizza.

I figured I had enough time to take a shower and get comfortable before the delivery person got there. So, I hurried upstairs and turned on the light in my bedroom. I grabbed my head and screamed bloody murder. Teddy was butt naked and asleep in my bed.

He sat up, shocked. "What's the matter?"

"I know your ass is not laying up in my bed! I know you have lost your mind!" I turned away, not wanting to accept what my eyes were seeing. "I can't believe you tried this."

"Calm down, Chantelle. It's not that serious. The couch was killing my back."

"That is not my problem. You have got to go."

"We were together thirteen years. We have history. That counts for something."

"It didn't make any difference to you when we were together. You didn't want a real woman. And whenever I look back at those years, they are nothing I want to repeat."

"Come on, baby, don't be like that. Lay down with me. Give me a chance to show you how much I love you."

"Oh, Lord, my God! If you don't get out of here!"

"All right, all right. I'll sleep on the couch," he said, scooting to the edge of the bed.

"No, I want you out of my house!"

"How are you just going to throw me out? I don't have anywhere to go."

Samuel's words rang in my ears. "Like I said, that's not my problem."

"Terri has my car. I can't leave."

I followed him downstairs, shouting. "I don't care! I don't want to hear it!"

Cursing under his breath, he pulled on his clothes and grabbed his duffel bag. I followed him to the door and slammed it behind him. I had barely taken two steps before the doorbell rang. I swung open the door, ready to shout him down again, but it was the pizza guy.

A couple of hours later, after stripping my bed, taking a shower, and filling my belly with pizza, I had calmed down. I was watching a *Law and Order* rerun when I heard the key turn the lock and footsteps running up the stairs. It was Terri.

"Mom!" she yelled as she reached my door. "Daddy said you put him out on the street!"

"Terri, this is between your daddy and me."

"He said he doesn't have anywhere to go."

"He'll work it out," I said, looking back at the TV.

Terri threw up her arms and stomped to her room. I shook my head. She would get over it, too.

***

The sound of someone banging on the door woke me up. It was barely daylight. I bumped into Terri as I stumbled out of my bedroom in my nightgown. If she hadn't ordered any food, it had to be Teddy. I snatched the door open, ready to curse him out, but it was Sheree standing there.

"I've been calling you since last night!" she said, half-hysterical. "Then I rush here and see Teddy out here sleeping in his car. I thought you got rid of him over a week ago. What is going on? Is this negro stalking you? I already called Lawrence, and he's on his way. I'm not trying to catch a case this morning!"

"Why don't you mind your own business, Sheree?" Teddy asked, getting out of his car.

Sheree turned toward him and put her hand on her hip. "Why don't you do the same, Teddy? You don't have any business here. Take your no-good broke ass back to Baltimore, where you ran to when you had fifteen cents in your pocket."

"Why are you so worried about me and Chantelle anyway?" Teddy asked her. "Don't you have somebody else's nerves to ride on?"

"Are you crazy?" Sheree shouted. "There ain't no 'you and Chantelle.' You left, remember?"

"You're the real reason we broke up!" Teddy said, pointing at her. "You were always in her ear and in her pockets."

Sheree grunted with disgust and took two steps toward him. I grabbed the back of her shirt.

"The devil is a liar! You messed that up by yourself with all your freaky-deaky nonsense!" she said, pointing a finger back at him.

Just then, Lawrence pulled into the complex ad up to my townhouse.

"Get back in your car, Daddy!" Terri hollered nervously.

Teddy stepped back, but he didn't go to his car. "I'm not bothering anybody," he said defensively. "I got a right to check on my child."

Lawrence came up behind him. "Hey, man, let me talk to you," he said, tapping him on the arm. We watched as Lawrence led him out of earshot.

"What in the hell is Teddy still doing here?" Sheree asked. "I thought you sent him on his way two weeks ago."

"We'll talk about it later," I told her, nodding toward Terri, who was tearing up.

After a few minutes, Lawrence went back to his car and stood there waiting. Teddy walked slowly up to the door.

"Can I talk to my daughter?" he asked.

Sheree took a step to block the door. I motioned for Terri to come out of the doorway where they could talk outside. Still wearing her short pajamas, she followed Teddy several yards down the sidewalk. Sheree and I watched him talk as Terri became more emotional. Less than ten minutes later, she came back to the door alone.

"I'm going to stay with Daddy," she said, tears flowing down her cheeks. "He needs somebody to look out for him. He don't have anybody but me."

Sheree and I went into the house behind her. "Your daddy is a grown man," I told her. "He's the one who should be taking care of you." Terri just shook her head and went up to her room. "Why don't you stay here until he finds an apartment?" I asked, trailing her.

She kept shaking her head. She was trying to pack all the things I had bought for her into the small suitcase she came with. I left the room and went back with another suitcase for her to use.

"Thanks for letting me come back," she said with her bags in hand.

"You're welcome, Terri. Anytime you want to come back, the door is open."

I trailed her down the steps and out the door, while Sheree stood guard. Teddy opened his trunk, put her bags inside, and gave me a long look before they got in the car and drove off, with Lawrence tailing them.

"He is a selfish bastard!" Sheree said. "He didn't need to take that girl with him. He still plans to use her to get to you."

"That won't happen," I said, closing the door. I should have been happy. The confusion was gone, but I was crying.

"I don't like to see you upset, Chantelle, but it's for the best."

"Maybe, except my life is torn up again."

"Come and stay with me and the kids for a few days. Lawrence is going out of town on business."

I shook my head no.

"Call Samuel, tell him—"

"No, the damage is already done. I need to be by myself."

"Is everything cool?" Lawrence asked, coming inside. I nodded slowly. He reached for Sheree's arm. "Baby, let's give her some space for a while."

"I'll stay if you need me," Sheree said, wrapping her arms around me.

"I'm good, sis, just tired. I'm gonna chill for the rest of the day. I'll call you later."

Nineteen

I poured all my energy into my work, putting in long hours to stay occupied. The extra effort paid off. Professionally, my life was great. After Mr. Levine was elevated to vice president of the company, Joanne advanced into his position as senior director, and she promoted me to fill her position as department head. Mama would have been beside herself with pride, and I would have taken her on a big trip to celebrate. Instead, I gave Sheree my red Corvette, and I bought myself a new silver 2014 BMW 750Li.

In my personal life, I couldn't win for losing. I felt lonely and used up at the same time. Sheree told me to get my mind right before I called Samuel. But with all the new responsibilities at work, two months passed, and I still hadn't picked up the phone. That wasn't the only reason though. After about month, just before school started, Terri showed up on my doorstep with a sad face again.

School started, and we had barely established a routine when I caught her sneaking food out of the house one evening. I knew the deal before I got to the window. Teddy was parked outside. I was standing at the door when she came back in.

"What's going on, Terri?"

"I took Daddy a plate," she said sheepishly. "He wanted to tell me that he got a new job, but he hasn't got a paycheck yet. He hadn't eaten dinner, so I offered him some food. I would have asked you, but I thought you might say no."

"I'm not the bad guy here, Terri. I'm not the cause of your daddy being hungry. He's a grown man. I hope there won't be a next time, but if there is, you need to let me know before you give him anything out of my house."

"I will," she said, rushing upstairs to her bedroom.

I went into the kitchen and pulled my wallet out of my purse. I had about a hundred in cash. I dug deeper for a pen and wrote a check for $1,000. Then I stomped outside.

"Why do you keep doing this, Teddy?" I asked, shaking my head. "Hanging out here in the parking lot. This doesn't make any sense."

"Chantelle, before we met, I never had a lady like you. I didn't appreciate you, and I didn't know how to treat you."

"We were together thirteen years, Teddy. You had time to learn. But, instead, when you got a little money in the bank, you took off."

"I guess I felt like I had something to prove."

"To whom?"

"I don't know—to myself and to my kids. I wanted to prove that I was the one providing for them and not you. I can't give up on us, Chantelle. I've learned so much, and I've changed. I'm a better man now. I can be a better man for you."

"Look, I'm happy for you if you're better; but from what I can see, you're down and looking for a way to get back on your feet. I've moved on, Teddy. I'm looking forward. I'm not interested in going backward."

"It's because of that other dude you're messing with."

"If you won't hear me, there's no reason to keep talking to you," I told him and walked back into my house.

Later that night, I peeped out the window, and I saw that Teddy's car was still there. The next night it was there. And for a week, most nights, it was there. I guess he hadn't gotten the memo that he couldn't con me anymore.

It was unbelievable to me that the man who would barely look at me for the last five years of our marriage was hounding the hell out of me now. Seeing him only made me miss Samuel more. As much as I wanted to call him and make things right, I hadn't cleaned up my house. But as the weeks passed and he didn't call me, my feelings were hurt. It was like another rejection from a man I had let get close to me. I started doubting if anything between us had been real.

***

The seasons changed. Summer turned to fall, and fall was approached winter. The one constant was Terri running in and out of the door tending to Teddy's needs. I was grateful for the few days of solitude and serenity when Terri announced that she was riding back to Baltimore with Teddy to spend Thanksgiving with his family. I had plans to spend the holiday at Sheree's house, and Aunt Betty was doing most of the cooking.

The weather had turned bitter by Atlanta's standards, and on Wednesday, November 27, the day before Thanksgiving, snow was in the forecast. I left work early, hoping to avoid some of the traffic, but it seemed most of Atlanta had the same idea. I sat in traffic for over an hour, watching my miles-left-to-get-gas display slowly go lower.

When I finally got off I-75, my nerves were fried, and I didn't feel like making any stops. But with bad weather coming and uncertainty about what might be open on Thanksgiving, I decided it would be wise to gas up the car before I went in. I drove one block to the Shell station where I usually buy gas.

The cold wind was whipping my legs as I swiped my card again and again at the gas pump. Then I heard the attendant's voice on the speaker say, "The outside card reader on that pump isn't working." Annoyed, I almost changed my mind and drove off before I reluctantly trudged inside to pay for the gas. I got at the end of the long line and tapped my foot impatiently. I had been waiting for about ten minutes when the lady standing behind me tapped me on the shoulder. I turned around, trying my best to be congenial.

She pointed toward the stand near the entrance where you can write your lotto numbers. "That guy over there is trying to get your attention."

I turned, and there he stood. It was Samuel.

"Hey, Miss Lady," he shouted across the store. He smiled. I didn't know how to react. I waved. He walked over, nodding his head, and half the people in the line were now tuned into the scene. "You're looking good. How are you?" he asked, not caring who was listening.

"Outstanding," I said in a low voice, looking back at him.

"All right then," he said, looking pleasantly surprised.

"You know I'm lying," I said, grinning. "I've missed you."

"Likewise, Chantelle. All you had to do was call me."

"After you kicked me to the curb?"

"That's not what happened."

"That's what it seemed like to me."

"I wanted you, baby. You were supposed to marry me. Then your ex came back."

"What did that have to do with us?"

"He was living at your house. I'm a mellow type of guy, but that was over the top."

"He wasn't there for me. I allowed it for Terri's sake."

He put up his hands in defense and changed the subject. "So, what's going on with you?"

"I'm good," I said, stepping up to the counter and putting my card down to pay for my gas.

"You know what I'm talking about," he said, removing my card from the counter and handing the cashier his own card. "I got this," he said, handing me my card.

"I'm working hard, trying to make it," I told him, heading out of the market after the transaction was done.

Samuel followed me to my car. "You switched cars. Nice. Pull the tank door open for me."

I opened the door, pushed the button, and stood beside the car. He started the gas pump and stepped closer to me. He stared at me for a few seconds before he asked, "Well? What about your stepdaughter and you ex?"

"My stepdaughter is staying with me. My ex has his own place."

Samuel nodded. Then he said, "Spend the holiday with me."

"Come on. I know you had plans before you saw me. You didn't expect to see me here buying gas."

"Yeah, I do. But the truth is I was hoping to see you here, and I was hoping to spend Thanksgiving with you."

"You let me go so easily. That shook me. I'm not ready to trust you or anybody else right now." I paused and stared back at him. "I feel like people want me when they need me, and when they don't, they block me out. I become invisible. I don't need that confusion in my life."

"You're not invisible, pretty lady, you hide. You're afraid to put yourself out there to be loved. Maybe you're the one who's oblivious to everyone around you. You're the one who doesn't want to be bothered. Life isn't something you protect yourself from. You can't get anything worth anything in this world if you don't take risks. Life is to be lived."

"Speaking the words of someone who hasn't been burned."

"That's not true. I just don't want to miss out on my future brooding over my past."

The pump clicked, signaling that the tank was full.

"It's freezing out here, and I don't want to keep you from wherever you were going," I said, opening my car door.

"Honestly, I do have other plans. I'll be with my family. I'm flying out to Chicago tonight. But I'll stay and spend the weekend with you if you want."

"No, you don't have to do that. I'm spending the holiday at Sheree's house. My Aunt Betty is cooking."

"I'm sure they won't mind if you bring somebody."

"I'm not sure if I'm ready for that," I said, getting into the driver's seat.

Samuel stepped back from the car. "You know I'm crazy about you, Miss Lady. I don't have time to play games or wait on you to get your life. I'll give you until Christmas to let me know what you want."

***

With my head bowed, I stared at all the food spread across the table. The sight and the smells were so familiar. I had seen it so many times while growing up. Aunt Betty was still thanking God for the blessings on our family over the past year when the sound of her voice faded as if someone had turned down the volume, and then I could hear Mama's voice talking to me. I closed my eyes, and the scene changed. I was back at Nicklewood in our old apartment. It was our last Thanksgiving together. I could hear the joy in her voice.

"Don't forget the apple cider, Chantelle," Mama said, placing the last dish on the table. "Spike it with a little cinnamon."

"I already did," I told her, carrying the pitcher in both hands. Then Sheree and Aunt Betty walked through the door. I could hear joy in my voice. I wanted that lightness of my youth again.

Then a gentle pat on my hand brought me back to the here and now.

"You're quiet today," Aunt Betty said to me. "What's on your mind?"

"Nothing," I answered, sighing. "Just missing Mama for a minute."

"I know, sweetie. I was thinking about her all day while I was cooking. No matter how hard I try, I still can't get the creamy texture of her sweet potato pie. One thing I do know is that she was so proud of you. And now you have accomplished all the things she wanted you to do."

"Yeah, I know that, Aunt Betty. Still, it would have been so special if she were here to share it with me. Maybe I wouldn't have made such a mess of my life marrying Teddy."

"Don't go there," Sheree said. "You weren't the one to blame in that mess. Teddy was. Besides, the heart makes decisions separate from the head."

"This is the day to be thankful," Aunt Betty interjected.

"I'm thankful for you, Aunt Chantelle," Monica said, grinning at me.

"Thank you, peaches," I said, blinking back a tear.

Aunt Betty clapped her hands. "Now, let's eat. We can't worry about woulda, coulda, shoulda. It'll give us all indigestion. Let's just thank the Lord that he brought us all through."

"Amen," Lawrence added.

Seeing the kids enjoy their meal and Lawrence sitting at the head of the table, I couldn't shake my melancholy mood. They were sharing their joy with me, but I didn't feel as if I had any of my own.

***

I sat around for the rest of the holiday weekend in a funk. I lied and told Sheree my stomach was upset and skipped our annual Black Friday shopping fest. Besides, it was partially true. I was upset through my bones to my soul. I was upset with Teddy, upset with Terri, upset with Jeremy and Julius, and—most of all— myself. Samuel was right: I subtracted from myself and gave it to others. Then I whined about my circumstances. I could finally admit that I was the creator of my invisibility. It wasn't so much that no one saw me; I was the one who was afraid to be seen.

By Sunday night, when Teddy brought Terri home, I had gotten an epiphany. To get my life, I needed to come out of the shadows of the darkness that Teddy was bringing to my doorstep. From now on, he was going to be invisible to me.

"How was your Thanksgiving, pumpkin?" I asked when Terri walked through the door.

"It was really good," she said, putting down her bag. "My mama was glad to see me. She said that she had missed me."

"That's great, baby girl. I'm happy for you."

"She made me promise that I would come back to Baltimore for the winter break and stay until after the New Year."

Normally, I would have resented her straddling the line between me and her mama, but I was over it. The fulfillment I craved would never come from the past. I had been there and done that. I was ready to look into my future. "I think that will be really nice."

She dashed up to her room, and on my way up the stairs behind her, I made a mental note to buy a new sofa.

***

"You look different," Joanne said curiously, inhaling the aroma of her morning coffee. Even though her schedule was busier, she still made time to have a break with me at least twice a week. "You must have had a great Thanksgiving weekend."

I knew she was wondering if I had seen Samuel. "The dinner was great, but I spent the rest of the weekend getting my head together."

"The wrinkle in your forehead is gone, so you must have gotten it all figured out," she said, sitting down. "Well, go on ahead, and give me the details."

"It's not all figured out yet, although I do have a plan. The problem is that I'm not sure if it will work out. I may have overplayed my hand."

Joanne took a sip of her coffee and sighed. "Is this problem you're talking about Teddy or Samuel?"

"I'm done with Teddy and his drama. I'm hoping that I can spend time with Samuel, quality time, out of Atlanta. I haven't been out of town in forever. I'm thinking about asking him to drive to Charleston with me for the weekend."

"Now, that's the report I wanted to hear," Joanne said, smiling. "That's just what you need. But why go to Charleston. It's too cool this time of year to enjoy the water. Why don't you go to the Bahamas? It's only a two-hour flight. You can put on a bikini and let your hair down, like in that movie *Stella Got Her Groove Back*.

"That sounds like a better plan than mine."

"Then do it," Joanne said, standing up. "You deserve it."

She was barely out the door before I pulled up Travelocity and Expedia on my computer. In less than thirty minutes, I had bought two tickets to Nassau and booked a beachfront villa on Paradise Island. The adrenaline rush to my heart gave me a jolt of hope that things could really work out, that I could have a man in my life who brought me joy instead of pain.

I grabbed my phone and called Samuel, anxious to extend my invitation. He didn't answer, and that brought me back down to earth a bit. I sent him a text, asking him to give me a call when he got a chance. I made a call to the beauty salon to get my hair braided, and then I called Sheree.

"What's up, sis?" she answered cheerfully, as usual. "Are you feeling better?"

"Yeah, I am. I hated missing our Black Friday shopping day."

"Mama and I cut it short. It wasn't the same without you."

"We can make up for it tonight or tomorrow. I just booked a trip to the Bahamas this weekend, and I need some bathing suits."

"Now that's what I'm talking about!" Sheree hollered through the receiver. "We have got to do this today."

I laughed, getting excited again. "I'm going to leave work early, and we can hit the streets."

"I'll be ready," she said.

After we hung up, I checked again for a text message from Samuel, but there wasn't one.

***

Sheree must have been watching for me through the window because she dashed out of the house before I could get out of the car.

"I'm so excited for you, sis," Sheree said. "I feel like I'm going on a trip. By the way, is Samuel going with you, or are you going by yourself?"

"I want Samuel to go with me, but I haven't talked to him about it yet. It was a spur-of-the-moment decision, and now I'm starting to second-guess myself. He hasn't returned my call. It's working my nerves, Sheree. What if he doesn't want to go? Every time I do something spontaneous, it blows up in my face."

"Don't start tripping," she said, patting me on the shoulder. "This is Samuel we're talking about, not Teddy. He'll call you. He's crazy about you. This trip is exactly what the two of you need to get your thing working again."

"I hope so. I can't let Teddy ruin this for me."

"Please. That negro is old news. Let's not even give him any more of our energy. We have to save that to find you all the sexy outfits for the Bahamas."

"Okay, but first, I've got to buy a new couch."

"Huh, why do we need to buy a new couch today?" Sheree asked, confused.

"I can't start fresh and snatch my new life with a sofa that smells like Teddy."

Sheree had no comment. She just held up her hand for a high-five. I pulled into the Z Gallery parking lot across from the mall. In less than 20 minutes, I had chosen a rust-colored leather sofa and arranged for it to be delivered in 48 hours.

"Now, can we get to the good stuff you need for the weekend?" Sheree asked, blowing impatiently. "Head straight to Bloomingdales. They've got everything you need, and I've got my discount."

"Absolutely," I answered, feeling as if I was getting my life back under control.

We walked through Bloomingdales, Saks Fifth Avenue, and the rest of the mall shopping for bathing suits, cute cover-ups, and sexy nighties.

Back in the car, I started having doubts. "I don't know, Sheree, this reminds me of the time we did the same thing when my marriage with Teddy was in trouble. I also remembered how it fell short of my expectations."

Sheree threw her head back before she responded. "I keep telling you, Samuel is not Teddy. Not all men are like him. You would have learned that if you had ever given any of the guys I tried to set you up with a chance."

"You would be shell-shocked, too, if you had been through what I went through."

"Believe it or not, me and Mama did go through it with you in a way. When you hurt, we hurt. It wasn't easy watching him dog you."

"I know that, and I appreciate you trying to fix me up. I never told you, but I thought Alex was fine. He was a good brother with a lot going on. I just wasn't ready."

"You were never going to be ready. That's why I give Samuel his props. He wouldn't take your no for an answer."

"That's true," I said, barely above a whisper. I never thought I would be begging him to let me say yes.

***

Later that evening after dinner, Terri was in her room watching TV or doing homework. I was in mine drinking a glass of wine and admiring my new swimsuits while I waited for the phone to ring. To my dismay, it didn't.

Two days later, I was near panic. Sitting on my new sofa, I called Samuel again. He answered on the third ring.

"I was getting worried," I told him, relieved he had finally answered. "Did you get my messages? I was starting to think you didn't want to talk to me."

"No, it wasn't that," he said casually. "I've just been doing some deep thinking."

"What have you been thinking about?" I asked, half afraid of what he might have concluded.

"I really like you, pretty lady, but I'm a practical man. I don't like to waste my time. My thinking is that you are not ready to move on from your past. You've got a big heart, but I have to admit I'm a selfish guy. I don't want to share my woman's heart with another man."

"Come on, Sam. I promise you, it's not like that. I've been calling to ask you to give me a chance to convince you that I'm serious about you, and I'm also asking you to take a trip with me to the Bahamas this weekend."

"Are you serious?" he asked, totally surprised.

"Absolutely, I am. I already bought the tickets."

"Wow, Chantelle. You've caught me off-guard with the invite. I mean, my mind was made up to walk away. That was a hard decision for me to make. Now, with this trip, you've given me a lot more to think about."

"Don't think about it. Just come with me. I really need to get away, and I really need to spend some time with you."

"Baby, if this decision was only about you and me, I wouldn't hesitate. I need you to give me a day or two to mull it over."

"I guess that's fair. You have been patient with me and my drama."

"I'll give you a call after I sleep on it, pretty lady. Have a good night."

When Samuel hung up, all the air went out of me, and I felt like a deflated birthday balloon when the party is over. If I had lost a good man over Teddy and his bullshit, I would probably take Sheree's offer to assist me in whupping his ass.

Chapter

Twenty

With the radio turned down, my thoughts drifted during the drive to work. I didn't want to take a chance that the music would drown out the sound of my cellphone if it rang. At the office, I couldn't concentrate on work between my prayers for Samuel to call.

Back at home, I couldn't have repeated one thing Terri talked about over dinner. The only voice I wanted to hear was Samuel's, telling me that he wanted to go on the trip with me. I climbed into bed early and watched TV with the volume muted. I fell asleep with my phone in my hand.

I woke up miserable. Sam hadn't called. I knew I wouldn't accomplish anything at work, so I picked up the landline phone, still hesitant to tie up my cellphone.

"Good morning, Joanne," I said, trying to sound animated. "I've got a ton of things to do before my flight tomorrow, so I won't be in today." I couldn't bring myself to tell her that Samuel probably wasn't going with me.

"I didn't expect to see you here today anyway," she said, excited for me. "Have a great weekend. You've earned it. I want to hear all the details when you get back."

"I will," I said, hanging up.

Once Terri was off to school, I started packing. I was determined to go whether Samuel went with me or not. I needed to get away from the drama that my life had devolved into. I wanted to go someplace where I could relax, pretend everything was great, and be invisible again.

An hour later, my suitcase was packed and sitting at the door. Then I started to get anxious about the plane ride. I had only flown once before, and that was on my honeymoon with Teddy. It made me think about the plans Mama and I had talked about and dreamed of all through my high school years. We were supposed to share the experience of our first flight together.

Those memories were too much to handle in my frame of mind, so I turned on the Lifetime channel to watch some movies to distract me and to ease my worries. My hair appointment wasn't until the afternoon, so I had some time to kill. But watching TV didn't help much. After a while, all the happy endings had gotten on my nerves.

Frustrated, I slipped my shoes on, grabbed my bag and keys, and headed out the door to get to the salon early. I had just started my car when my cellphone rang. My heart nearly stopped. It was Samuel.

"Hello," I answered timidly. I wasn't ready to hear any bad news.

"I'll meet you at the airport," he said plainly. "What time is the flight?"

"I'm glad you decided to come with me. It's at 8:45."

"What airline?" he asked bluntly.

"Delta, but both of us don't need to pay for parking," I said, feeling insecure about him showing up and coming with me. "I'll pick you up."

"What's the matter? You don't trust me to be there on time?"

"Not entirely," I said, laughing nervously. "I just don't want to go out of my mind waiting for you, thinking you've changed your mind."

He laughed and said, "I know the feeling." Then he hung up.

After a long exhale, I realized that I had barely been breathing for the last twenty-four hours. I took a deep breath and drove to the beauty salon.

My appetite returned, and my stomach started growling as soon as I walked into the salon.

"You're right on time, Chantelle," Roger said, hot curling another client's hair.

"You look like you're busy," I said, touching my belly. "Do I have time to get something to eat before you finish?"

"No, no, honey," he answered. "Nakita is ready to take your hair down. You can order something from Twisted Soul Cookhouse and have it delivered. Nakita, give her a menu."

I looked through the menu and ordered a fried chicken sandwich that had jalapeño cheese and a cranberry maple glaze.

Roger heard me on the phone and hollered over to me. "Go on and get the fries with it, girl. You are gonna be here for a while."

***

I set an alarm before I went to bed, but I woke up before it went off. I was anxious about flying, and whether Samuel would change his mind. I turned on the radio to relax while I got dressed. It didn't take long since I didn't have to do anything to my hair. I checked the clock. It was time for Terri to get ready for school. I peeked into her room before I left. She was yawning as she sat on the side of the bed.

"Give me a hug, sweetie. I'm heading to the airport," I told her, walking over to the bed. She stood up, and I wrapped her in a tight hug. It suddenly occurred to me that we didn't hug each other enough. "I've left you some money on the kitchen table. Sheree is going to check on you until I get back. You know my rules. No one is allowed in this house while I'm gone, and that includes your daddy." I looked her in the eye for emphasis.

"I got it," she said, half-whining. "You can trust me."

I hurried down the stairs, grabbed my suitcase, and hopped into the car. It was still dim outside; the sun was just rising. I was grateful that the morning rush hour wasn't in full effect yet. The closer I got to the airport, the more excited I felt. I turned off on the exit and drove toward the long-term parking lot. I caught a shuttle to the Domestic Terminal South. I glanced at my watch, and it was 7:00.

I figured it would be easier for Samuel to find me in the atrium area before the security screening. I found a seat that gave me a clear view of the entrance.

Forty-five minutes later, panic was creeping up on me. My leg jumped up and down to my accelerated heartbeat. I couldn't help but be afraid that Samuel might not show up. Thoughts of him changing his mind at the last minute had me nerve-racked. I was just about to freak out when I saw him walking toward me.

"I love your hair," he said, smiling.

I smiled back at him. "For a minute, I thought you were going to stand me up."

"No way, pretty lady," he said, putting his suitcase next to my suitcase. "I wouldn't dare miss a weekend at the beach with you looking all sexy in a swimsuit."

"That's a relief. I had my doubts."

"I did, too, but I'm over it. There's no way I'm going to let another man get in the way of what I want."

When he said that, I felt that I could breathe again. "Come on, let's go before we miss the flight."

It was a long walk through the concourse to get to our gate. As we walked down the long hallway to the connector to board the plane

I reached for Samuel's hand. "I've only flown once before. My mama and I planned to do a trip together after I graduated from high school. We were going to LA. She passed away before we got to go."

Samuel put his arm around me and said, "I hate that for you, but I'm here with you. And the fact that you booked first-class seats will make it even better."

I smiled at him. "I thought since it was our first flight together, we might as well go first-class."

Once we were on the plane, he guided me to the window. I hesitated. "I don't know if I want to see how far I am from the ground. Are you sure you don't want the window seat?"

"I'm good," he said. "We can switch later if you want, but it's amazing to see the world from up in the clouds."

I sat down, fastened my seatbelt, and closed my eyes until the plane was high in the air. I was tired from worrying for the last two days and planned to sleep until we landed, but the flight attendant was beyond attentive. It seemed as if she checked on us every ten minutes.

About an hour outside of Atlanta, raindrops splashed against the window, drawing my eyes to look. I was amazed. It looked like a waterfall pouring out of the clouds in the distance. For the rest of the flight, I couldn't tear my eyes away from the window.

***

It was around noon when we landed in Nassau, and it was beautiful. The flight was only three hours, but the stress of the last few days still had me tied in knots. I needed to relax. The taxi we hired to drive us to the cottage didn't help at all. The cabbie drove as if we had robbed a bank and he was the getaway car.

"The first thing I need to do after we get settled is find a spa near here," I told Samuel as I unpacked my suitcase. "I need a massage."

"You don't have to go to a spa," he said, running his hand across my back seductively. "I can give you a massage."

I ignored his overture and kept unpacking. "I appreciate that, but I need to unwind for real."

He walked out of the bedroom, and a couple of minutes later, he yelled back to me, "This place is perfect. It has a grill on the patio facing the ocean. Why don't we stock up with some food and drinks? There's a grocery store close by. We passed it in the taxi. I can cook up something for you while you relax and enjoy the view."

"Why don't I get a massage while you do the shopping?" I asked, walking into the living room.

The look on Samuel's let me know that he had a problem with my suggestion. It sounded crazy to me as soon as I said it. I had gone through a ton of drama to be alone with this man, and as soon as we landed, I was trying to get away.

It hadn't occurred to me until I got to the cottage, but the flashbacks of my beach weekend in Charleston with Teddy were filling my head. That trip had turned into a disaster. It had me wondering if this trip might turn out the same way.

Samuel brought me back from my musing. "Are you serious?" he asked, confused.

"No, no. I don't know what I'm talking about. I'm just stressed out. I wanted us to have this weekend, then I was afraid that you were done with me. And now you're here, and I don't know what I'm doing."

"Calm down, pretty lady," he said, wrapping me in a tight hug. "We're here, and we're going to have a great time. The first thing we need to do is go get something to eat, buy some food for the house, and get us some good strong liquor to drink."

That made me laugh, and my tension began to fade.

It was a ten-minute walk to the store. I don't know what I expected, but it wasn't much different from grocery stores back in Atlanta. We bought enough food to prepare our meals for the weekend and some food that was already prepared. The only thing that felt odd was doing this with Samuel. It hit me that we hadn't spent that much time together. With all the bags from shopping, we caught another taxi back to the cottage.

We got settled in and ate a late lunch.

"How do you feel?" he asked while we sat at the table.

"I'm winding down. I could use a power nap."

"Go on and get a nap. I'm going to do to some exploring.

***

The nap did me a world of good. I felt so much better. I got up, brushed my teeth, and went to find Samuel. He was sitting on the patio drinking a beer. He smiled when he saw me come through the door.

"I've been waiting for you, baby. Let's take a walk on the beach. I've seen couples do that in a hundred movies."

"So have I," I said, smiling.

"Can we agree to leave Atlanta in Atlanta and enjoy this paradise?" he asked seriously, taking my hand.

"Absolutely. Yes, we can."

We walked on the beach for a long time, and Samuel told me about his childhood on the South Side of Chicago. His parents met in the military, and he had a brother and a sister. His father left the army after ten years and opened up a mechanic shop, while his mother stayed in the service. With both his parents working or away, it made him, his brother, and his sister very independent.

His parents grew in different directions over the years until the only thing they had in common was the children. After his sister, the youngest, graduated from high school, his father sold his business and moved out of state. His mother retired from the military and joined the police force. Samuel said he went into the military to help take care of the family.

"While I was in the military, my mom met another guy, but she wouldn't take the step to marry him. I was angry at my dad for years; but when I came home and saw a smile on my mom's face where the tears used to be, it made me happy. I felt like I could live my own life, so I got married. When my marriage went sour, I felt sure that I could meet another lady who could make me happy. When I saw you, something inside told me you were that lady."

"Wow, that's really special," I said, admiring his resiliency. "After my divorce, I thought I would never be happy again. I guess I stayed in a bad relationship too long. That's why being with you scares me sometimes. When we're together, it's amazing. But I'm afraid things will change, and I'll be back where I started."

"You don't have to worry about me hurting you, pretty lady. I would never do that."

I held his hand tighter as we made our way back to the cottage.

When we got there, Samuel said, "I made shish kabobs while you were resting. Open up a bottle of wine while I get the grill fired up."

We ate dinner and finished the bottle of wine as we watched the sunset. Samuel massaged my neck and back, removing any remnants of tension.

"Let's take a shower," I said, standing on my feet. "I want to show you how much I appreciate you being here and cooking dinner for me."

"You don't have to ask me twice," he said, taking my hand. "I like it when you take charge."

"Maybe so, but only when it comes to you. You do something to me, and I like it."

We took a hot shower, and then I gave him the massage that I thought I wanted when we first got to the cottage. He showed me his appreciation with kisses from my head to my toes. We made love and then sat on the patio, drinking in the moon with glasses of Hennessey. We made love again, and I fell asleep with a feeling of comfort and satisfaction I had never known.

***

Samuel and I spent most of the next morning and the afternoon walking in downtown Nassau and feeding our faces at local eateries. I bought souvenirs for Sheree, Aunt Betty, and the kids. We hired a cabbie who drove us around the city. Samuel wanted to see where the real Bahamians lived. It was just like Atlanta: Some parts had beautiful, impressive houses where the well-off lived, and then there were other parts where hardworking folks struggled to keep a roof over their heads. After the tour, the taxi dropped us back at the cottage.

I looked in the fridge. "Are you hungry?" I yelled out to Samuel.

"No, I'm cool," he said, turning on the TV.

"Do you want to go to Atlantis?" I asked, walking into the living room. "We can check out the casino, or I saw a brochure about a boat ride."

"You don't have to entertain me, Chantelle. I'm fine here enjoying myself with you."

"I just don't want you to get bored."

"I'm not bored. Come on over here and sit with me. I'm gonna find us a movie to watch."

Samuel turned on some futuristic action flick. I tried to get into, but after he fell asleep in the middle of it, I went out on the patio to watch the waves hit the shore. It was so peaceful. I wished we could have spent a whole week there instead of just the weekend.

I didn't know what time it was when Samuel woke me up on the patio and led me to the bedroom. I felt as if I was the star of one of those romantic Lifetime movies.

***

The next morning, we laid in bed long after we were awake. Samuel finally got up around 11:00 to make breakfast. "I need some food to soak up the liquor from last night," he said, pulling on his pajama bottoms. "I still feel like I'm buzzing."

"I don't want to move," I told him. The truth was I was dreading going back home. In my relationships, reality had never been kind.

"Our flight isn't for another five hours, but we need to pack and get a taxi to the airport."

"Don't remind me," I said, climbing out of bed. "The pounding in my head now that I am standing is telling me to lie back down."

Samuel laughed. "I'll have you some coffee and scrambled eggs by the time you get out of the shower. And why don't you put on your bikini; I haven't even seen you in it. Besides, I want to take some pictures of you on the beach."

"I don't know if we have time for all that," I said, heading into the bathroom.

I couldn't help but smile to myself, thinking about modeling my swimsuit on the beach. Samuel always made me feel so special, but after being treated as second-class by Teddy for so long, it felt odd to me.

Out of the shower, I took my braids down and put on the sexy turquoise two-piece that Sheree had picked out. I chose the sheer flower-print cover-up and strutted into the kitchen.

"How do I look?" I said, striking a pose before I slid down into a chair at the table.

"You're blowing my mind," he said, grinning.

I took a swig of my coffee to hide my face. I was blushing like a teenager.

It didn't take us long to eat the eggs and toast. We both knew we didn't have much time left before we had to pack up our things. Samuel changed into his trunks and grabbed his camera as we headed to the beach.

Samuel insisted I take off the cover-up for the photos. "You don't need to be shy," he said. "These are for my eyes only."

I danced and splashed in the ocean, showing off for the camera, feeling as if I was a contestant on *America's Next Top Model*. Sheree would have been proud. When Samuel put his camera down and joined me to frolick in the water, it was like a fantasy come true. I wrapped my arms around him and stood on my toes for a kiss.

"I hate to be a killjoy, but it's time for us to pull our stuff together," he said, running his fingers through my braids.

I nodded and reluctantly followed him back to our cottage. We took turns washing the salt and sand off our skin and packing. We cleaned up the kitchen, placed the key on the table, and went outside to wait for our taxi.

***

My mood began to sour as soon as we went through airport security. It signaled the end to my fantasy weekend. When we boarded the plane, I closed my eyes and pretended to be sleep. I didn't know if Samuel sensed the change in the vibe between us. He was unusually subdued and drank two beers during the flight. After landing, we went to the baggage claim area and watched the conveyor turn without talking.

Once we had our luggage, I forced a smile on my face and asked, "Where are you parked?"

"I didn't bring my car; I took an Uber."

"Okay," I said as casually as possible. "I guess we're riding together." Samuel walked behind me to the shuttle area for long-term parking.

I was trying to adjust my mood when I saw the woman again. Mama. She was riding the escalator. I knew better than to chase her. It was a sign that a major decision was approaching in my life. I could feel the wrinkle creep onto my forehead.

Everything had been perfect. That scared me. I couldn't get over the feeling that it wouldn't last, that something would go wrong. I knew my paranoia would only sabotage our relationship, but I couldn't control my emotions. The fear of being hurt again was more powerful than I realized.

"Is something wrong, Chantelle?" Samuel asked as we waited for the shuttle.

"No. It's probably the letdown of coming home after a great weekend."

"I get that, but why would that affect us? It's like you're giving me the cold shoulder again."

"It's not you; it's me."

"Don't' flip on me, Chantelle. I thought we had gotten over the mind games."

"We have. I'm just tripping."

Samuel nodded, but he didn't say anything else until we were putting the luggage into my car. "It's late. I'll drive," he said, opening the car door for me. "I can crash at your place tonight. I'm off tomorrow."

"Okay," I said, turning on the radio, hoping it could help me shake my funky mood by the time we got to my townhouse.

***

Everything thing looked normal when we pulled up. The light upstairs in Terri's room was on. We got out of the car, but before we got to the door, a dark figure rushed at us and grabbed Samuel from behind. For a moment, I thought we were being robbed. Then, in horror, I saw it was Teddy.

"What the fuck!" Samuel roared, pushing him off. "What is your problem, man?" he yelled when he saw it was Teddy. Looking drunk and out of his mind, Teddy charged toward him again. They wrestled until Samuel pushed him off a second time.

"Stop it!" I screamed. "What do think you're doing?"

"I'm fighting for you. You need to know how much I want you in my life."

"I don't want you, Teddy!" I shouted at him.

"What do I have to do to prove to you that I love you?" Teddy shouted back.

"I don't care. I don't love you!" I said, turning away from him. Curtains moved, and blinds were opened in the windows in the cul-de-sac. We were making a scene.

Then Terri burst out the door, jumping between Teddy and Samuel. "Don't touch my daddy!"

She hollered.

I dug out my cellphone from my handbag and dialed 911. I held it up where they could see it and yelled, "I called the police." Teddy froze.

Samuel came and stood by me. "It's over, man," he said. "Chantelle is with me. Stop making a fool out of yourself."

Teddy opened his mouth to speak, but no words came out. He put his hand in his jacket pocket, and I thought things were about to get ugly. Then he took it out, threw both hands in the air, and ran back to his car.

"Daddy!" Terri shouted.

His tires screeched as he sped away, as the sounds of sirens grew closer.

"Let's go inside," Samuel said, picking up our luggage.

Terri rushed by us and ran upstairs to her room. "She'll be all right," he said, closing the door behind us.

***

I laid in bed and called out sick from work the next morning. I was physically exhausted and emotionally drained. It had taken nearly a half hour to explain to the cops that my ex-husband ambushed us but that I didn't want to press charges. I assured them, and Samuel, that I would file for a restraining order on him as soon as possible.

"Are you hungry?" Samuel asked, sitting up in bed.

"My stomach is kind of upset, but I need to eat something," I answered. "I stocked the fridge before I left, but I don't know what's down there. Terri has probably been feeding Teddy all weekend."

"No problem. I'll drive your car and pick up something."

"That sounds good," I said, hoping that Terri would be dressed and gone to school by the time he got back. I crawled out of bed and pulled on my robe. I bumped into Terri on my way downstairs to the kitchen. "You're getting an early start," I said, seeing she was already dressed.

"Yeah, my ride has to be at school before 8:00." She grabbed her coat from the closet and headed out the door.

The cool air from the open door revived me. "Okay. Well, have a good day," I said. She didn't respond or look back. Unsure of where my cellphone was, I went into the kitchen and dialed Sheree on the landline.

"Welcome back!" Sheree squealed. "How was your weekend?"

"The weekend was great. I wasn't ready to come back."

"That's what I'm talking about," she said. "Are you at work this early?"

"No, I called out."

"Oh, shit. It must have been a helluva weekend."

"Are you working today?"

"Yeah, I go in at 10:00. What's up?"

"Nothing, just wondering if you can take a break and hang out for a few."

"You know how I roll," she said with a laugh. "I'm a manager now. I can take breaks whenever I want. Lawrence is still after me to quit, but working gets me out of the house."

"All right. I'll be there around lunchtime."

Samuel came in the door as I was hanging up. He had bought breakfast sandwiches and coffee from Starbucks. It was evident that my funky mood was contagious, and I could tell from Samuel's facial expression that he had caught it. So much for the glow of our trip shining throughout the week.

"What do you have planned for this morning?" he asked casually.

"I'll probably run by the mall and try to catch up with Sheree."

"Don't you think you need to get that restraining order handled?"

"I will," I said, knowing that possibly might not be true. "It's you I'm worried about. He came after you, not me."

"Can you honestly say he has never been violent with you?"

I thought back on the time he pushed me out of the way when I caught him getting off to porn in his office. I wasn't sure if that qualified. "No, I don't have any reason to be afraid of him."

"If you say so," he said, getting up from the kitchen table. "My Uber ride is here. Some of us still have some studying to do."

I waited at the foot of the stairs while he got his suitcase. He gave me a quick hug without a kiss before he walked out the door.

Watching the car drive off, I remembered the words he had said to me the day I invited him for the weekend: that I wasn't ready to let go of my past.

***

Thankfully, I was wearing sweatpants and a hoodie under my coat. My body hadn't adjusted to the cold temperature after relishing the 80-degree days in Nassau. Trying to avoid the chill, I jogged into Bloomingdales to find Sheree. I was about to catch the elevator to her office when I saw her in the Versace area.

"I should have known I'd find you here."

"What can I say? My birthday is coming up. I might have to treat myself."

"You always do," I said, laughing.

I followed her to a dressing room where there were chairs on the outside. "So, what's going on with you?" Sheree asked on her way inside the changing room.

"I didn't tell you before I left, but when I called Samuel to invite him to go with me, he practically broke up with me," I said, plopping down in one of the chairs.

"You're kidding!" she said, sticking her head out of the dressing room door.

"I wish. He was tired of the Teddy drama. He was done. When I asked him to go with me, he said he needed some time to think. He didn't call me back until the night before the flight. He met me at the airport."

"Wow, that's deep," she said, taking a seat beside me. "What happened in the Bahamas?"

"The cottage was great. We were within walking distance to the beach and had a great view."

"And how was the loving?" she whispered.

"It was the best part of the trip. We didn't do much else."

Sheree held up her hand for a high-five. "Now, that's what I'm talking about. So, what's the problem?"

Sometimes it made me angry that Sheree could read me so well. "How do you know there's a problem?" I asked, smirking.

"I can't count the times you skipped work to hangout with me for no reason, because it has never happened."

"Okay," I said, sighing. "Samuel rode back with me to the townhouse from the airport. When we got out of the car, Teddy jumped him."

"What the hell?" Sheree asked, her eyes wide with shock.

"He called himself fighting for me."

Sheree shook her head. "I bet he couldn't bust a grape."

I sniggled. "No, he couldn't."

"So, now what?"

"Sam wants me to put a restraining order on him, except I don't think it's necessary."

Sheree stared at me as if I wasn't making sense. Then she said, "This craziness has been going on for almost six months. It's time to end it. I'm with Sam. Put a restraining order on his ass. If he comes around again, have his ass locked up."

A short line gathered outside the dressing room, and I didn't want them all listening to my business, so I stood up. "I hear you. I'll get out of your hair and let you do some work."

She stood up and gave me a hug. "Call me when you leave the police station," she said as I walked away.

*****

I didn't think it was necessary, but I did file the restraining order. I didn't want to have to lie about it to Samuel. In the parking lot, I reached for my phone and called Teddy.

Without saying hello, he said, "I'm sorry, Chantelle."

"I've filed a restraining order against you, Teddy. We are done. I want to be there for Terri, but if you insist on coming around to see her, she won't be able to stay with me."

There was silence on the phone for almost a minute. I could hear him breathing. Then he said, "I won't bother you anymore." Then he hung up.

Instead of driving home, I went by Home Depot, had an extra house key made, and headed over to Samuel's place. I was relieved when I saw his car parked outside. I parked beside him, rushed up to the door, and knocked.

Hey, what's up?" he asked, surprised to see me.

"I missed you. I was wondering if you would pack a few more things in your bag and come stay with me for a while?"

His face relaxed into a wide grin. "I think I can do that." I put my arms around him, and he pulled me close.

I looked up at him. "From now on, everything will be about us."

"That's all I wanted to hear, pretty lady."

I sat down in the living room and waited for him to pull some things together. On the drive back to my place, I kept checking my rearview mirror until he parked his car next to mine. I gave him the extra key I had made, and he unlocked the door.

I made space for him in my closet and cleared out one of the drawers in the dresser. It felt great to watch him put his things away. I had taken the step I never thought I could make again, the one toward commitment.

***

Terri wasn't disrespectful to Samuel. We ate meals together, but she avoided him as much as possible. I'm sure there was some resentfulness left for me as well. She and I rarely watched *Love and Hip-Hop Atlanta*, *RuPaul*, or *Real Housewives of Atlanta* together anymore. Sheree and Aunt Betty advised me to let it be, saying that you can't make a teenager happy, no matter how hard you try.

I raised the subject of college applications with Terri, hoping to find something we could do together. That was when she told me she wanted to apply to Morgan State University in Baltimore. I felt a tinge of betrayal that she wanted to go back there to school instead of Spelman or another college in Atlanta. Just before the school winter break, she announced that she was going to Baltimore for Christmas and wouldn't be back until after the new year. On the day she left, I gave her a card with money in it. Teddy was going to drive them to Baltimore, and I wasn't sure if his financial situation had gotten better.

When I got home from work the next day, Samuel surprised me with a decorated Christmas tree. We spent evenings watching the lights blink, drinking wine, and listening to The Whispers. I was happier than I'd ever been since Mama passed. Introducing Samuel to my family and eating Christmas dinner with us all together was so special. Samuel and Lawrence got along great. I felt the joy of the holiday, realizing that I had been going through the motions for a long time.

The new year brought me a clear vision of myself, not only in my personal life, but in my professional life as well. When Joanne asked me about making the presentation for our division in the annual meeting, to her surprise, for the first time, I said yes. I was moving out of my comfort zone to the spotlight. I was done hiding. I was ready to be seen. The cocoon I had shrouded myself in hadn't protected me from the pitfalls of life. It was time to spread my wings and fly.

It was never a lack of confidence or low self-esteem that kept me shrouded. Basically, I had been blind to my own self-worth.

And because I couldn't see it, I had settled for less than I deserved. Even worse, when I was offered more, my doubts forced me to turn it away.

Chapter

Twenty-One

Samuel and I ate dinner with my family every other Sunday, and we always had a good time. Lawrence suggested we go out on the town and do something special together for Valentine's Day. When we agreed, Lawrence made reservations at the Capitol Grille. I even took Sheree's suggestion and was wearing a new sexy red dress for the occasion.

Sitting in the restaurant, I thought about how far Samuel and I had come in our relationship. It felt good to be able celebrate with someone who truly loved me. Lawrence ordered champagne, and just as we were about to toast, Samuel got down on one knee and proposed in front of everybody. I could feel all of the eyes in the entire restaurant were on me.

Holding my hand, he said, "I knew from the first time I saw you I wanted you to be my wife. It took me a while to show you that I meant that and that I love you. Hopefully, I have convinced you enough to say yes." With his other hand, he reached into his pocket and pulled out a small box. "Chantelle, will you marry me?"

I had no doubts. "Yes! Yes, I will!"

"Finally!" Sheree cheered, clapping her hands.

"A toast to Samuel and Chantelle," Lawrence said, raising his glass.

I took a big swallow of the champagne. "Did you know about this?" I asked Sheree.

"Only because Sam wanted a little help picking out the perfect ring," she said, smiling.

The diamond facets sparkled when I held up my hand to admire my ring. "It is perfect."

Samuel slid back into the booth beside me and kissed me passionately, like he did in private, but we had the attention of the whole restaurant.

"I feel embarrassed," I whispered to Sheree.

"No, don't be. It's inspiring," she said, raising her glass again.

I looked around the room, and quite a few glasses were raised to toast. I couldn't believe it; I was the center of attention.

*****

After the evening of the proposal, Samuel and Sheree were pressuring me to set a date for the wedding, but I kept stalling. One night when we were lying in bed, out of the blue, Samuel said, "Now, that we are engaged. Let's make a baby. No more condoms and no more pills."

"You're crazy, Samuel," I said, laughing.

"No, I'm being real. If we're gonna have a baby, we don't have time to wait."

Those words reminded me of Mama. They made me stop and think before I responded. My first instinct was to argue and disagree. That's the way I had behaved with Samuel since the day we met. I had to stop myself. This man was offering the thing I had begged for from Teddy for so many years, a child of my own.

"Okay," I said, surprising him. He was so used to coaxing me throughout our relationship. "But I want us to get married first."

"Now, you're talking," he said, pulling me on top of him. "Just tell me when. You know Sheree is itching to plan the wedding."

"Let's just go to Vegas and elope," I said softly. "I don't think we need to make a big deal out of it. I don't need a big ceremony to say I love you."

"My lady, I want a big ceremony. I want all of Atlanta to know I love you. I want you to walk down a long aisle where I can see you take those steps to be my wife."

"You need time to plan that type of wedding. You can't do it in a few weeks. Besides, I'm about to be overloaded with senior year activities for Terri, including pictures, prom, and class trip. I don't see how I can plan a wedding with all that."

"Don't worry. When Sheree and I were picking out your ring, she told me to give her the date, and she would handle it. We can get married in June, after Terri graduates."

"All right." I said, giving in. "June is fine with me."

"There's one more thing we need to talk about," he said, sounding serious. "I want us to buy a house. My apartment is too small. We need our own place."

"This can be our own place for a while."

"Your living here, or me living here where your ex slept doesn't sit well with me."

"Okay," I said, sighing. "We can start looking for a house."

***

The next three months were a whirlwind. Samuel and I found a house in Lawrenceville, not far from Sheree. After the closing, Samuel invited his family to visit for a weekend, for a housewarming, and for an opportunity to get to know me before the wedding. Just to keep things less awkward, I encouraged Terri to spend the weekend with one of her friends who lived nearby.

Before they arrived, Samuel told me a lot more about his family. I knew his parents met serving in the army and were divorced, but he told me they hadn't seen each other in 20 years. His mom had become a police officer, and she had worked her way up to captain. His father, after being in the military for so long, couldn't get used to staying in one place. Last they heard, he was driving trucks cross-country.

Despite Jimmy, Samuel's brother, being a senior manager at Boeing, he was afraid to fly. He and his wife, Beverly, would be driving down. Beverly was self-employed. She made jewelry and taught African and modern dance. The two of them had left Chicago at daybreak and would get into Atlanta that evening. Samuel's mother, Sandra, and his sister, Sebrina, were flying in. They had an early flight that Friday, so I took off work to go with Samuel to meet them. Being at the airport always reminded me of Mama, so my feelings of melancholy were mixing with my anxiety over whether his family would like me.

I recognized Sandra and Sebrina as soon as they came down the escalator. There was a strong family resemblance. His mom wasn't heavy, but she was sturdy. Sebrina was tall, with a body like Jackie Joyner-Kersey. Samuel said his mom was retired now, but she still carried herself as if she were still in charge. It only took one glimpse to see that Sandra was a sharp dresser, and every hair was in place.

Sebrina wore her hair in braids and was dressed more conservatively in a blazer and a denim skirt. In her horn-rimmed glasses, she looked like a college professor. Samuel said she had dropped out of law school after her second year and had become a paralegal. She liked her independence and had never married. It was obvious that she was close to her mother. They walked almost shoulder to shoulder toward us.

Samuel rushed up to meet them. I watched them wrap their arms around Samuel, and there was no doubt that they were very protective of him. This visit was for me to pass their test of my suitability to be accepted as his wife.

"You must be Chantelle," Sandra said, looking me straight in the eyes. "Come on and give me a hug," she said with outstretched arms. "We're practically family."

I could smell her scent of Chanel No. 5, the same scent that Sheree bought for Aunt Betty. Belying her outer appearance, she was as warm and inviting as a down comforter in the dead of winter. "I'm so glad to finally to meet you," I said, feeling somewhat relieved.

"Show me so love, too," Sebrina said, coming between us and giving me a quick but tight hug. "This is all we brought, so let's get out of here. I'm hungry."

"That's nothing new," Samuel said, teasing her as he led the way to the parking garage. "Why is it that the people who can't cook are always wanting something to eat?"

Sandra laughed loudly. "Isn't that the truth."

"You are not gonna worry me this weekend, Sam," Sebrina said, joking. "I am going to enjoy myself. And, Chantelle, I hope you are better than the company you keep."

I had to laugh. "I'll try my best."

"Well, good," Sebrina said, laughing. "I need to see what kind of watering holes y'all have down here."

"Hold your horses, little girl," Sandra said. "We didn't come here just for you to get your party on. We are here to celebrate your brother's engagement and welcome Chantelle into the family. It's too early for her to see your questionable side."

"Come on, Mama," Sebrina said. "From what Sam has told me, she done see it all."

Samuel held up his hands just as we approached his car. "I'm going to need you two to keep it mellow and respect my lady."

"I don't mean no disrespect," Sebrina, said. "You know I keep it cute, but she's gonna be family, so I might as well keep it real."

I grabbed the door handle to let Sandra get in the car, but before I opened it, I said, "Neither of you have to tiptoe around me. I want to be comfortable around you, and I want you to be comfortable around me. If there's anything you want to know, just ask. If there's anything you want to say, just say it. I'm cool with it."

"That sounds good by me, Chantelle," Sandra said. "And that goes both ways. We all live in the same world, and ain't nothing new under the sun."

"Can we all just get in the car?" Samuel said, popping the trunk.

"You the boss," Sebrina said, giving him her bag and climbing into the backseat on the driver's side.

I got in after Sandra lifted herself up into the SUV. I heard Samuel exhale after he got in and pushed the ignition.

Sandra reached up and tapped him on the shoulder. "Find me a little gospel music on that radio, baby. I got to thank the Lord for our safe passage."

"No problem, Mama," he said, smiling.

"And find us a nice place to get some seafood," Sebrina hollered. "It's Friday, so you know we need to eat some fish."

Sandra hummed to "God Is" by the Reverend Walter Hawkins on XM radio, while Sebrina murmured, "Yes, yes, yes," over and over. I smiled to myself, looking out of the car window, and Samuel laughed and shook his head.

***

After we dropped off Sandra and Sebrina's bags at the house, we found a seafood restaurant and filled ourselves full of fish. Samuel drove around for a while to give Sandra and Sebrina a tour of the city. When we got back to the house, Sandra wanted to watch the evening news. Sebrina stretched out on the sofa next to her and dozed off. When the news ended, I was about to surf the channels to look for a movie, but Sandra said she was beat and ready to go to bed.

"I'll show you where your room is," I said to Sandra. Thankfully, Samuel and I had prepared their beds and bathroom the day before.

"Put on some music or something," Sebrina said. "And I know you got something to drink around here. I need to wet my whistle."

"I'll get you a beer," Samuel said with a chuckle.

Samuel put on an Earth, Wind, and Fire CD and got a deck of cards to play tonk with Sebrina. I sat on the floor near the coffee table way past midnight laughing while they played cards and cracked jokes on each other between beers. Just when I stood up to call it a night, a horn beeped outside. It was Jimmy and Beverly pulling in the driveway.

"It's about time!" Sebrina exclaimed. "I could have gotten here faster on a bike."

We all followed Samuel to the door. "What's up, bruh!" Samuel said, grabbing Jimmy's hand and pulling him in close to bump shoulders.

Jimmy blew a long breath. "Man, I'm telling you, that drive was no joke. I'm glad to finally get here. Beverly complained the whole way."

"Hey, he was driving too fast for my taste," Beverly said, moving forward to give Samuel a hug. Then she looked at me and smiled. "I guess you're Chantelle. Anything you want to know about this crazy bunch, just ask me."

"Close your mouth until you brush your teeth," Sebrina said, grabbing her in a hug.

Jimmy and Beverly looked like the odd couple, just as Samuel said. Wearing a wrinkled button-down shirt and dress pants, Jimmy reminded me of a door-to-door salesman. I'd met a lot of men like him. They never relaxed, even when they were far away from the job. It was obvious that Beverly was the laid-back one. Her natural hair was cut close, and she was dressed in an oversized t-shirt that hung over one shoulder and yoga pants.

"You guys want anything to eat or drink?" Samuel asked.

"Hell, no!" Jimmy exclaimed. "All we want is a place to crash."

"Speak for yourself," Beverly said. "Point him to a bed, Sam. He can't even see straight right now. I don't know how we got here in one piece. As your mama, says, 'it must have been King Jesus.' "

"I'm kind of beat myself," Samuel said, laughing. "We'll let you ladies have it."

"That's fine," Beverly said, waving her hand. "Now, can a girl get a glass of wine around here? I'm parched. And which way to the bathroom?"

"It's the door down that hall on the left," I said, pointing the way. "Make yourself at home. I'll open a bottle."

I got a bottle of chardonnay and three glasses. I nixed the thought of a cheese ball and crackers. What I wanted was to follow Samuel to bed. By the time I popped the cork and poured the wine, Beverly was back from the bathroom.

"Oh, yes! I feel so much better," she said, grabbing a glass and sitting on the floor.

"You are not about to keep us up all night," Sebrina said, chuckling. "I know you probably didn't help drive and slept most of the way."

Beverly laughed. "There you go. All up in other folks' business again. I just wanted to chill with my sisters for a few minutes."

"I'm on my last leg, but I'll stay up for a few," I said, hoping to bridge the gap that would lead me to my bed in the not-too-distant future.

"Well, since I'm on a time limit, I might as well be blunt," Beverly said, turning toward me. "From what I've heard, you have a lot of baby daddy drama going on. What's up with that?"

"You're out of place, Bev," Sebrina said, jumping in. "I appreciate the fact that you care about my brother, but you ain't blood. Don't get it twisted. My brother is a grown-ass man, and I trust him to make an intelligent decision about who he wants to be with."

With that interaction, my last leg was kicked out from under me. Beverly wasn't as mellow as she looked. "Well, on that note, I'm going to have to see you ladies in the morning," I said, standing up. "Help yourselves to more wine or food in the fridge."

I climbed the stairs, took a quick shower, and slid into bed beside Samuel. He was in a deep sleep and didn't wake. I lay beside him thinking about the happenings of the day, and it finally dawned on me what my family drama must have felt like to him.

***

Samuel was still asleep when I dragged myself out of bed before 8:00 the next morning. I was determined to be a good host to his family, even if it killed me. I was surprised to find his mom in the kitchen sitting at the table sipping a cup of coffee. Wearing a housedress, she looked less intimidating. When she saw me, she got up and took eggs and bacon out of the fridge. "No, I can't let you cook. You're company," I said, attempting to take the food from her hands. "I'll make breakfast for everybody."

Sandra pulled the cartoon out of my reach. "Chile, you don't have to wait on me. I know my way around a kitchen. You probably can't half see with those bags under your eyes. Go on and rest yourself. Sit there at the table, and we can talk."

"Okay," I said, preparing myself for a grilling.

"You know, Sam is my middle baby," she said, turning on the stove. "Jimmy went his own way, but Sam was the one I could rely on to hold the house together while I was working. He's loyal, but at the same time, he's practical. I knew from the way he talked that he was crazy about you. I know my son, and he'll be good to you like he is to everybody in his life. The question is, How good will you be to my son? He's seen his share of nonsense, and I'd prefer that he not have to deal with anymore. From what Sam told me, you're a good woman; but you have ties that can't be broken."

"Miss Sandra," I said respectfully. "I want to assure you that I love your son, and I will do everything in my power to make him happy." Before I could say anything else, Samuel walked into the kitchen.

"That sounds good to me," he said, kissing me on the cheek before he went over and hugged his mom. "You need any help?" he asked her.

"No, go on over there and sit with your bride-to-be."

We sat in silence, listening to her hum a medley of gospel tunes. It made me think of how much my mama loved all the old Motown hits. Then Sebrina came in and went straight to the fridge.

"I am starving. What else you got to eat in here?" she asked, staring at the shelves.

"Hand me that milk, and I'll stir up some pancakes," Sandra told her.

"How about some grits?" Sebrina said, looking over at me. "We're down South, so I know you got to have some." Then she started searching the cabinets.

Samuel laughed and stood up. "Get out of the way. You wouldn't know what to do if you found them." He brought down the box of grits and got a pot to boil them in.

In the next fifteen minutes, Sandra was putting eggs, bacon, and the first batch of pancakes on the table. Samuel was stirring grits, and Sebrina was getting plates and silverware. I got up to make some toast and pour the orange juice.

"I'm ready for this feast," Beverly said, dancing into the room, with Jimmy following behind her. He was more casual in a polo shirt, but he was still wearing dress slacks.

Sebrina sucked her teeth. "Conveniently showing up after all the work is done again."

"You're not going to worry me this morning," Beverly said, stretching her arms wide and showing off the wide sleeves of her silk caftan. "I feel great this morning. I'm ready to eat and check out the ATL."

"Everybody sit down! I'm ready to say grace," Sandra fussed, pulling out her chair on the other side of Samuel.

When she finished, I spoke up. I had decided that I wanted to give a statement before Beverly or anyone else felt the need to interrogate me. "Listen, everybody, I'm so glad that you all have come to Atlanta to visit with us. It gives me the opportunity to get to know Samuel's family and for you all to get to know me. I understand that you may have heard some things about me, and they may have given you a distorted picture of who I am."

"Baby, you don't have anything to explain," Samuel said, caressing my arm.

"That's right, Chantelle," Sandra said, interrupting him. "We don't think nothing bad about you. We just want to see Sam happy. If he's happy, then we're happy."

I gave her hand a thankful squeeze and kept talking. "One thing I've learned is that it's always good to clear the air. Then there are no misunderstandings. My ex put me through a lot of drama. I helped raise his children, and then he walked away when he didn't need me anymore. When I met Samuel, I had given up on being loved or loving anybody. He changed that for me. Then out of the blue, after more than two years, my stepdaughter and my ex came back to Atlanta. I let my stepdaughter move back in with me to finish high school. My ex has been a pain in the ass for me, and for Samuel, but we can handle it. Are there any questions?" I asked, looking around the table.

"I don't have any," Jimmy said, glancing over at Samuel. "From where I sit, it looks like bruh chose a woman of substance and ambition."

"Is that what you did?" Sebrina asked him, laughing.

"And what is the reason that you don't have a man?" Beverly snapped at Sebrina.

Sandra raised her arms up. "Everybody here use your mouths to eat, and be quiet!"

Except for the sounds of eating, it was silent at the table. Then Samuel said, "I've got a whole day planned for you guys in the ATL, so put on some comfortable shoes. Chantelle has some work she has to get done, so we'll catch up with her for dinner."

"Now that's what I'm talking about," Sebrina said.

I rubbed Samuel's leg under the table, grateful for him making an excuse for me. I'm sure my face showed how tired I was, and I could use a few hours alone to get some more sleep.

After breakfast, Samuel and his mom cleaned the kitchen and loaded the dishwasher. They moved around as if they had gone through the process a million times. There was no doubt that so much of his character had come from his mother. Once everything was all back in its place, Samuel got his family together, and they headed out. I stood at the door and waved as they all climbed into his big truck. When they were gone, I headed straight back to bed, too exhausted to call Sheree and give her an update on how things were going.

The tour Samuel gave his family around Atlanta left them subdued for the rest of the evening. Jimmy insisted on treating us all to dinner at a high-end steakhouse in Buckhead. It wasn't too far from my old townhouse, so I silently prayed that Teddy wouldn't be lurking anywhere around. We had a good time at dinner, and the three bottles of wine we drank probably helped smooth out our dispositions.

***

I beat Sandra to the kitchen the next morning. I made coffee and put out some bagels and cream cheese. Sandra came downstairs dressed to impress and ready to go to church. I had showered just in case. Samuel came out of the shower while I was putting on my dress. He put on a suit and went with us.

It was the first time Samuel had gone to church with me, and it was the first time I had gone in a month of Sunday's. We got there a bit late, but I could see Aunt Betty sitting on the second pew with the sisters; and Sheree, Lawrence, and their kids were seated midway toward the front.

Sandra said she enjoyed the service. Afterward, we waited outside for her to meet my family. Surprisingly, Aunt Betty was the first to come out.

"It's so good to meet you," Aunt Betty said, holding her arms wide to give Sandra a hug. "Your son has been a godsend. I prayed for Chantelle to meet a good guy to share her life with."

"I'm glad I came here. I feel comfortable that my son has a good woman now," Sandra said, smiling over at me."

"I can assure you he has," Aunt Betty said as Sheree and Lawrence came out. "Here's my daughter and her husband. Sheree and Lawrence, this is Samuel's mother."

"It's a pleasure to meet you," Sheree said, smiling.

"Likewise," Sandra said, eyeing Sheree. I was sure she noticed a kindred fashionista standing before her.

"What are your plans for the rest of the day?" Lawrence asked Samuel. "We'd love to take you all to an early dinner."

"My sister, my brother, and his wife are waiting at the house," Samuel answered.

"They are all welcome," Lawrence said.

"Thank you for the invitation," Sandra said, "But we have to get our things together so we can fly back home this evening. We'll definitely have to do that when we come back for the wedding."

"I'll look forward to that," Aunt Betty said.

Samuel hugged Aunt Betty and Sheree. "We probably need to get back and check on my other folks," he said.

"I'll call you later, Chantelle," Sheree said as I walked to the truck.

I nodded back.

"You have a nice family," Sandra said, clicking her seatbelt. "Where's your stepdaughter? I wanted to meet her."

"She's hanging out with a friend this weekend." I answered as casually as I could.

"I guess we'll meet her next time," Sandra said warily.

"Terri's a good girl, Mom," Samuel said, turning on the radio. "She'll be going to college in the fall."

Sandra didn't say anything but started humming to the song playing on the radio. I could tell she had her reservations about Terri living with us and what that meant. There was nothing I could say to reassure her about the situation. I was hoping for the best myself.

Sebrina, Jimmy, and Beverly were up and ready to go out and get something to eat when we got back to the house. They had to wait a few minutes while Sandra packed her things. Their flight was at seven, so they needed to be at the airport around five.

We had an early dinner at Soulful Taste Restaurant. Sandra wanted to see if the fried chicken in Atlanta was as good as hers. We had a pleasant meal, and neither Sebrina nor Beverly made snappy remarks at the table. I guess all the fears of me being the questionable, crazy, space cadet who was going to drag Samuel into my country, ghetto, never-ending drama were allayed.

I felt a rush of relief myself as we waved goodbye to Sandra and Sebrina as they went through airport security. They were good people, and I felt as if I had gained their approval. Jimmy and Beverly didn't ride with us to the airport. They wanted some time to themselves to explore the city. They were going to spend another night at the house, with plans to leave at daybreak the next morning.

Twenty-Two

Taking the week off from work after Samuel's family came to visit was the best thing I could have done. To get ready for Terri's graduation, we had to shop for the perfect dress and shoes and for the particular hair Terri wanted for a weave. I scheduled hair appointments and nail appointments for a couple of her friends. It was a happy time for her, and her excitement was infectious. I remembered that moment in my own life, the feeling that I was about to embark on a fantastic and joyous journey.

It was also a little sad for me to think about. Thoughts of how I felt back then were marred, knowing I would lose my mother soon after. I reflected on how my whole world was turned upside down. I wondered if Mama had survived how much different my life would have been. Would I have even met Teddy? Would I have even married him? And if I did, would I have stayed after the twins showed up? I shook my head to clear out all the negative thoughts. This was a day to celebrate.

I looked at my reflection in the mirror. I smiled. I had come along way, and the child I had helped raise was about to graduate from high school.

"Hurry up. You don't have time to be late," I called out on my way downstairs.

"I'm almost ready," Terri shouted from the bathroom. "We have plenty of time to get there."

I checked my watch and sat down to wait. Samuel had decided to skip the ceremony in case Teddy showed up. He didn't want to spoil the day for her; she already had one disappointment to deal with. Terri had called her mama and invited her to the graduation; but a day later, her mama called back and told Terri that she couldn't get off work to come.

It was after that when Terri informed us that she wanted to spend the summer in Baltimore to get settled before she went to Morgan State in the fall. I made my peace with it. Children grow up and go on with their lives. What was most important to me was that she was a confident and outgoing young lady.

Sitting in the crowded auditorium, I could see so much of myself when I saw Terri walk across the stage and get her diploma. The anticipation of finding her place in this world, while ignorant to the challenges that would come into her path. I prayed that her dreams would come true, as I'm sure my mama prayed for me.

I suggested that we go to Gladys Knight's Chicken and Waffles for dinner to celebrate. It was more of a nostalgic thing for Sheree and me, having celebrated our high school graduation, but Terri and Monica didn't have a problem with eating chicken. My hope was to sit at the same table when we got to the restaurant, but it was already taken.

"Congratulations, Terri," Sheree said, handing her a gift bag after we had eaten.

"Thank you, Aunt Sheree," Terri said, smiling.

"What is it?" Monica asked.

"It's a new iPhone," Sheree told her. "That way Terri won't have a reason not to keep in touch. There's a gift card in there, too. Use it to get some things you need when you start college."

"I will," Terri said, smiling.

"Girl, do you remember the day we graduated?" Sheree asked. "I was so glad to get out of Grady High. I was going to take over the fashion world."

"Yeah, I remember," I said. "All I could think about was me and Mama going out to LA."

"It's not all like we planned, but it's all good," Sheree said, holding up her hand for a high-five.

"It definitely is," I said, slapping her hand. "Anybody want dessert?" I asked.

"No," Terri said quickly. "I was wondering if we could leave soon. I'm going out with some of my friends tonight."

"Okay," I said, signaling the waitress for the check and wondering if one of those friends might be Teddy.

***

Terri left town a few days after her graduation. It was only two weeks until the wedding, and I wanted her to stay; but she said her mama had planned a graduation party for her in Baltimore. At first, I had the blues, those same feelings of being used and then rejected. But then it all changed. I enjoyed having the house alone with Samuel. Bricks tumbled down each day from the wall I had built around myself. I even cried when he left for his guard weekend with the reserves.

It was also the day of the final fitting for my wedding dress. I took the pregnancy test to eliminate the question that had been stuck in my head for more than a month. When the positive sign appeared, my hands began to shake. "Mama, where are you?" I murmured in the bathroom. I rushed to the window of my bedroom, hoping to see a glimpse or a shadow of her walking along the street or half-hidden behind a tree, but she wasn't there. I looked up in the sky for a cloud or some sign, but there was none. So many emotions began to bubble up in me making me feel sick.

I got dressed and drove around looking for Mama until it was time to meet Sheree and Aunt Betty at the bridal shop. I had lost track of time, and Aunt Betty and Sheree were already seated at the boutique waiting for me. They had insisted that I let them buy my wedding dress. They looked so happy and satisfied chatting together and looking at dresses. The shadow of worry and pity I had seen on their faces because of me over the years had gone away.

"I hope the dress still fits," I said uneasily, walking over and giving them each a quick kiss.

"Why wouldn't it fit?" Sheree asked, puzzled. "You look so nervous."

I couldn't hold the words in my mouth any longer. "You won't believe this. I'm pregnant."

They both looked stunned for a minute. Then Sheree raised her fist and hollered. "Yes! Now that's what I'm talking about. This the best news I've had in years!"

Aunt Betty teared up and hugged me so tight. It felt like Mama was holding me. "I'm so happy for you, sweetheart. This makes me so happy. For so long, I felt like I let Frances down. I didn't protect you like I wanted to."

"Don't think that, Auntie," I said, hugging her tighter. "You were there for me. I'm the one who made some bad decisions. I never wanted to make you feel bad. Without you and Sheree, I wouldn't have been able to make it, and now everything is all right."

"Won't He do it?" Sheree said, dancing and shouting like she was in church.

"Stop showing out," Aunt Betty told her, giggling through her tears.

The boutique attendant, who had been standing to the side witnessing our drama, stepped forward with a bottle of wine and glasses. "Welcome back to Winnie Couture," she said, smiling. "Your aunt and sister can relax with a glass of wine while we get you into your dress."

"Thank you," I told her, handing Sheree my bag.

The dress fit perfectly, and when they saw me, Aunt Betty started crying again and Sheree threw her hands up praising the Lord. I wanted to shout, too. I felt like I finally had the life I wanted. I was getting a second chance at happiness. When I turned to look in the mirror, I could see Mama's reflection sitting next to Aunt Betty smiling at me. I smiled back. I didn't need to turn or try to chase her; I had finally gotten peace.

***

The music began to play, and the door of the sanctuary opened. My heart jumped when I saw all the people seated inside. Sheree nodded, and Monica walked forward slowly as she scattered the rose petals along the aisle in the church. She was almost ten and already a beauty, but she had insisted on being my flower girl. Sheree smiled with motherly pride when Monica reached the front of the church.

Sheree had been the best matron of honor on earth. As always, she had been there for me every step of the way. Even while we waited for Lena and Doreen to walk up the aisle, she fanned my face to keep me from sweating up my makeup. Once my bridesmaids were in place, I stepped into the doorway.

Looking straight ahead, I could see Samuel at the front with his eyes focused on me. Aunt Betty was sitting on the front row teary-eyed. Samuel's family was seated on the right. Sandra wore an approving smile. I gazed around at all the familiar faces from Spelman and from Supreme.

And then I saw him.

Teddy was sitting in an aisle seat of a pew near the back. I shivered. Sheree saw him, too. She grunted, handed me my bouquet, took my arm, and walked beside me up the aisle.

Samuel's eyes locked onto mine, and I couldn't look away. He was everything I wanted and needed. After we said our vows and Sheree's pastor pronounced us man and wife, I felt a rush of joy, as if I was born again. Then we kissed. Sheree was the first one to clap, and then the room filled with applause, and the organist started to play. Samuel reached for my hand. We jumped the broom and strolled back down the aisle. I glanced over to the pew where Teddy had been sitting, but he was gone.

I did my best to hide my nervousness while the photographer took pictures. At the reception, I couldn't relax or eat, thinking Teddy might come in at any time and make a scene. After about an hour with no sight of him, I breathed a sigh of relief. Sheree did a toast.

"Chantelle, my mama and your mama are sisters, and you and I are sisters in every sense of the word. Seeing you so happy with Samuel, and knowing how much he loves you, thrills me to no end. You deserve all the good that life has to offer. Here's to a new beginning." We raised our glasses and drank champagne. "Now, it's time to party!" Sheree yelled.

Samuel pulled me to the dance floor, and a sinking feeling in my chest rose up into my mouth and I blew it out. It didn't matter whether Teddy came in or not. I was free, free to be happy with this man who adored me.

"I have a surprise for you," Samuel said, pulling me close on a steppin' jam.

"You're everything I'll ever need," I said, smiling.

"You planned a trip for me, and since we didn't talk about a honeymoon, I planned a trip for you." My eyes widened, and my mouth fell open. I couldn't speak for a moment. "We leave for LA tonight." I still couldn't speak, and my feet had stopped moving. "If we get out of here in an hour, we'll just have time for you to pack."

"I love you!" I said, resisting the urge to scream with happiness. "I'm so glad you didn't give up on me."

"It's us now," he said, pulling me close.

I wanted to tell Samuel about the baby right then, but I had decided to tell him when we got home.

A half hour later, we went around the room, thanking our guests before we made a quick exit. I knew Sheree would keep the party going and handle the business when it was over. The valet was waiting with Samuel's car.

When we got back to the house, my bags were sitting inside the door. I opened the note on top. It was from Sheree. "Have a ball, sis. I've packed everything you need. You deserve this more than anyone else I know." My eyes filled up until they overflowed.

"Sheree is good people," Samuel said, reading the note in my hand.

"She's the best."

"Let's get changed. Our ride will be here in a few minutes."

We took quick showers and put on jeans. In the car on the way to the airport, I still hadn't caught my breath from the day, when my phone vibrated in my blazer pocket. I pulled it out and saw a text from Teddy: "You were the best thing that ever happened to me." I put the phone back in my pocket. There was nothing left to say.

Epilogue

The honeymoon in Los Angeles was a dream come true. I knew Samuel had probably planned it because of what I had told him about Mama and me never getting to make the trip after my high school graduation. It was incredibly thoughtful, and there's no way I could express how much it meant to me. Samuel booked us a suite at the Indigo Hotel downtown near the Walt Disney Concert Hall. It had a modern décor and a wonderful view of downtown L A.

We could have the spent the whole week in our room loving on each other, but we wanted to see as much of LA as possible. I thought it would be easier to get around for a full tour if we hired a guide. We spent hours riding in the car, and Samuel complained that the traffic was even slower than in Atlanta. But at least with our guide we didn't have to drive.

The first day of our agenda was to hike our way up the Santa Monica Mountains on a trail that would lead us near the Hollywood sign to get a close photo of it and a great view of the city. It turned out to be a lot more of a challenging climb than we had thought, but we made it, and the outlook of the landscape was more than worth the effort.

Our second day in the city was more laid back. We went to Beverly Hills and drove down Rodeo Drive and saw all the beautiful homes lined by palm trees. I got a kick out of seeing so many sights I had seen in quite a few movies. We perused all the designer stores, and I bought Sheree a dress from Versace's that I knew would make her holler.

Samuel thought I was kidding when I mentioned that I wanted to go to Universal Studios, but we both loved it. The movie sets were fantastic, and the shows with the special effects were amazing. We rode the Flight of the Hippogriff rollercoaster, and for the first time in my life, I lifted my arms and enjoyed the ride. Being at the park reminded me of the days when Sheree and I would hang out at Six Flags. I made a silent promise that we would do it again with Monica and Lawrence Jr.

We spent the next few days checking out the best restaurants, and Samuel wanted to see the real part of LA, including Skid Row. I wasn't mentally prepared to see the living conditions that so many people had to endure. The poverty, homelessness, hopelessness, and stench were overwhelming. This was real suffering. I realized that, for the better part of my life, I had been living in a protected bubble. Inside the car, I leaned closer to Samuel, knowing I was blessed and ashamed that I had pitied myself for so many years.

The people on Skid Row in LA and in so many other cities are the invisible people. They are the people most of us don't see or smile at. They aren't acknowledged, neither are the issues that brought them there. It made me think of the Luther Vandross song that says don't fall too far down where you can't pick yourself up.

On our last day, we went to the Hollywood Walk of Fame. We saw more names than I could count. The special one I really wanted to see was Marvin Gaye, in memory of Mama. It took a while to find it, but we finally did on the 1500 Block of Vine Street. I took a picture that I would frame. That evening, we went to Venice Beach to watch the sunset.

We walked along the beach for a while until we found a somewhat secluded spot on the sand. That was when I told Samuel about the baby.

He just stared at me for a minute, and then a smile spread across his face. "I love you, pretty lady," he said, pulling me to his chest. "I knew you were worth the trouble."

"I can't even argue with you," I said with a laugh. "I'm just glad you didn't give up on me."

"I couldn't, even when I wanted to."

"I love you, Mr. Goodman," I said, giving him a sensual kiss.

"That's all I need to hear," he said, kissing me on my forehead.

"There's something else I want you to know. Having this baby means so much to me. It's a new life after going through so many changes. But you are the one who helped me change my perception of myself. I thought no one really saw me or knew who I was inside or out. When you saw me, you forced me to see myself. I had to pull back the veil I had hidden under. I learned to value myself. I just want to give you as much as you have given me."

"You already have," he said, holding me close.

We sat there for hours watching the sunset. Red rays streamed from the sun as it sat on the ocean, blended with the darkening blue sky, painting a portrait of pink and purple hues above a golden fire. The beauty and the sound of the waves taken together were magnificent. It was beyond romantic. It was like a religious experience.

***

My wedding was six months ago, and I've decided to take time off from work until our baby is born. It still amazes me that Samuel can't take his eyes off me and that he always reaches for my hand. I have regained all that I had lost: I have a new husband, a new home, and a baby soon to be born.

Lying in bed rubbing my belly, I wonder why it took me so long to get to this point. Then I smell bacon frying in the kitchen. Samuel turns on the radio, and I hear Marvin Gaye. Through the window, a cloud shaped like a bird floats high in the sky. I can almost hear Mama singing.

The End